Solomon's Scrolls

A North & Swiftwater Adventure

BY

RICHARD TURNER

ISBN: 978-1-988141-28-2

Solomon's Scrolls

A North & Swiftwater Adventure

1

La Rochelle, France
October 13, 1307

Marc Grenier stared nervously into the night and held his breath. A second later, a flaming arrow flew up into the darkened sky before disappearing behind an old windmill. Grenier gripped the hilt of his sword tight in his hand and clenched his jaw. A fiercely loyal subject to the crown, Grenier initially didn't want to believe the rumors leaking from the king's court were true, but now there could be no doubt. To his disgust, King Phillip IV of France had secretly signed a warrant for his arrest, along with all the other members of his chivalric order.

"What's wrong, Papa?" asked Henri, Grenier's bright-eyed, six-year-old son.

Grenier looked down at Henri and ran a hand through his curly hair. "It's time to leave, my son," he replied bitterly. The king's treachery cut deeper than any of the dozen wounds Grenier had sustained during his time in the Holy Land.

"Why must we leave, Papa?"

"Because we have been betrayed. Come, my son; we must make haste before the king's men arrive."

Henri peered into the dark. "Papa, who fired that arrow?"

"A friend did. Now, no more talking, my child. Grab your things, and join the rest of the family in the courtyard."

"Yes, sir."

"Henri, be quick. We don't have any time to waste."

The boy nodded and took off, running.

Grenier strode purposefully down the tower's stone stairs and into the courtyard. He waved at the young man holding the reins of a tall, black horse hooked up to a fully loaded cart. Like Grenier, the horseman wore warm clothing from head to toe.

"Is it time to go, my lord?" asked the man, his breath hanging like fog in the cold night air.

"Yes, Andre, it is time. Please see to the cart."

"As you wish," said Andre, bringing his right hand up to touch the brim of his worn leather cap.

Grenier took the reins of his horse in his hands and patted his steed's neck. "I'm sorry, Josephine, but this is one trip you won't be making with me."

Young Henri and his mother, cradling a sleeping child tight in her arms, walked into the yard. Hesitantly, she asked, "Marc, are we sure the king's men are on their way?"

Grenier nodded sadly. "Huguette, my spy within the king's court, was adamant that the king had signed a warrant a week ago for the arrest of everyone in my order all across France this very morning. And not two minutes ago, a signal arrow was launched by my old friend Louis Darras, warning me that riders are approaching. It pains me to say it, but our lives are in grave danger." Grenier picked up his son and placed him beside Andre on the cart's bench. Next, he helped his wife and daughter up onto the cart.

"What about the servants?" asked Huguette. "Surely the king's men will torture them to learn where we have gone."

Grenier shook his head. "No, I released them from service to our family just after sunset. I made sure they were paid well and are already on their way to safety." Grenier hauled his large frame up onto his horse's saddle. He took one last look around his ancestral home, sadly knowing he would never step foot inside the manor again, and gently tapped his horse's sides. His mare walked onto the dirt road leading to the Bay of Biscay.

"Papa, look," said Henri.

Grenier looked over his shoulder and saw his son pointing to the east. Flames lit up the horizon. Anger boiled up inside Grenier's chest. The fires could only mean one thing. The king's assassins had arrived and were burning down the homes of anyone they suspected of helping him and his family. Grenier tapped his horse again and urged her to pick up her pace. Since learning of the king's plot, Grenier had been feverishly planning their escape. Having grown up in the region, he knew the roads to the bay like the back of his hand. With riders closing in, Grenier knew he couldn't afford to waste a single second.

The cold, gray light of dawn greeted them as they left the trail and rode out onto a creaky, wooden pier. Dozens of seagulls hovered in the air, looking for something to eat—the unpleasant smell of saltwater mixed with the city's garbage filled the air. A small ship with one mast sat silently on the dark water. A barrel-chested man stood on the docks, his arms crossed, waiting for them to arrive. Grenier halted his horse and dismounted. He rubbed his hand along his horse's neck and gently patted her one last time.

"My lord," said the man in greeting.

Grenier smiled and offered his hand. "It is sad that we must meet again under these tragic circumstances, my old friend."

"That it is." The ship's captain snapped his fingers, and six young men jumped onto the pier to quickly unload the cart.

"Tell me, Jacques, do you think we have sufficient provisions for the journey?"

Jacques flung his head back, laughing. "I should say we do. I couldn't believe the list you sent me when I read it. As you can see, there is barely room on board for all the provisions you asked me to bring."

Grenier took a cursory look at the ship. His friend was right. Wooden boxes of all sizes and barrels of provisions took up almost every spare inch. There was barely any space on the deck for anyone to walk around.

"My lord, I've never started a voyage with so many supplies. Where are we going, China?"

Grenier opened a pouch on his saddle and handed the captain a worn, cloth map. "Here. Study this before we depart. I've marked the route I'd like you to take."

Jacques nodded and walked back onto his ship to find a lantern.

"Papa, will we ever see France again?" asked Henri.

Grenier picked up his son in his arms and held him close. His heart ached, but he knew he had to tell his son the truth. "I doubt it, Henri, but you never know. Things change, and thankfully, God doesn't let kings live forever."

"Where are we going?"

"Far, far away. So far, the king's men will never find us."

"Henri, quit bothering your father and come join Sarah and me belowdecks," said Huguette.

"Yes, Mother," he replied dejectedly.

Grenier placed his son down. "Do as your mother says, and by the time the sun rises, we'll be far away from these shores." He watched his son take his mother's hand and climb onto the ship's cluttered deck.

"Sire, I think I hear riders approaching," reported Andre, looking to the east. He drew his sword and stepped in front of Grenier.

"Damn," uttered Grenier, reaching for his sword. "I prayed we'd be long gone before any of the king's men arrived."

"Don't worry, my lord; I'll delay them long enough for you to escape."

"No, Andre, I must do this. Go with my family and promise me you'll protect them from harm."

The younger knight shook his head. "Sire, I don't mean any disrespect, but you're not the man you used to be. You can barely see out of your right eye and aren't half as fast as you used to be.

On top of that, sir, you haven't drawn your sword in anger in over a decade. No, sir, I will deal with these bastards while you look after your family."

Knowing his young apprentice was right, a lump formed in Grenier's throat. He wasn't the man he once was. Grenier hesitated for a moment.

Andre's voice grew insistent. "Please, sire, go now."

Grenier cursed as he jumped from the pier down onto the waiting ship.

"My lord, what the hell's going on?" asked Jacques.

"We have to set sail," he replied.

"Now?"

"Yes, now, before it's too late."

"What about your man? Surely, we can't leave him behind."

Grenier's tone grew tense. "He knows his duty. Now, do yours."

"Yes, my lord." Jacques let out a piercing whistle. Everyone on deck stopped what they were doing and looked at their captain. "Weigh anchor and prepare to set sail."

"No, we're too late," said Robert Junot, leaping from his horse. In front of him stood a man with his sword drawn. Junot looked past the swordsman at a ship slowly sailing away from the pier. His body shook with rage. Junot's prize was getting away, and he could do nothing about it.

Three other knights joined Junot on the dock. A man with a deep scar running down his face and long, scraggly black hair spat in Andre's direction. "Sire, shall I deal with this dog?"

Junot shook his head. "No, Mathieu, he is mine."

Mathieu bowed his head slightly. "As you wish, sire."

"Now, young man, you will tell me where your lord is going, or I will make sure your death is a particularly unpleasant one," said Junot to Andre, slowly unsheathing his sword.

"I'm sorry, my lord, but even I do not know where he is going," replied Andre politely.

Junot's face contorted. "You're lying!"

"No, my lord, I am not. Only my master knows where he is going. He never told me what he planned to do once he left these shores, and I never bothered to ask."

Junot bared his stained teeth. "You damned fool. I'm going to make you pay for your foolishness."

Andre brought his sword up and respectfully saluted his foe. "So be it. My life is in God's hands as it always has been."

Junot stepped forward and brought his sword up. He edged closer before slashing at Andre's head.

With countless hours of practice under his belt, Andre saw the move coming and easily parried the blow to one side. Then, with a flick of his wrist, Andre sent his blade toward his opponent's neck. Junot, the wily veteran, leaped back, avoiding the thrust.

"I see your master has taught you well," said Junot. "Tell me, boy, have you taken your vows to be a knight yet?"

Andre lunged at Junot's face with his sword. Only to have his lunge blocked. "No, sire, I have not."

"Then you are innocent and have no reason to die. Lower your weapon and become a member of my order. I could use a man like you."

Andre shook his head. "Never!"

Junot let out an exasperated sigh. "Fine, have things your way."

"I shall," Andre replied, slashing at Junot's stomach.

Junot blocked the attack with lightning-fast reflexes and drew a hidden knife from his belt. A fire burned in his eyes as he jammed the blade deep into Andre's side, twisting the knife from side to side, trying to cause the maximum pain and damage to his opponent's innards.

Andre gasped and collapsed to his knees. Sweat poured down his ashen face. He knew his wound was mortal. His breaths became labored as he prepared to die.

"My son, you were a worthy adversary," said Junot, raising his sword above his head. "For that, I'll grant you a swift death."

From the back of the ship, Grenier watched in horror as his young apprentice's head fell from his body. Blood gushed like a fountain as the headless corpse tumbled onto the pier. Grenier clenched his fists tight. The assassin picked up Andre's head and held it up in triumph. He ensured that Grenier could see him celebrating the young man's death.

"Papa, who was that man?" asked Henri.

Grenier looked down and saw his son standing by his side. His heart ached that Henri had been on deck to witness Andre's death. Grenier's voice couldn't mask his sadness. "You've never met him before, Henri."

"Do you know him, Papa?"

"Yes."

"Who is he?"

"He's my brother,"

Henri gave his father a puzzled look. "I don't understand. Why have I never heard of him before?"

"He's not my real brother. But he once was a member of my order and my closest friend when I served our king in the Holy Land."

"Papa, I don't understand. If he was your friend, why did he kill Andre?"

"Because that man has fallen from grace and embraced the king's greed over his vows to help and protect others. Today is going to be a long day, so please head below and try to get some sleep."

Henri stamped his foot. "Papa, do I have to?"

"Yes. Now do as you're told."

"Yes, Papa." Henri lowered his head and reluctantly walked away to join his mother and sister.

Jacques walked over to Grenier's side, holding the cloth map in his callused hands. "Sire, I've been a sailor all my life and never seen such a detailed map."

"Yes, it's almost a work of art, isn't it?"

"These lands to the west, are they real?"

"Yes. Why do you ask?"

"Unless you know something I don't, this is the first time anyone has accurately mapped land west of Hibernia."

Grenier smiled. "And your point is?"

"Sire, we're risking everything on this journey; how can you be certain that map isn't a forgery?"

Grenier patted his friend on the shoulder. "Trust me; it's not."

"Sire, I'm not trying to be difficult, but how can you be so confident?"

"Because my father traveled there once before and, on his deathbed, he left me this map. Our future, my friend, lies in the lands of the mists."

2.

Present day – The Democratic Republic of the Congo

An early-morning mist blanketed a long mountain ridge covered in tall, lush trees.

In a small clearing, a young female mountain gorilla stirred from her sleep and stretched her arms over her head. She yawned loudly before rolling over onto her side. A yellow-and-white butterfly sat perched on a fern, and she reached out to touch it, only to see it flutter its wings and fly away. She went to chase it but accidentally poked her older sister in the ribs, waking her. Unimpressed at being woken up, the older sister pushed the child away and flashed her displeasure by baring her teeth. The younger sibling jumped back and ran off on all fours, looking for some berries to eat when her mother woke and lazily reached over, grabbing hold of her. She hugged her child tight and, despite her objections, started to groom her head.

One hundred meters away, on a small hill, something crawled slowly through the underbrush to get a clearer view of the gorillas. Careful not to make a sound or sudden movement, a man hidden under a camouflaged ghillie suit stopped moving and made himself comfortable. He cautiously slid out a spotter scope and focused it on the head of the family, a four-hundred-pound silverback. He studied the gorilla for a few seconds before scanning the rest of the troop. He was happy to see that all eight family members were still alive.

"*Blackjack, this is Red-One. Do you read me?*" asked a man with an Australian accent in the scout's earpiece.

"I hear you loud and clear, over," replied the Congolese scout into his radio.

"*Good. I don't think the police know we're coming, so keep a close eye on the gorillas for us, and let me know if the silverback makes any sudden moves.*"

"Roger that. As far as I can tell, we're the only ones out here."

The Australian chuckled. "*The cops are probably all still in bed.*"

"Maybe, maybe not."

"*Wait a second; John's getting a call.*"

The scout rested and sipped some water from his CamelBak while he waited.

"*Crap, I just got word that the cops know we're here and have sent some people to try and stop us. Somebody must have talked.*"

"Bob, don't worry. If you pick up your pace, you should be here long before the cops arrive."

"*Jesus, man, what did I tell you about using names over the radio?*"

"Sorry, I forgot."

"*Don't do it again. We're on our way.*"

A pair of battered, green Land Rovers came to a sliding halt on a muddy trail. Two men, one white and the other black, dressed in camouflaged uniforms, got out of the lead trucks with their scoped hunting rifles and warily looked around. When they were satisfied that they were alone, they waved for six Congolese men carrying machetes to join them.

The Australian hunter looked at a slender Congolese man with short white hair and said, "Okay, Chance, take the lead."

"Yes, sir," replied Chance, who turned and passed on his orders to his men in a mixture of French and Swahili.

"Well, John, what do you think?" asked the black hunter. A middle-aged lawyer from Los Angeles, he had joined his friend on several illegal hunts throughout Africa and Asia over the past decade. "Do you think today will be the day?"

"Let's hope so, mate," replied the man's partner, loading a round into his rifle. "Because I don't relish the thought of spending a single day in some cesspit of jail in the Congo."

"I hear you. Let's get to work."

The two poachers fell into line behind Chance and his men as they hacked their way through the thick jungle foliage. They continued for almost an hour in the oppressive humidity until Chance raised a hand and asked John to join him.

"Why have you stopped?" asked John irritably, wiping the rivers of sweat from his face with a soaked handkerchief.

Chance pointed at a gorilla's footprint in the wet ground and whispered, "Sir, we're close. We'll scare off the gorillas if my men keep cutting a path through the jungle. You and Mister Gordon must take the lead now. We'll stay back until you've shot the silverback. Okay?"

John wondered if their guide was afraid to go any further. It didn't matter either way; John had paid a ton of money for a once-in-a-lifetime chance to bag a silverback, and he wasn't going to waste this opportunity. He nodded his head and waved for his friend to join him. "Ready?" he asked, wiping the sweat from his brow with the back of his hand.

"Yeah, let's do this," replied Bob with a glint in his eyes.

Both accomplished hunters, the men stepped out onto a narrow game path and crept toward the clearing. Anticipation built in their chests, thinking about killing a gorilla that weighed as much as the two poachers combined. They had no intention of carrying out the dead animal's carcass as a trophy. A photo of them standing next to the silverback's body would suffice. Chance and his people would keep it as payment for their services. The hundreds of pounds of gorilla meat would bring in much needed cash for the impoverished farmers. A buyer in China had already paid for its hands.

John slowly raised a hand and got on one knee. He looked over his shoulder at his accomplice. Then, barely above a whisper, he said, "I think we're almost there."

"Do you want me to take the lead?" asked Bob.

John nodded and pointed at the jungle off to their right. "The winds are coming from the north. I doubt they'll pick up our scent until it's too late."

"Right." Bob stealthily stepped off the path into the thick rainforest. He watched every step, careful not to step on any twigs or branches that might alert the gorillas to their presence. They crept forward until they were near the edge of the treeline and then got down on all fours. The gorilla pride was less than one hundred meters away, unaware that death stalked them.

John keyed his radio. "Blackjack, this is Red-One. We're in position. Are we still alone?"

"No," replied a voice above their heads.

"What the hell!" uttered John, scanning the trees. At first, he couldn't see who had spoken to them. Then, the camouflaged shape of a man appeared, sitting on a tree branch, waving at them. Then, the man shifted the weapon in his hands and aimed his M4 carbine at the two poachers.

"Who the bloody hell are you?" demanded John.

"My name is Captain Connor North, and you two morons are under arrest."

The poachers got to their feet, unsure what to make of the man in the tree.

"You don't sound Congolese," said Bob. "Hell, you sound American to me. So legally, you have no jurisdiction in the Congo."

North kept his carbine trained on the hunters. "You're right. I am from the States, but you're dead wrong about whether or not I have the power to arrest you. As a member of the Congolese anti-poaching task force, I have the powers of a peace officer, which means I could shoot both of you dead where you stand, and no one would bat an eye over your deaths. But I'm a nice guy, so I'll give you two a chance to surrender first."

John spat on the ground. "That'll be the day, boy."

Bob looked around. "Where's your backup, cop?"

North shrugged. "Beats me. I suspect they're arresting your helpers. And before you try asking your spotter to take a shot at me, you should know that he's one of us. Sergeant Makosso is one of our best men who's helped bring down at least ten poachers in the past year alone. Now quit talking. Place your guns on the ground, and get on your knees with your hands on your heads."

"Come on, man, you don't need to do this," pleaded John. "If you look the other way for five minutes while we walk away, I promise we'll make it worthwhile."

Connor chuckled. "I'm sorry, but I don't take bribes."

"Trust me; we can make you a rich man."

Connor's voice turned cold. "You're wasting your time. I don't care about your money. Now, place your guns on the ground!"

A short burst of gunfire cut through the air. For a brief second, Connor raised his head to see who had fired the shots. Bob saw his opening and sprinted into the jungle while his partner raised his rifle to fire. Connor, acting on instinct, fired two rapid shots into John's right shoulder. The man cried out and staggered back, holding his left hand over the bloody wound.

"Idiot," said Connor, jumping down to the ground. Then, before John knew what had happened to him, Connor disarmed and cuffed him to a tree.

"For the love of God, man, don't leave me here," pleaded John.

Connor quickly cleared John's rifle and tossed its bolt into the jungle, rendering it useless. "I should leave you here for the animals to feast on, but Patrice and his men will be along soon enough to take you into custody."

The sharp crack of a rifle ended the conversation. Connor spun on his heel and raced down a game path toward the gunfire. He activated his radio and, in French, asked, "What's going on, Patrice?"

"*Sir, we're pinned down, and Matisse has been hit,*" reported Patrice, the lead Congolese police officer on the team.

"Hang on. I'll be there in a minute." North dug his heels in, angry that Matisse, a trainee peace officer barely out of his teens, had been shot on his first mission.

Another loud shot echoed through the valley.

Connor turned a bend in the trail and spotted the escaped poacher aiming at Patrice's men. He slid to a stop and swung up his M4 to his shoulder. Connor focused on the hunter's head but hesitated. Ten years in an overcrowded African jail was a more fitting outcome. He lowered his aim and gently pulled back on his trigger. The M4 recoiled as the bullet left the barrel. The round hit the man square in the hip. The poacher yelped and dropped his rifle. He fell to the muddy ground like a sack of potatoes.

"Don't even think about going for your gun," Connor warned as he approached the hunter with his weapon trained on the man's head. Connor kicked the hunter's rifle out of reach and ignored the man's pleas for medical aid while he cuffed him.

"Captain North, is that you?" called out Patrice.

Connor stood and waved a hand in the air. "Yeah, it's me. How's Matisse doing?"

Patrice jogged up the rise to Connor's side. "He's doing okay, sir. Luc has stopped the bleeding with a field dressing, and a jeep is on its way."

Connor smiled. "Well done, Sergeant. I couldn't have done any better."

"Thank you, sir."

Connor swiped some of the camouflage face paint from his face with his dirty scarf. "Don't forget; I'm only here to help with your training. You're really in charge. So, what do you intend to do now, Sergeant?"

Patrice glanced down at the bleeding poacher. "I'll have Luc stop this man's bleeding and arrest him. I take it there's another man up the trail waiting to be arrested, too?"

Connor nodded. "That is correct."

"Does he also need medical attention?"

Connor grinned. "What do you think?"

Patrice shook his head, brought two fingers to his mouth, and blew a piercing whistle. "Luc, get your lazy behind up here. You have a lot of work to do."

3.

Can anything be more relaxing than a hot shower after a month in the jungle? Connor thought, holding his head under the water, letting it slide down his back. He stood there with his hands on the metal wall until the water turned cold. Connor turned off the tap, grabbed a towel, and dried himself off. He walked over to the sink, reached for his toothbrush, and looked at the steam-covered mirror. Connor wiped the condensation from the glass and studied his reflection. His black hair was longer than when he was an officer in the Marine Corps, but not by much. Black stubble covered his angular face. Connor's ice-blue eyes were as sharp as ever, even if the bags under his eyes said he needed a few days off.

Patrice opened the door to the converted ISO trailer, letting a cloud of steam escape. He saw the condensation on the mirrors and groaned. "Captain, please tell me you didn't drain all the hot water again?"

"Sorry, Sergeant, but you know me. I like to take long, hot showers."

Patrice shrugged. "Hot or cold, I still need a shower."

"It should be lukewarm by now."

"Whatever, sir." Patrice started to disrobe. "Oh, before I forget, there's a man here to see you."

Connor raised an eyebrow. "Did he say who he was and why he wants to see me?"

Patrice shook his head. "I have no idea. But he sounded American to me."

"American?"

"Yes. He's waiting for you in the mess tent."

Curious, Connor wrapped his towel around his waist and finished brushing his teeth before heading to his trailer to get changed into a clean uniform. First, he slid on his rank insignia of three spears to show he was a Captain in the eyes of his employer, the Congolese government. Next, Connor slapped on a Velcro white patch with the word trainer embroidered on it so no one would mistake why he was there. He took a brief second to look in the mirror to ensure his green beret sat straight on his head. Connor wasn't a big fan of berets but wanted to ensure he looked presentable. Lastly, he picked up his dog tags and held them momentarily while looking at the tarnished wedding ring suspended from the metal chain. Connor stared at it for a few seconds, thinking of his late wife and how desperately he missed her. He slipped the chain over his neck and hid it under his combat shirt.

Connor walked outside and made his way through the maze of white trailers to the mess tent. He opened the wooden door and stepped inside. His eyes were instantly drawn to a slender, bald, black gentleman wearing a light-gray suit with a yellow bowtie, sitting alone at a table near the back of the tent. He had silver-rimmed glasses and looked to be in his early sixties, with a salt-and-pepper goatee. The man's right hand rested on a worn, brown-leather briefcase. To Connor, he looked like either a schoolteacher or perhaps a bureaucrat from the embassy.

The man stood and smiled. "Captain Connor North, I presume?" The man's accent reminded him of someone from Boston.

"Correct, and that would make you Henry Stanley," said Connor, alluding to the famous meeting between Henry Stanley and Doctor Livingstone in 1871.

The man laughed. "A good one, Captain, but only half right."

Connor removed his beret, walked over, and offered his hand. "When in Africa, you have to try that line at least once a month, or why come here in the first place?"

The man shook Connor's hand firmly. "Indeed. Well, good day, Captain; my name is Henry Knox, and I've come a long way to speak to you," he said, handing Connor a business card.

Connor read the card and raised an eyebrow. "A lawyer. I hope I'm not in trouble. If this is about that parking ticket I got before flying out here, I swear the cheque is in the mail."

Knox smiled. "That's an old joke as well. But I'm not here to collect any money."

"If I'm not in trouble, then why are you here?"

"Let us take a seat, and I'll tell you why I came all this way to speak with you."

They poured themselves some coffee and sat back down at Knox's table.

"You're a hard man to find, Captain. I knew you were in the Congo but had no idea you were working so far away from the capital."

"I go where the job takes me."

"Would you mind if I called you Connor?"

"Not at all."

"Thank you."

"I, however, think I'll continue to call you Mister Knox because it suits you. So, what brings a gentleman like you to the Virunga National Park?"

Knox sipped his coffee and looked into Connor's eyes. "You do."

Connor sat back. "Me?"

"Most definitely." Knox cleared his throat and looked carefully around the tent. "Connor, I have been retained by a wealthy gentleman who, for now, wishes to remain anonymous."

Curious, Connor leaned forward. "An anonymous client. The plot thickens."

"My client asked me to tell you he would like to meet you in his home in the United States three days from now."

Connor furrowed his brow. "Why three days?"

"He did not say. Nor did I ask."

"Sir, six months ago, I signed a one-year contract with the Congolese government to train a couple of anti-poaching teams, and I happen to like my job. So, it's going to take something more than a clandestine meeting to get me to leave my people on such short notice."

"Connor, I spoke with your bosses in Kinshasa, and they are prepared to release you from your contract without incurring any financial costs."

Connor scrunched his brow. "Really. How much did that cost?"

"A paltry sum compared to some of the deals I have conducted over the years elsewhere in Africa."

"Sir, I don't care about the money. How much do you know about illegal wildlife trafficking?"

Knox adjusted his glasses. "Probably not enough."

"Well, sir, here are the cold, hard facts. It's estimated that poachers all across the globe make upwards of twenty billion dollars a year from the illegal slaughter of some of the world's most endangered species. There are less than nine hundred mountain gorillas left here in the Congo. If we don't take steps to protect them, they will go extinct by the middle of the century."

"So, you're an idealist. Now, try being a realist. Who do you think pays for most of the anti-poaching operations in Africa?"

Connor could see that Knox had done his homework. "International donors do."

"Precisely. You may have signed a contract with the Congolese government to train its people, but they're hard up for cash. Did you know the funding for your position came from an anonymous donor in South Africa who regrettably died in her sleep last week?"

"No, I did not." Connor narrowed his eyes. "Sir, where are you going with this?"

"What would you say if I could guarantee you three years of additional funding for your position, with no strings attached? Other than you agree to meet with my client."

Connor ran a hand over his chin and thought about the proposal for a minute. Then, finally, he got to his feet. "Okay, I'll do it, but only on the condition that you'll fly me straight back here once we're done."

Knox smiled and held out his hand. "A wise decision, Connor."

Connor shook the lawyer's hand, wondering how wise his decision truly was.

4.

Logan International Airport – Boston

The loud squeal of the Learjet's tires touching down woke Connor from a fitful sleep. He rubbed his tired eyes, sat up in his chair, and stretched his arms over his head, yawning loudly.

"We're here," said Knox, glancing out of a window at the rain.

Connor shook his head to wake up. He bought up his watch and tried to focus his tired eyes on the time. It read five-thirty in the morning. He looked over at Knox. "Don't get me wrong, Mister Knox, I truly appreciate flying home in style, but why did we have to land so early in the morning?"

"My client is a busy man. He has probably been out of bed for the past two hours reviewing his financial reports."

Connor ran a hand through his hair. "Well, that's his problem, not mine."

"May I have your passport?" Knox asked, holding out a hand.

Connor handed it over and looked down at his disheveled clothing. In contrast to his impeccably dressed host, he wore well-worn boots, green military-style cargo pants, and a khaki sweater to finish off his outfit. Unfortunately, he hadn't had the time to buy any decent clothes before they left Kinshasa.

The plane taxied to a private hangar and was met by an overly friendly customs agent who boarded the jet and told awful dad jokes while he checked everyone's passports and the flight manifest before letting them carry on.

Knox handed back Connor's passport and reached for his cell phone. It only rang once before a man answered the call. "Sir, we've just landed," Knox reported. "Yes, sir, I can see the limo from here. We'll be there shortly."

"A limo! I could get used to this," said Connor, picking up his small pack and throwing it over his shoulder. "It's true. The rich do travel differently than the rest of us."

Knox slid his phone into a pocket and smiled. "Well, Connor, are you ready to meet your mysterious benefactor?"

Connor swept into a theatrical bow. "Lead on, sir."

They made their way from the plane to a waiting glossy black limousine. Connor was relieved to see a carafe of coffee and some warm croissants for them in the back. He and Knox helped themselves to an early breakfast as the limo driver drove out of the airport onto a nearly deserted road.

"Where are we going?" asked Connor, brushing some crumbs from his sweater.

"The seaport district," replied Knox.

"Is it a nice part of town?"

"Very much so. My client recently purchased a penthouse suite in one of the more exclusive towers overlooking the harbor."

"How exclusive?"

"The cheapest apartment goes for just over two million dollars."

Connor let out a low whistle. "Thank God I'm still okay with second-hand ISO trailers and communal bathrooms."

Knox cleared his throat and sat back in his chair. "Connor, can I give you some advice?"

"Sure. What is it?"

"When you meet your benefactor, I want you to think with your brain and not your heart."

Connor narrowed his eyes. "What are you getting at?"

"Just remember to remain calm."

Now Connor was perplexed. Who the hell was he going to meet? He thought about bailing on the whole idea for a brief moment, but the proposed multi-year funding for his anti-poaching team was too good a deal to pass up.

The limo parked in the exclusive tower's underground garage. Knox and Connor got out and made their way to the nearest elevator. Knox pressed the button for the penthouse, and as the car rose, he hummed along with a song from the seventies coming over the speakers. Connor wished he could feel as calm, but Knox's warning had him on edge. Why did he have to tell him to remain calm? Calm about what? The elevator slowed, and the doors parted. They stepped out onto a blue carpeted floor. Connor glanced to his left and saw a blond-haired man in a dark suit standing outside a closed door, eyeing them. The noticeable bulge in his jacket warned he was armed.

"Follow me," said Knox.

Connor placed his hands behind his back and walked a pace behind.

"Good morning, Mister Knox," said the guard with a strong Southern accent. "He's expecting you."

Connor smiled. Outward, he projected the air of normalcy while inside, his guts told him to be wary.

The guard spoke into a mic in his right jacket sleeve. "Sir, Mister Knox and his guest are here. Should I let them in?" The guard heard the reply in his earpiece, nodded, and unlocked the door.

"Remember what I said," whispered Knox to Connor. "No matter what happens next, I want you to stay calm."

Connor nodded at the guard in greeting and followed Knox inside the penthouse suite. Right away, the hair went up on the back of his neck. Something oddly familiar about some of the pictures and paintings in the apartment made him wonder if he knew the occupant.

"Good morning, Connor," said an unwanted voice.

Connor spun and scowled at the one man in the world he had hoped never to cross paths with again, his former father-in-law,

Jason Hamilton. "Son of a bitch," snarled Connor. "I've been set up!"

Hamilton raised his hands. "Connor, it's not what you think. I haven't asked you to come here so we can yell at each other over Rachel's death. We've been over that, and it's high time we both moved on."

Hearing Hamilton mention his late wife's name only fueled Connor's anger. "I told you at her funeral that I never wanted to see or speak to you ever again, and I goddamn meant it." He faced Knox and angrily shook his head. "I'm out of here!"

"Wait, Connor," urged Knox, stepping in his path. "I called you an idealist in Africa. Now be a pragmatist and listen to what Mister Hamilton has to say."

"Please, Connor, I'm begging you to stay," said Hamilton. "Just give me an hour of your time, and I'll make it worthwhile."

"I shot the last man who said that to me," Connor replied coldly.

"Of that, I have no doubt. Please, one hour, that's all I'm asking for."

In all the years Connor had known Jason Hamilton, he had never heard him beg for anything. Perhaps something was wrong. Were Rachel's younger twin sisters in trouble? "Okay, you've got your hour and not a second more, Jason." Connor deliberately used Hamilton's first name, as there was no way in hell that he was going to call him Mister Hamilton.

"Please let us move into the dining room where we can talk."

Connor eyed Hamilton. It had been just over two years since his wife had been laid to rest after a motor vehicle accident while Connor had been deployed overseas, involving a car driven by her father and a speeding truck. Hamilton hadn't changed much. He'd put on a few pounds around his waist, and his well-trimmed beard and hair were nearly all white.

Connor asked, "Before we begin, are Sarah and Kelly okay?"

Hamilton nodded. "Yes, both are doing well. Why do you ask?"

"Because I care about them, that's why," responded Connor curtly.

As they entered the dining room, Connor immediately noticed a wide-open wall safe and chuckled. "I take it this means someone robbed you." He wanted to add that it couldn't have happened to a better man but kept his mouth shut.

"Unfortunately, yes," said Hamilton, taking a seat at a polished, oval mahogany table. Connor and Knox joined him.

"Have you told the police about the robbery?" asked Connor.

"No, and I don't intend to, either, because I know who did it."

Connor shook his head. "If you know who has your possessions and you don't plan on involving the police, I fail to see where I could be of any value to you."

"You may not, but I do. Connor, how much did Rachel tell you about our family history?"

"Not much, other than you originally came from France. Your family moved to England during the French Revolution and then on to the United States in the 1850s."

"That part is correct. But there is far more to the story than that. My great-grandfather, Donald Hamilton, was the son of a very successful businessman. And like so many men of his generation, he traveled the world looking for adventure before he took over the reins of his father's shipping business. Eventually, he ended up in the Holy Land, helping at an archaeological site in Jerusalem. That is where he met a free-spirited French woman called Rosemary DuFour. He stayed there a whole year and fell deeply in love with her."

Connor interrupted. "This is all very interesting, but what does any of this have to do with me?"

"I'm getting to that. Please be patient. You must first understand the past to grasp what is happening in the present."

Connor raised a hand. "Okay, but if I have to sit here and listen to you talk for an hour, I'd like a cup of coffee."

Hamilton stood and exited the room to return five minutes later with a serving tray with three cups on it. "Now, where were we?"

"The Holy Land, sir," said Knox, handing around the coffee.

"Yes, in the summer of 1914, my great-grandfather and his new bride returned to the States so she could meet the rest of his family. Unfortunately, that summer, World War One broke out, and Rosemary's brother, Peter, fled to France, taking everything of value with him. When Rosemary and Donald reached out to her brother for her notebooks and journals so they could carry on her work after the war, their requests were brushed aside. So, after a few years, they gave up, and Donald focused on running his father's shipping empire."

"The same one you and your brother, Mark, own today."

"Correct, again. I wasn't made aware of Rosemary's other journals until about a year ago, so I reached out to Rene DuFour, Peter's descendant, to see if he would be open to returning the journals so I could perhaps carry on my great-grandparents' work when I retire."

Connor was becoming intrigued. "And?"

"He said no and then sent someone to steal what little I had from my great-grandparents."

"How can you be sure it was him?"

"Because the thieves took nothing else but two journals and a few small trinkets that once belonged to Rosemary Hamilton. Why only take those specific items but leave behind close to seven million dollars in jewels belonging to my late wife?"

Connor got up and examined the open safe. Hamilton was right; barely anything had been touched or removed. He had to agree that it looked like a targeted burglary. He faced Hamilton. "Were any of these trinkets, as you call them, expensive?"

Hamilton shook his head. "Not really. It's the detailed notes Rosemary took while helping to unearth a tomb dating back to around the time of the First Crusade that I suspect Rene was after."

Connor gave Jason a questioning look. "I still don't understand why you won't involve the police. You know who did it and where the stolen items are, so why not make the call? Hell, I know I would if I were in your shoes."

"No, Connor, I'd rather keep the authorities out of this family matter and deal with it myself."

Connor sat down and drummed his fingers on the table for a minute. "If you're thinking what I think you are, you've got the wrong man; I'm not a thief. I wouldn't know how to open a locked safe if you placed it in front of me with the owner's manual open to the page on how to open a safe. No, siree, you're barking up the wrong tree."

Hamilton smiled. "I'm sorry if I gave you the impression that I need you to break into Rene's home. No, I already have a person lined up for the job. I need you to ensure that she gets in and out of Rene's house alive with all of Rosemary's books in her hands."

Connor raised an eyebrow. "She?"

"Yes, the best person for the job happens to be a woman. Does that trouble you?"

"No." Connor looked over at Knox. "Did you know this before flying to meet me in Africa?"

Knox nodded. "Yes, I did. Who do you think recommended Ms. Swiftwater to Mister Hamilton for the job? After all, she is the best at what she does."

Connor wagged a finger. "Mister Knox, I'm beginning to think you're not a real lawyer."

Knox grinned. "Oh, I can assure you that I am a real lawyer. In my line of work, you get to meet a lot of less-than-respectable people. A great many of whom owe me favors."

"So, you want me to act as Ms. Swiftwater's bodyguard while she steals your stuff back?" said Connor to Hamilton.

"Yes. That's precisely what I want you to do."

"Why me, Jason? Aren't there dozens of close-protection companies on the East Coast that could supply you with a trained person to babysit Ms. Swiftwater?"

"I suspect there are, but I want you. Rachel always had faith in you, and if she thought you were the best at what you did, then who am I to argue? I need you, Connor. Please don't say no."

Connor glanced over at Knox, who sagely nodded his head. Connor stood and started to pace. Rachel filled his thoughts. He stopped and faced Hamilton. "For the love of God, I know I'm going to regret agreeing to this. So, I have one request to make, and it's non-negotiable."

"Go ahead," said Hamilton.

"Regardless of the agreement Mister Knox and I made before coming here, I want you to commit to financing the team I worked with in the Congo for the next ten years. That includes the Congolese anti-poachers and anyone the government hires to train the next generation of peace officers."

Hamilton didn't even bat an eye. "Done."

Connor was stunned that Hamilton hadn't objected since the cost for ten years would easily exceed two million dollars. "All right, I guess I'm your man."

"Thank you, Connor," said Hamilton. "That's a massive load off my mind."

"So, when do I get to meet Ms. Swiftwater?"

"You'll meet her tonight," said Knox. "I've arranged for a private plane to take you from Boston to Paris, France. There, you will be met by Yuri, a man with many, shall we say, unique talents. He'll give you everything you need to infiltrate Mister DuFour's home and get out undetected."

"And what happens if we run into trouble?"

"Then, Connor, you're on your own."

5.

Connor bound up the steps and boarded a blue-and-white Bombardier Global 7500 airplane. He handed his pack to the plane's flight attendant, a woman in her mid-thirties with flaming-red hair, and sauntered into the jet's luxurious passenger compartment. He immediately noticed the plane's only other passenger, Ms. Swiftwater. She sat in a green leather seat, sipping from a flute of champagne. She had a runner's build, a tanned complexion, short black hair, and piercing, mahogany-brown eyes. Connor noticed that Swiftwater had a slightly turned-up nose and slender lips and didn't wear any makeup on her attractive face. She wore comfortable shoes on her feet, gray slacks, and a loose-fitting white sweater. Although her clothes weren't high-end, Ms. Swiftwater gave off the aura she was used to the better things in life. Connor guessed she was in her late twenties.

"Good evening, Mister North," said Swiftwater, getting to her feet and offering her slender hand in greeting.

"And a good evening to you, too, Ms. Swiftwater,".he replied, shaking her hand.

"Please, call me Kim."

Connor smiled and let go of her hand. "And you can call me Connor."

"Shall we?" she said, motioning at the plane's comfortable seats.

"Why not? We've got a long flight in front of us."

They sat across from one another. Kim reached for an open bottle of champagne and topped off her glass; when she went to pour Connor a drink, he placed his hand over the empty flute.

"Thanks, but no thanks," he said firmly. "I don't drink."

Kim furrowed her brow. "Not even expensive champagne, especially when someone else is paying for it?"

Connor shook his head. "Not now, not ever. I haven't had a drink for over a year, and I want it to remain that way."

Kim placed the bottle down. "Sorry, I didn't know."

"How could you? We've just met."

Connor saw Kim eyeing his casual clothing. She took a sip of champagne. "So, you're my insurance policy should anything go wrong."

Connor chuckled. "I hadn't thought about it that way, but I guess I am."

"I know I'm good at my job; what makes you so special?"

Connor wasn't used to strangers asking him about his qualifications and was slightly irritated, but he could see why Kim would be wary. He smiled and said, "Where do I begin?"

"I've always found that it's best to start in the beginning."

The flight attendant locked the front door and told her passengers to buckle up for the plane's departure. A few minutes later, the jet taxied down the runway and lifted off into the night sky.

Connor waited until the attendant was busy at the front of the plane and then smiled at Kim. "Let's see now. I was practically born with a rifle in my hands. My father was an Alaskan State Trooper, and he and I would go hunting when he wasn't at work. So, from a very early age, I learned to respect the rifle I was carrying. Over the years, we hunted almost everything on four legs. By the time I was in my teens, I was an expert marksman. If you can believe it, aside from a school trip to Washington DC, I never left Alaska until I joined the Marines."

"Why did you join the Marines and not the Army?" queried Kim.

"Family history, I guess. My father was a Marine for a few years, as was his father, and so on, all the way back to the Revolutionary War. Being a bit of a traditionalist, I thought it was the right thing to do and enlisted. After four years at the Naval Academy in Annapolis, I was commissioned as a second lieutenant and joined the Fifth Marine Regiment in Camp Pendleton, California. It didn't take me long to realize that I liked being a Marine and requested to be transferred to the Marine Special Operations Regiment, which later became the Marine Raider Regiment. The training there was damned hard but very rewarding."

"I take it you must have served overseas a couple of times?"

Connor nodded. "I was deployed overseas several times to Iraq and the Philippines before I resigned my commission and sought work elsewhere."

"If you were happy being a Marine, Connor, why did you leave?"

Connor felt his throat tighten. "In a word, Rachel."

"By the pained look on your face. I take it she was someone special."

Connor nodded. "She was the most beautiful and caring person I have ever met, and it may sound corny, but for the two of us, it was love at first sight."

Kim smiled and sat forward. "Where did the two of you meet?"

"In Hawaii. I was on leave and met her at a luau, of all things. She was with a few of her friends, but my eyes were instantly drawn to her."

"It sounds quite romantic to me."

"There was only one problem, her father."

"And who was that?"

"A certain Mister Jason Hamilton."

Kim almost spat out the champagne in her mouth and placed her flute down. "No way! You just made that up."

Connor smiled and shook his head. "No, I'm afraid it's all true."

Kim's eyes lit up. "Oh, this is getting good. What happened?"

"A month after we met, Rachel told her father about me, and he arranged for us to meet at their summer home in Southampton, New York. At first, he seemed like a nice guy, but when he and I went for a walk alone the night before I was due to fly back home, he offered me one hundred grand to walk away and never see or speak with Rachel ever again."

Kim shuffled in her seat. "Let me guess, you turned him down and ran off with Rachel to get married anyway?"

Connor nodded. "That's exactly what happened. When I told her what had happened, Rachel was livid, so we flew to Vegas and eloped. Of course, Jason and my parents were none too happy that we'd chosen to get married that way, but it was our decision, not theirs. And then one day, while I was deployed overseas, Jason picked Rachel up from the airport, and on the way home, a driver ran through a red light and smashed into the car." Connor's voice cracked. He paused for a second before continuing. "Rachel was killed outright, and yet somehow Jason managed to walk away without a scratch. To the best of my knowledge, the man who killed my wife fled the scene of the accident and has never been caught."

"Oh God, that's so horrible. I'm sorry."

Connor paused to compose himself. "At Rachel's funeral, I told Jason to his face that I never wanted to speak with him for the rest of my life. It wasn't long after that that I started to drink. It got so bad that I couldn't start my day without a few stiff drinks to control my shakes. The Corps offered me a choice: attend rehab or resign my commission. I was so angry at the world that I couldn't think straight and resigned. A few months later, I ended up in Africa, teaching people how to track illegal poachers."

"And your alcoholism?"

Connor chuckled. "I was posted to one of the remotest places in all of Africa and found that I didn't need it to help me get through the days anymore. Instead, I had a job, great people to work with, and a purpose back in my life. So, in a way, you could say, I found myself again in my work."

"That's quite some story."

Connor opened a bottle of water and took a long drink. "And it's all true. So, what's your story?"

Kim pointed at herself. "Me? You want to hear about little old me?"

"Yes. I told you all about me. So, don't hold back."

"I was born at the Eagle River First Nations Reserve in Alberta, Canada. The name on my birth certificate says Kimi, but I prefer to be called Kim. My twin sister, Kaya, and I never really knew our parents, as they died in a house fire when we were only a year old. With no other place to go, our grandparents took us in and tried their best to look after us. It was a hard life as my grandparents were poor and could barely look after themselves, let alone two children. By the time we were teens, Kaya and I were a pair of hellraisers. Every weekend, the police would bring us home to our grandparents, who would lecture us and tell us we were grounded, but that never stopped us. As soon as they were asleep, we'd climb out of our bedroom window and be gone until the sun came up."

"You sound like you were quite the handful."

Kim nodded. "Yeah, I know. But wait, it gets better. At sixteen, we ran away and headed south. We slipped across the border at a reserve and took a bus to Houston, Texas, aiming to get as far away as possible from our old home. But we were as green and as stupid a pair of teenage runaways could be, and it didn't take long for us to fall in with the wrong crowd. Kaya got into drugs, and to pay for her habit, she became a prostitute. As much as I tried to help her, we slowly drifted apart. Then, a few months later, I met a man called John Jurado, who saw something in me and took me under his wing. And before you get the wrong idea, he never mistreated me or asked anything from me. John insisted that I finish my education and taught me how to act in polite society and break into safes without getting caught. We started with, you know, small safes hidden in people's walls, and then moved onto commercial centers and finally high-security compounds." and

"Sounds like you've had an interesting life so far."

"Everything was going great until one night when I found John dead at his desk. The doctors told me he'd died of a brain aneurysm," Kim's voice cracked. "I was heartbroken and didn't know what to do. That was until I found a note he had written before his passing. In it, he told me to be proud of who I was and where I came from. And to carry on pushing the boundaries of my newly chosen profession. Someone had to be the best, and he wanted it to be me. So, I carried on as he asked and eventually made my way to New York, where I met Mister Knox and your father-in-law."

Connor made a *T* with his hands. "Whoa! Time out. You knew Knox and Jason before tonight?"

Kim smiled. "Yes. I've been working on and off for them for the past year and a bit."

Connor sat back. His head was swimming. "Let me get this right. My ex-father-in-law is involved in illegal activities?"

Kim hesitated before answering. "Yes and no. Also, it's probably not what you think."

"Okay, what is it, then?"

"I'd rather Mister Hamilton explained it to you than me. He isn't as one-dimensional as you believe. In fact, he's quite nuanced. I know it's not my place to tell you what to do, but from what I've heard, I think you should give Mister Hamilton another chance."

Connor snorted. "That'll be the day."

"And why do you call Mister Hamilton by his first name? It's not very respectful."

"Because I know it pisses him off, and it'll be a cold day in hell before I call him Mister Hamilton again. Besides, who are you to lecture me about respect? By the sounds of it, you weren't too respectful to your grandparents."

Kim pursed her lips. "People can change. I know I was an awful teenager and should have shown my grandparents the respect they were due. However, I think your reason for being disrespectful to Mister Hamilton is pretty juvenile."

In the blink of an eye, tension filled the cabin.

Connor's neck muscles tightened. He leaned forward and looked into Kim's eyes. His voice turned cold. "Yeah, well, when he kills a person you love, you can lecture me all you want. Until then, you can keep in your lane, and I'll stay in mine."

Kim narrowed her eyes. "I thought you said your wife died in an accident."

"That's how her death was listed, but I know better. I heard from a family friend that Jason had been drinking that day and should never have been behind the wheel of his car. Although I don't have any evidence, I'm positive Jason used his money and influence to ensure his blood alcohol level was never brought up during the investigation."

"That's a big assumption if you ask me."

"It sure is, but I also believe it to be true."

"I've seen the pain in Mister Hamilton's eyes when he talks about his daughter. He's hurting, too."

Connor clenched his fists. Who was this woman to tell him how to feel? "I don't care, Kim. I hope the bastard dies of a broken heart. But let's get one thing straight between us. I'm here to make sure you survive the mission and nothing else. So, let's agree to leave the past in the past."

Kim nodded and raised her hands. "Hey, I'm sorry if I upset you. But I don't see the world through your eyes."

"Has anyone ever told you that you say sorry a lot?"

35

Kim chuckled. "All the time. It's a habit I picked up from my grandparents."

Connor unclenched his fists and glanced out the window at the half-moon. It reminded him of the first night he and Rachel met in Hawaii and how her short, blonde hair glistened under the moon's silvery light. His heart ached for her. Connor knew that one day he would have to come to terms with her death. He couldn't continue being angry for the rest of his life, but he wasn't sure how to let go of the past. Connor closed his eyes and leaned his chair back. He was tired of talking. He just wanted to be alone with Rachel.

6.

Paris, France

Connor sat in his seat and watched as their jet taxied to a private hangar. A blue-coated French customs agent met them. The man boarded the plane but never spoke with Connor or Kim. Instead, he hurriedly stamped their passports and then turned to leave. Out of the corner of his eye, Connor noticed the flight attendant slipping the agent a couple of hundred Euros. He smiled to himself, grabbed his small pack, and walked to the exit. As he left, he glanced over at the attendant. "I take it that was his tip for being so efficient?"

"You can take it any way you want, Mister North," she replied dryly. "Please watch your step and have a nice day."

Connor shook his head and climbed the stairs onto the hangar floor. He stopped and looked around. Aside from the plane, the building appeared deserted.

"I wonder where Yuri is," said Kim, placing her luggage at her feet.

"I haven't a clue," Connor said, checking the time. "Knox said he'd be here when we arrived."

Kim went to dig out her phone when a man driving a forest-green Land Rover Defender drove inside the hangar and stopped in front of the plane. The driver's door opened, and a slender man walked toward the plane. He had looked to be in his mid-forties with black stubble on his angular face and a ponytail that hung beneath the collar of his rumpled Hawaiian shirt.

"Bonjour, and welcome to France," said the man, with a noticeable Russian accent. "I hope you had a pleasant flight."

"Not too bad, Mister—?" replied Connor.

"Yuri, please call me Yuri," the man said, offering his hand in greeting.

Connor shook the man's callused hand. "Yuri, is that all?"

Yuri smiled. "For now, it's just Yuri, Mister North."

Connor wasn't surprised that Yuri knew his name. "If you know who I am, I doubt I have to introduce Ms. Kim Swiftwater to you."

"Enchanted, Ms. Swiftwater," said Yuri, taking Kim's right hand and bringing it to his lips. He delicately kissed the back of her hand and smiled. "It's too bad that you are here on business, Ms. Swiftwater, as I could have shown you the sights of Paris at night. I know you would have loved it."

Kim gently pulled back her hand. "I'm sure you could have. But as you say, we're here on business, so why don't we get down to it?"

"Pity. Another time perhaps, *ma belle*?"

Kim forced a smile. "Another day, maybe. So, what have you got for us, Yuri?"

Yuri tossed a set of keys at Connor. "Everything you will need is in the back of the Rover."

"Like what?" he asked.

"Mister Knox's list was quite detailed. There's more state-of-the-art gear than you could possibly use, along with your costumes for tomorrow night's charity gala."

"Costumes?" stammered Connor.

Yuri nodded. "Yes, didn't Mister Knox tell you? Monsieur DuFour is holding his annual children's charity event at his chateau tomorrow evening. Your invitations are with your costumes."

"Safe houses?" asked Kim.

Yuri dug out a piece of paper and handed it to Kim. "These are the addresses of your safe houses. I'm sure I don't need to tell you never to use them twice. Before leaving here, you'll need to memorize their locations and then destroy that note."

Kim scanned the paper and handed it back. "Here, you can burn it if you like."

"Really?" Connor queried. "That was kind of fast. Don't you think you should read it over a couple more times to be sure?"

Kim tapped a finger on the side of her head. "Trust me. I have a near-eidetic memory. I only need to read or hear something once, and it's stored away in my head for life."

"If you say so." Connor wasn't convinced and scanned the note himself. He pretended to look like he was capable of instant memorization as well.

"From here on out, don't use your personal cellphones or credit cards," warned Yuri. "Both are far too easy to track. In your Rover's glove compartment, you'll find two disposable phones and several credit cards. Please use them wisely."

"Since we're attending a charity gala tomorrow night, I hope there's some loose cash in there, as well," said Kim. "Because I've only got a couple of hundred bucks on me."

"But of course. There's twenty K in fifty-Euro bills with your costumes. I'd love to come with you, but as I have other things to do, I wish you both luck at the roulette table."

Connor was starting to feel out of place. Private jets, a thief who could easily be on the cover of a fashion magazine, and twenty thousand dollars in petty cash. It all seemed quite surreal to him. He was more at home roughing it in the jungles of the Philippines or Africa. But, on the other hand, he was impressed that Knox and Yuri seemed to have thought of everything.

Yuri continued. "If there are no further questions, I have just one more thing to give you."

"And what's that?" asked Kim.

"These," said Yuri, handing them a pair of forged Canadian passports.

Kim went to hand hers back. "Yuri, I already have one of these."

"I know. But Mister Knox thought that if you're going to be working undercover, you'll need a new one. Canadian passports draw less attention than American ones do internationally, and if you look inside, you'll see you're siblings."

Kim flipped open her new passport and shook her head. "Miss Stephanie Wright. How cute."

"Darcy!" said Connor, reading his profile. "Really? Do I look like a Darcy?"

Yuri shrugged and gave them a wave goodbye. "I'm a busy man, so I'll say good luck and hope our paths cross again another day."

"Can we drop you off somewhere?" asked Connor.

"No, thanks, that won't be necessary. My other car is parked outside." Yuri waved goodbye and walked out of the open hangar doors.

Out of curiosity, Connor and Kim followed their contact and watched in awe as he slid into the passenger seat of an expensive white Maserati MC20. The driver, a young blonde-haired woman, winked at them before putting the car in gear and speeding off.

"That car must have cost a fortune," mused Connor.

"A quarter of a million dollars, easy," said Kim. "I like the finer things in life too, but that car is an obscene waste of money if you ask me."

Connor nodded. "That's for sure."

Kim looked back at their Rover. "Shall we get to work?"

As far as Connor was concerned, the sooner the assignment was finished, the sooner he could go back home to Africa. He flashed the Rover's keys in the air. "Why not? I'll drive while you navigate."

"I wouldn't have it any other way."

Their first stop was at a safe house on top of a café on the outskirts of Orleans. The aroma of freshly brewed coffee was far too enticing to Connor. So, the second he and Kim had finished unloading their vehicle, he headed downstairs and returned with two coffees and toasted baguette sandwiches. They ate at a small, round, wooden table while they studied a map of Chateau Sainte Croix, where DuFour was hosting his party tomorrow evening. Constructed in the mid-1600s, the chateau was one of France's largest, privately owned estates. Aside from the elegant, four-storied building containing a large ballroom and twenty majestic bedrooms, there was a tall hedge maze and two long stables for DuFour's two dozen prized horses.

"That's some place," noted Connor. "It must cost him a small fortune to keep running year-round."

Kim picked up a tourist brochure and passed it to Connor. "That's why his company allows tours of the grounds during the spring and summer to help pay for the upkeep."

"Smart thinking."

"The problem with those tours is they don't let you explore the third floor, where DuFour keeps his safe."

Connor chuckled. "To use your parlance, you've already cased the joint, haven't you?"

Kim smiled. "Yes, I have."

"When was that?"

"About a month before Mister Hamilton was robbed."

Connor shook his head. "Just a second. Let me guess, Jason was planning to rob DuFour before being beaten to the punch?"

Kim raised her eyebrows. "Maybe."

Connor didn't like playing games and got straight to the point. "He was, wasn't he?"

Kim nodded. "Yes, Connor, he was."

"That slimy bastard!" snarled Connor. "He's nothing more than a white-collar crook. I knew I shouldn't have agreed to come along."

"Well, you're here now, so erase any thoughts you may have of leaving me from your mind. As for Mister Hamilton, he's not the person you think he is, either."

Connor went to open his mouth but decided to drop the subject altogether. He needed to focus on the mission at hand, not on Hamilton. Connor got to his feet, undid the hasps on a large plastic container, and flipped open the lid. Inside, he found a treasure trove of non-lethal weapons and equipment, from small containers of pepper spray to expandable batons and so much more. Yuri was right. They probably had more equipment than they could ever use.

Kim opened another box and chuckled.

"What's so funny?" Connor asked, straining his neck to see what was in the container.

Kim held up a red-and-yellow harlequin costume. "I think this is for me."

Connor cocked his head and smirked. "Somehow, I think it suits you. Is there one there for me?"

Kim dropped her outfit and pulled out a black-and-white jester's costume. "I see Mister Knox has a good sense of humor."

Connor swore under his breath.

Kim tossed Connor his costume, along with a silver face mask and a jester's hat. "Somehow, I think it suits you, Connor."

"Swell," muttered Connor. He checked out his get-up and then tossed it onto his bed.

"Don't worry. It's not like anyone will know who you are under that outfit."

"That's not what's bothering me."

"So, what is?"

"The robbery. I'm not a thief, so I have no idea how hard it will be for you to break into DuFour's safe. I may be retired, but I still think like a Marine officer, meaning I want to know precisely what we're getting ourselves into. Are you sure you can get in and out of his office without being detected?"

Kim sat down on the edge of her bed and looked Connor in the eyes. "Don't worry. I know I can pull this off."

Connor could see the confidence on her face but had doubts. "How can you be so positive?"

Kim leaned back and brought out a slender device from the costume box that looked like an ordinary cellphone. "Because I have this."

"What is it?"

"It's a highly sensitive thermal scanner. With this, I'll be able to see which keys DuFour last pressed when he entered his code into the control panel next to his safe."

Connor scratched his head. "I get what you're saying, but how will you know which sequence to press them in?"

"That's a good question."

"And the answer is?" asked Connor, wishing Kim would get to the point.

"I've studied DuFour for months and have learned that he's a creature of habit. Even though he changes his password daily, everything he does relates to his family history. Tomorrow night is his late sister's birthday, so I'm betting he'll use that for his code."

"How do you know he changes the code to his safe daily?"

"A disgruntled former guard sold me the information."

"Okay, I can buy that. And if he doesn't use tomorrow's date. Then what?"

Kim smiled. "Then get ready to run."

7.

Chateau Sainte Croix

Connor gently applied the brakes, slowing the Rover. He joined a long line of expensive cars being guided to a gravel parking lot just outside the chateau by a group of young people in yellow vests carrying flashlights.

"It looks busy," noted Kim.

"Is that good or bad for you?" Connor asked.

"Good. The more people there are, the easier it will be for me to hide among the partygoers."

"That makes sense. What would you like me to do while you lose yourself among the attendees?"

"I suspect everyone will be on their toes at the start of the evening, so we should join in the fun, play some games, and lose the money we were given. Then, sometime around midnight, I'll slip away and make my way to the third floor. When I do that, you should move to the front doors and be prepared to run like hell for our car. If all goes well, which it should, and I have what I'm after, I'll make my way to you, one way or the other."

Their vehicle was the next in line to park. Connor drummed his fingers on the steering wheel. In the Marines, he was used to knowing the people he worked with and rehearsing the operations they were involved in until they knew every minute detail. Tonight, however, he barely knew Kim, and that made him nervous. "Kim, I know I sound like a broken record, but please tell me you've got this in the bag. I'm used to being in charge, not backup."

Kim reached over and gently patted her accomplice's hand. "Connor, I've got this. This is real life, not the movies. DuFour's office won't be guarded by laser beams and pressure-sensitive tiles on the floor, forcing me to act like an acrobat. We'll be on our way back to the States before DuFour even knows he's been robbed."

"God, I hope so."

Connor parked their Rover and generously tipped their valet fifty Euros. He and Kim slipped on their masks and hats and chuckled at each other's ridiculous-looking costumes before walking toward the brightly lit chateau. In the courtyard, a troupe of medieval-style musicians merrily sang and danced to a top-forty song as if it had been written in the 1400s, much to the amusement of the people waiting to enter the chateau.

Connor counted no less than six security cameras covering the courtyard and didn't doubt there were plenty more hidden from observation. He gently nudged Kim and indicated with his head at one of the surveillance devices.

"It's okay," she whispered. "I'm not worried about them, and neither should you."

Connor had to admire Kim's sang froid. He'd been under fire more times than he cared to think about, but tonight he almost felt like a raw recruit. His partner, on the other hand, seemed oblivious to it all. But Connor couldn't shake his training. Overconfidence, more often than not, led to disaster. He'd have to be extra alert tonight.

"*Bonsoir*," said a broad-shouldered man with a thick neck in a long-tailed butler's uniform at the front entrance.

"Good evening," replied Connor.

"May I please see your invitations?" asked the man, switching to English.

"Certainly," responded Kim, handing the man their invitations.

The man scanned them and then handed them back. "Good

evening, Mister and Miss Wright. On behalf of Monsieur Rene DuFour, I welcome you to tonight's festivities. I hope you have a pleasant evening."

"I'm sure we will," Kim said, sliding their invites into a pocket of her baggy pants.

Connor nodded at the guard and strolled inside with Kim on his arm. *So far, so good*, he thought. The air seemed alive. Dozens of people dressed in flashy costumes stood in small groups, sipping champagne and laughing loudly. At the same time, others huddled around tables playing cards and roulette or tried their luck with the dice. Melodic chimes came from a side room packed with classic arcade games. Everywhere Connor looked, everyone seemed to be having a good time.

"Where should we begin?" asked Kim.

"I don't know about you, but I rarely gamble, so why don't we take a quick walk around and see what the stakes are at each table? I'd hate for us to blow all of our money in the first hour."

Kim nodded. They slowly wove their way through the boisterous crowd, checking out each table they passed. The lowest was fifty dollars a hand for Texas Hold'em poker, all the way up to one hundred thousand Euros for one spin on a super-sized roulette wheel in the high-stakes room.

Connor leaned over and said into Kim's ear, "I hope you're good at poker because I suck. I'd play blackjack, but they want a grand per hand."

"Come on, let's quit playing it safe and see how lucky we can be tonight," she replied, steering Connor over to a table. She sat while Connor stood behind her. Kim bought five thousand Euros in chips and waited for the first hand to be played.

"Champagne, monsieur?" asked a young woman in a black tuxedo carrying a silver tray.

Connor smiled, took a flute, and placed it next to Kim. He tipped the server well and asked, "Would you happen to have any mineral water?"

"But of course, monsieur. I'll get some for you right away."

"Merci."

Connor turned back to see Kim place her cards down and win two hundred Euros. Maybe tonight wasn't going to be all doom and gloom after all.

Rene DuFour stood before a hall mirror as he adjusted his comically oversized, polka-dot bow tie. For this year's event, he'd decided to go dressed as a clown. He wore large, shiny, red shoes on his feet and a baggy, multicolored costume, complete with a brightly colored wig and a bulbous, red nose.

"Not too shabby, if I do say so myself," said DuFour, checking himself out in the mirror. At forty-one, Rene DuFour was at the top of his game. Handsome, with short, reddish-blond hair and deep-blue eyes. He had never married, preferring the detachment of a bachelor's lifestyle. DuFour had a muscular build and liked to ride his horses for an hour every day before breakfast. Fluent in five languages, DuFour's aerospace company, Hera Enterprises—named after the Greek goddess of air and the stars—was on the rise, with offices throughout Europe, North America, and the Far East.

The door to DuFour's office opened, and a tall man with a scarred, bald head and dragon tattoos on his neck walked inside. He brought up his watch and pointed to it. "Sir, you're going to be late to your party if you don't hurry up."

DuFour spun around, nearly tripping over his novelty shoes. "That is where you are wrong, Jean, my old friend. I am only fashionably late. After all, it is my party."

"Yes, sir," said the man wryly. Jean Vallin was there for the money, not to be DuFour's friend, and was never afraid to speak his mind or express disdain regarding his boss' eccentricities.

"How are we doing so far?" inquired DuFour.

"The last time I checked, we were one million Euros in the black. So, if things keep going as they are, by midnight, your late sister's charity will be at least ten or twelve million Euros richer than it was this morning."

"Excellent." DuFour slipped his wig over his head and adjusted his round, red nose. He winked at Vallin and tiptoed over to his safe. He pretended to hide what he was doing as he keyed in today's date to secure the safe.

Vallin tutted and shook his head. His boss' buffoonish theatrics were beginning to wear on his nerves. Finally, he took a deep breath, unable to restrain himself anymore. "Sir, how many times do I have to tell you that your security codes are far too simple to break? A child could break them. One day, someone's going to rob you blind."

DuFour smiled mischievously at his head of security. "I know; why do you think I do it?"

"Sir, some days I wonder if you're brilliant or borderline insane."

DuFour snapped his fingers in the air. "Why be boring? Why not be both?"

"Yes, sir, why not?"

"Come, my old legionnaire, let us mingle with the crowd and see if we can't help them lose all of their money here tonight."

"Shouldn't I stay upstairs with the security team in case something goes wrong, sir?"

"No, that's the last thing I want. Besides, unlike you, I want something to go wrong."

Two hours after arriving, Kim was up ten grand but knew that wasn't the object of the night's festivities and lost it all in under ten minutes. Connor, envying Kim's winning streak, strolled over to a blackjack table and quickly lost five thousand Euros before he was forced to admit to himself that his skills lay elsewhere.

Suddenly, his stomach rumbled loud enough for people standing next to Connor to hear, so he quickly filled a small plate with a tasty assortment of canapés and rejoined Kim.

"Now what?" Connor asked, offering the canapés to Kim. "It's only twenty-two hundred hours. We still have two more hours to kill."

"We still have five grand left, so let's go and play some arcade games to waste some time," suggested Kim.

"For two hours?"

Kim shrugged. "Unless you can think of something better to do, it's all we've got right now."

Connor didn't. "Okay, you win. Lead on."

Off to their right, the crowd grew noisy. Connor and Kim turned to see what the commotion was all about. The revelers parted as a man dressed as a clown made his way through the party, shaking hands and laughing at his own jokes. Behind him hovered a rough-looking gentleman in a dark blue suit with a dark scowl on his face and anger in his dark eyes. *This was a man to be wary of*, thought Connor.

"Bonsoir, bonsoir," said the clown, holding his hand in greeting.

"Good evening, sir," said Connor, firmly shaking the man's hand.

The clown pulled his hand back and pretended to be in pain. "That's quite the grip you've got there. I take it by your accent that you're American?"

Connor almost blurted out yes without thinking when he remembered his fake passport. "No, sir, I'm Canadian."

"Oh. I love Canada. Where did you grow up?"

A lifelong hockey fan, Connor smoothly replied, "Edmonton, Alberta, sir."

"I've never been there. Is it a nice town?"

"I like it."

"So, what do you think of tonight's soirée?"

Connor glanced around at the partygoers. "It's quite impressive."

"Mon Dieu, where are my manners? My name is Rene DuFour, and you are?"

Connor was stunned to be speaking to the man whose house they intended to rob. "Wright, Darcy Wright, sir."

DuFour looked past Connor at Kim and smiled. "And who might this be?"

Kim smiled and gently shook DuFour's hand. "My name is Stephanie. I'm Darcy's sister. It's a pleasure to meet you, sir."

"Oh no, the pleasure's all mine. And please call me Rene. Are you having a good time tonight?"

Kim nodded. "We are. I just wish my brother and I had brought more money to lose tonight at your charity event."

"Oh, dear. How much have you lost already?"

"I think about fifteen thousand Euros."

DuFour chortled. "That's nothing, *mes amis*."

"Maybe not to you, but to my brother and me; it's almost all the money we brought here tonight."

DuFour snapped his fingers in the air. A split-second later, a young man in a long-tailed tuxedo ran over. "*Oui, monsieur?*"

"Jean-Pierre, please give my new friends thirty thousand Euros."

The man bowed and hurried off to get the cash.

Kim said, "Sir, I think there may be some kind of misunderstanding; my brother and I aren't looking for a loan."

DuFour smiled. "It's not a loan. I want you to have fun while you're my guests. But please ensure you lose all that money in the casino before leaving tonight. My late sister Bernice's charity and I would be most appreciative."

Kim was stunned. "If you say so."

"I do. Please excuse me; I have several hundred other guests I need to speak to tonight. Have fun, Ms. Wright." DuFour waved goodbye and headed straight for a packed roulette table.

Connor felt a chill creep down his spine as DuFour's bodyguard walked past him and locked eyes with him. The man let off an aura of trouble. The less he saw of him, the better.

"Sir, your money," said Jean-Pierre, holding a tray with thirty thousand Euros in chips.

"Merci," Connors replied, tipping the young man one hundred Euros.

Kim eyed the money. "I've got to tell you; this is the last thing I expected to happen to us tonight."

"Yes, it's almost surreal. By the way, what charity should we lose money for?"

"Childhood cancer." Kim looked around the room. "Now that we're sitting pretty, shall we try our luck at the roulette wheel or back at the card tables?"

"It's your call. Unfortunately, I'm lousy at both."

Kim saw an empty spot at the roulette table. "Come on, Connor, let's try something new."

8.

Connor watched the roulette dealer scoop up the last of their money. Even though it wasn't theirs, the thought of losing thirty grand so quickly stung. It was the same salary he'd been making back in the Congo, and that was for a whole year's service.

"It's nearly time," whispered Kim.

Connor's senses instantly heightened. He knew from experience that no plan survives contact with the enemy. And since it wasn't his plan, he was extra nervous. "Okay, good luck. I'll be waiting for you by the front doors."

Kim winked. "See you in fifteen."

Connor stepped aside to let Kim fade into the party. He waited until she reached the bottom of the stairs before turning around and eyeing a gray-haired man carrying a tray packed with champagne flutes. "Here goes nothing," said Connor under his breath. He headed straight for the server and, at the last second, pretended to look at his watch. The two men collided, spilling the drinks everywhere.

"Oh, I'm so sorry," said Connor, steadying the shaken server.

"It's all right, sir; I should have seen you coming."

"Nonsense, it's all my fault." Connor bent over to help pick up the glasses. If someone was watching the hall with surveillance cameras, he'd just bought Kim ten seconds.

"Now," said Kim, taking the stairs two at a time. She sprinted as fast as she could and reached the third floor with one second to go. Kim paused to catch her breath. She glanced up and down the corridor and thankfully saw she was alone. She adjusted the earpiece hidden under her hat and whispered, "So far, so good. I'm on the third floor, and there's no one in sight."

"That's excellent news. Good luck," replied Connor.

"See you soon."

Kim wrapped a scarf around her face and then slipped a hand into a pocket on her costume, activating a powerful surveillance jamming device. Combined with the thermal shielding stealth fabric her outfit was made from, she was almost invisible to any of the building's surveillance cameras. To anyone watching, Kim would look like a blur or a ghost moving down the hallway. Kim moved slowly but deliberately down the hall until she found DuFour's office. Kim tried to open the door, but as expected, it was locked. Undeterred, she dropped to one knee and dug out her lockpicking tools.

"It's like stealing candy from a baby," said Kim, quickly opening the door. Before slipping inside the dark room, she held her breath and waited for a few seconds to see if an alarm would sound. Next, Kim reached for a small, red-filtered flashlight in a pocket and switched it on. She moved the light around the office, stopping at a painting of DuFour's sister. Her heart started to race. She edged over and ran the light around the picture frame, looking for switches that might trigger an alarm. When she didn't find any, Kim exhaled. Feeling safe, she gently removed the painting from the wall and delicately placed it on the carpeted floor.

Kim brought out her thermal scanner and turned it on. "God, if you're listening, if I'm ever going to screw up big time, please don't let it be today."

She took a long breath and scanned the keypad on the wall beside the safe. A wide smile crept across her lips as a series of numbers and letters shone brightly on the thermal screen. She quickly typed in the date and heard the safe click. Kim's stomach felt as if it were filled with thousands of butterflies. She was used to being scared and nervous, but this felt different. Warily, she opened the safe and looked inside. Her eyes widened when she spotted four old red leather books and several piles of paper on a shelf by themselves. Kim retrieved a stack of books from a nearby desk. She weighed them in her hand and judged they were the same weight as the four she was about to steal.

Kim tapped her earpiece. "Standby, Connor."

"Roger that."

Kim nibbled on her lower lip, praying there wasn't an overly sensitive pressure-sensitive device inside the safe. She brought up her replacement books and paused. It all seemed far too easy. Kim shook her head and chided herself for doubting herself. She placed her left hand over the four journals while she brought the fake ones over in her right. "Here goes nothing," Kim said, switching the books in under a second flat. She held her breath, expecting an ear-piercing alarm to rip through the house. When only silence greeted her, she knew the most challenging part was behind her and prepared to close the safe. Kim couldn't believe her luck when it all came crashing down. Kim cursed when she spotted a tiny, red light flashing on and off in the back of the safe.

Kim instantly stashed away Hamilton's books in the oversized pockets on her costume and spun on her heel. She almost made it to the door when she saw a sliver of light coming through the crack at the bottom of the door and heard voices. Instantly, Kim knew she wasn't going out the way she had come in. She rushed to the far windows and flung them open. She popped her head out and saw in the light of a silvery moon that it was too high for her to jump without breaking a leg. Kim's only avenue of escape was an old lead drainpipe secured a few meters away from the window. Kim leaned out, desperate to reach it, but, to her dismay, she found it was just out of reach.

Behind her, the door flung open, and two men rushed inside, brandishing their pistols.

Kim had no choice; she screwed up her courage and dove out the window, aiming for the drainpipe. A split second later, her fingers touched the cold metal. Kim wrapped her hands around the pipe and gripped it firmly. The tube creaked loudly but thankfully didn't break under her weight. Knowing that she had seconds to reach safety, Kim rapidly climbed hand over hand down the pipe.

"Stop!" yelled one of the guards, shining his flashlight on Kim.

A shot rang out from above, missing the side of her head by millimeters. Kim swore and let go of the pipe, landing on the wet grass. She rolled over and then got to her feet, running. Her ridiculous-looking hat fell off and landed behind her. Another shot tore through her baggy costume next under her armpit. Adrenaline surged through Kim's veins. She'd never been shot at before and didn't like it one bit. With her heart pounding in her ears, Kim sprinted into the maze and vanished into the dark.

"Help!" Connor heard Kim's trembling voice in his earpiece and instantly looked back at the stairs. She was nowhere in sight. He clenched his jaw when he watched DuFour's bodyguard hurry his boss out of the room. The game was up, and Kim was in deep trouble.

"Maze...I'm in the maze. Please help."

In a flash, Connor's training kicked in. He took to his heels and raced out of the chateau and across the courtyard for his parked Rover. Connor ripped off his hat and mask as he ran. It was a race to see who would get to her first. Connor prayed that it was him.

Kim stopped running for a moment and realized she was lost. The light from the moon helped somewhat, but it was still quite dark inside the maze. She could hear voices calling out to one another, but they sounded as lost as she was. Kim cursed and tossed her mask away so she could see better. She ripped off her gloves and reached for her only means of defense, a small container of pepper spray in a pocket on her costume. "Think, girl, think," said Kim, desperate to find a way out of the maze before being caught. An image of her sister flashed in her mind. As children, they'd spent hours every fall chasing each other through corn mazes in a local farmer's field. A voice in her head reminded her that if she placed her right hand on the wall, she'd never get lost and eventually find the exit. Kim put her right hand on the hedge wall and crept forward.

Connor spotted his Rover and picked up the pace.

He was almost at the entrance to the parking lot when two guards came into sight. One was speaking into a Motorola. The other man saw him coming and raised his hand. "*Arretez, Monsieur!*" ordered the man.

Connor had no intention of stopping. Instead, he grabbed his concealed collapsible baton and extended it with a sharp flick of the wrist. The closest guard spotted the bat and went for his concealed pistol. Connor slid to a halt and smashed the metal rod hard on the guard's right arm, shattering it. Then, before the man knew what hit him, Connor swung the baton around and hit him on the side of the head, knocking him out cold.

The second guard dropped his radio and fumbled for his sidearm, only to get smashed in the stomach. The man moaned and dropped to his knees in agony. Connor brought the rod up and hit it on the stunned guard's head, sending him to the ground, unconscious.

Connor dropped down, quickly rifled through the guards' jackets, and took their pistols. He collapsed his baton and sprinted over to his car. Connor jumped in, started the vehicle, and activated his earpiece. "Kim, where are you?"

"*I don't know. I'm trying to find the exit.*"

"Keep going. I'll be there soon."

"*Hurry!*"

Connor shifted his Rover in reverse and slammed his foot on the accelerator. Rocks flew behind the vehicle as the tires tried to grip the gravel road. He spun the wheel around in his hands and changed gears. In seconds, like a charging cheetah, he drove out of the lot and sped toward the maze.

"Report!" bellowed Vallin as he stormed into the chateau's security office.

"Sir, we have an intruder trapped inside the maze," reported a heavyset man.

"Where? Show me."

"Uh, I can't." said the man, pushing his half-eaten sandwich to one side.

Vallin wasn't known for being a forgiving man. "Why not?"

The guard wiped his lips with the back of his hand. "Sir, everything happened so fast that I forgot to launch our drone."

"Well, what the hell are you waiting for?" Vallin hauled back and struck the guard on the side of his head. "Do it, and then ask for a situation report from our security teams."

"Yes, sir," stammered the man, scrambling for his Motorola.

Vallin ground his teeth. His reputation as a man who was good at his job was at stake, and that was the last thing he needed to be tarnished.

"The drone's away, sir."

Vallin looked up at the row of computer screens. The drone hovered over the hedge maze, sending back a thermal image of the labyrinth. He spotted three figures. One was halfway through the maze but moving slowly. The two others moved as fast as they could in the dark.

"Vector our men onto the thief," ordered Vallin.

"Yes, sir."

Vallin glanced at the other screens and saw a Land Rover speeding down a road toward the back of the château. He grabbed hold of a radio handset and called for the men at the parking lot to respond. When no one answered, Vallin gripped the Motorola tight until his knuckles blanched. Anger boiled inside him. Swearing at the top of his lungs, he smashed his radio down on the table, breaking it. Vallin grabbed the surveillance operator by the collar and hauled him to his feet as if he weighed nothing, raising the man until he was inches from his face. "Send a team of men on motorbikes to the far exit of the maze and then activate the Chateau's fireworks."

"But, sir, Monsieur DuFour said not to fire them until he gave the word," stammered the fat man.

Vallin slammed the man against the wall, painfully knocking the wind from the guard's lungs. "I don't care. Do it what I say, or you're going to need an ambulance once I get finished with you."

"Yes, sir," said the man, quivering in his boots and struggling to catch his breath. "I'll do it right away."

Vallin threw him into his chair. "I'd be quick if I were you, as I'm starting to lose my patience with you."

The guard typed in a command on his keyboard, activating the fireworks. Outside, the dark night sky lit up with sparkling explosions as dozens of rockets shot up into the air and exploded.

Good, thought Vallin. That should mask the sound of any gunfire.

Connor saw the fireworks explode over the chateau, sending waterfalls of gold and silver sparkles down onto the roof. In any other situation, he might have enjoyed the wonderous display of lights. But now wasn't the time. He kept his foot jammed down on the gas pedal and sped past the chateau and the maze. Connor brought the Rover to a screeching halt and turned the vehicle around until the trunk faced the maze exit.

"Kim, can you hear me?" he asked.

"*Yes.*"

"Standby. I'm going to make an exit for you. Just look for the lights and then run like hell."

Kim's voice was tight. "*Connor, there's a drone right above me.*"

"Don't worry. Just get ready to run." Connor placed one of the pistols he stole from the injured guards on the passenger seat and looked over his shoulder. Connor revved his engine with one foot on the brake and one on the accelerator until it roared. He lifted his foot off the brake and felt the Rover jump back. In a heartbeat, the vehicle picked up speed and easily smashed through the hedges. Connor flipped on the high beams and jumped out of the Rover with a pistol in his hand. He moved aside and looked up, trying to spot the drone.

Kim heard the crash and saw the bright lights just off to her left. She let go of the hedge wall and ran as fast as her feet would go. She turned a sharp corner and let out a surprised cry when she ran headlong into one of the men hunting her. The man was equally surprised; however, Kim reacted first and jumped back. She brought up her can of pepper spray. The guard's eyes widened when he saw the spray bottle. He went to knock the can from Kim's hand but was a fraction of a second too slow. Kim pressed a button on top of the container, shooting a stream of burning irritants into the man's eyes. The man screamed in pain and reached up for his burning eyes. Kim saw her opportunity, kicked the guard's feet from underneath him, and ran for her life.

"Easy does it," said Connor, as he laid his pistol's sights on the hovering drone. He held his breath and gently pulled back on his weapon's trigger. He felt the recoil in his hands as the pistol fired, and the bullet shot toward the UAV. In the blink of an eye, the round struck home, shattering the drone. It wobbled in the air for a few seconds before plummeting to the ground and breaking in half.

"Connor!" yelled Kim.

"I'm here!" he cried out. Connor lowered his pistol and ran to the front of the Rover. Over noise from the idling engine, Connor didn't hear Kim clamoring over a hedge and dropping down next to their vehicle. She saw him, threw her arms around him, and hugged him tightly.

"Thank God you're here," said Kim.

"We're not out of here yet," he replied. "Get in."

Connor went to jump into his seat when the second guard crawled over the hedge, dropping to his feet right in front of him. Both men eyed each other for a milli-second before going for their weapons. At this range, it was impossible to miss. Unlike his opponent, Connor didn't bother to bring his arm up and fired his pistol from his waist, sending two bullets into his adversary's thighs. The man instantly dropped to the wet ground, rolling from side to side in agony. Connor kicked the guard's gun away from his hands and got into the Rover. He thrust the gas pedal down and shot out of the maze. Connor spun the wheel around, rapidly switched gears, and drove down a narrow trail into a darkened forest behind the chateau, heading hopefully for safety. Connor switched off his vehicle's lights to avoid being seen.

He glanced over at Kim for a second. "Are you okay?"

"I am now," she replied. "How are you doing?"

"I'll be okay when we get out of here. Did you get what you were after?"

Kim nodded.

"Thank God. What happened back there?"

"I must have triggered a silent alarm. Before I knew it, a couple of guards burst into the room, and I had nowhere to go but out the window."

"I hope whatever Jason wants is worth it."

"So do I," said Kim poking a finger through the hole in her costume.

"Damn," uttered Connor, glancing up at the rearview mirror.

"What's wrong?"

"We've got company."

Kim looked back and saw a pair of headlights closing in from behind.

"Hang on," said Connor, turning the wheel hard and leaving the trail. Right away, the Rover bucked up and down on the rough ground.

The motorbike riders were undeterred by the sudden change and continued their pursuit. Connor had hoped the uneven terrain would force their pursuers to slow down. Instead, they grew closer by the second. A burst of automatic gunfire hit the back of their vehicle, shattering the driver's side rear lights. Another shot hit the rear window and carried on through their windshield.

Kim cried out and instinctively ducked down in her seat.

Connor could see that the men chasing him were professionals. The riders split apart, intent on taking them from both sides. Connor knew he had seconds to do something before they caught up with them and forced them to stop. Up ahead, the trees thinned, and he could see a small clearing. A plan quickly gelled in his mind. "Kim, when I hit the brakes, I want you to run to the nearest tree and take cover. Okay?"

"Why? What are you going to do?"

"There's no time to talk. Just do as I say."

Kim bit her lip and nodded.

Connor waited a couple more seconds, hoping the motorbike riders would get closer. "Now!" he yelled, slamming on the brakes and throwing open his door.

The closest rider hadn't anticipated the move and sped headlong into the open door. With a loud thud, the man flew over his handlebars and tumbled through the air end over end until he hit a tree trunk and slid to the forest floor.

Kim opened her door and ran toward a thicket.

With anger and adrenaline coursing through his body, Connor leaped from the Rover with his pistol at the ready. He spotted the second rider raising his compact submachine gun to fire at Kim. Connor never hesitated. He fired twice, hitting the man in the side of his chest. The dead man fell off his bike and lay facedown on the cold earth.

Connor swore. He'd killed people before, but that had been on military operations with clear rules of engagement or in self-defense in the Congo. Killing a man over some old notebooks pissed him off. But he had no choice; it was him or Kim. Connor placed his weapon on safe and whistled for Kim to come back.

"Is he dead?" Kim asked, walking past the motionless rider.

"I hope so," replied Connor. "Now, let's get the hell out of here before anyone else comes after us."

Kim gently placed a hand on Connor's arm. "I'm sorry, I never thought it would come to this."

"Jason did. That's why he hired me."

"We should get going."

"I agree. Where's our second safe house located?"

"It's in Paris. If we don't get stopped by the police, we should be there in about an hour."

Connor climbed back into his seat and waited for Kim to join him. They drove off in silence, fully aware that their lives had changed as of tonight, and perhaps not for the better.

9.

Vallin kicked the door to DuFour's office wide open. He stormed in, carrying a blood-stained motorcycle rider's helmet, and slammed it down hard on DuFour's desk. "Four, we lost four good men today, and for what?" he roared.

If Vallin's anger was supposed to intimidate DuFour, the ex-legionnaire was sadly mistaken. The businessman looked up from his computer with a bored expression. "Let's not exaggerate things, Jean. We have two men with broken bones and one with non-life-threatening gunshot wounds. We only have one man dead. It's a small price to pay for what I'm after."

Vallin started to pace like a caged animal. "Ahmed was married. Are you going to tell his widow that he died for nothing?"

DuFour wagged a finger. "I never said that. His death is unfortunate, but this is why I insist that all of my employees have life insurance in case something tragic occurs to them."

"Jesus, man. What are we going to tell the police?"

"Nothing."

Vallin stepped back, confused. "Sir, you were robbed, and we have a dead body downstairs."

"Jean, do I have to think of everything? Be creative for once in your life. Make Ahmed's death look like an accident in which his body was burned beyond all recognition. And then make sure you bribe the usual officials in the coroner's office and the local police department so they don't come sniffing around here."

Vallin paused and stared at his boss. "And the injured men?"

"A traffic accident for the two with broken bones and a negligent discharge for the man who failed to clear his pistol before cleaning it. Just make sure they're paid well to keep their mouths shut. Honestly, Jean, I can't believe I have to do your job as well as mine."

The veins on Vallin's neck bulged. He clenched his fists tight and glared at his employer. "That's the last thing you need to do, sir. I bloody well know how to do my job. If you would take me into your confidence and let me know why you deliberately left your safe vulnerable tonight, I might be able to anticipate your future moves and help you."

"Jean, take a look in my safe and tell me what has been removed."

Vallin walked over to the safe and peered inside. He was surprised that none of DuFour's jewels, or five million in Euros in neat stacks, had been stolen. As far as he could tell, the only things missing were two of DuFour's old books, along with the two recently acquired books from America.

"Sir, I don't get it. Are you and Mister Hamilton playing some kind of childish game I'm not privy to?"

DuFour got out of his chair and poured himself and Vallin a small glass of sherry. He gave one to his head of security and then took a sip from his glass. "You asked if Hamilton and I were playing a game. If it is, it's a game of chess, and at this moment, I'm thinking at least two moves ahead of him, and he doesn't even know he's being played for a fool."

Vallin placed his drink down and shook his head. "Sir, I still don't understand what's going on here. I'm used to clear and concise orders, not childish mind games. So, what aren't you telling me?"

"As you know, a short while ago, I had a man steal some books and handwritten notes from Jason Hamilton because I needed to see what was written in them. Regrettably, Hamilton's journals, like mine, were filled with an undecipherable type of shorthand. I'd hoped Hamilton's books contained the key to decoding my four journals. But, alas, it wasn't meant to be."

Vallin shook his head. "I'm still not following you."

"Jean, look around. I allowed myself to be robbed tonight. If I can't decipher the books, maybe someone else can."

Vallin scrunched his forehead. "What the hell are you looking for, sir?"

"Riches and fortune, Jean. Riches and fortune."

10.

Paris - Safe House

Kim sat at a dining room table with a warm, red blanket around her shoulders. She held a cup of hot chocolate in her hands and sat there, staring ahead, as Connor unpacked the suitcases and containers of equipment provided by Yuri.

"How are you doing?" asked Connor.

Kim looked over. Her eyes glinted with tears. "I've been scared before, but never like that. My God, I could have died tonight."

"Not while I'm around," said Connor, giving her a reassuring smile.

"I knew what I was getting into when I agreed to steal back Mister Hamilton's books. Naively, I didn't factor in the lengths DuFour would go to stop anyone from getting their hands on these books. Most of the places I've robbed were deserted. Sure, the odd security guard was walking about, but they were never a threat like tonight."

Connor glanced at the four red-leather-bound notebooks and wondered what made them so important that people would kill to keep them a secret. "Kim, I wouldn't beat myself up if I were in your shoes. Unlike breaking into a rich man's home to steal his jewels, DuFour is clearly a step above what you're used to. No matter how good you think you are in life, there will always be someone better than you."

"What about you? Would you have come knowing the risks?"

Connor smiled. He was as troubled as Kim by the night's events, but his experience allowed him to suppress his feelings. "Come on, Kim, look at me. No one hires me for my looks."

Kim laughed. "True enough."

"Hey, that's not a nice thing to say," he replied, feigning being hurt.

A timer on Connor's watch beeped. He flipped open a secure laptop on a small wooden table and pressed the power button. A minute later, Jason Hamilton and Henry Knox's faces filled the screen.

"Good morning," said Hamilton. "I'm glad to see you both alive."

"As are we," replied Kim somewhat sarcastically.

"Is there something wrong?"

"Yeah, I almost died tonight. You might have warned me that DuFour had more security on the grounds than an army base. Yet, when I toured the chateau last month, I barely saw a guard. And none of my informers ever mentioned the extra security we saw last night.

"Sir, I can answer that," said Knox.

"Please do," said Kim.

Knox cleared his throat and adjusted his glasses. "The short answer is we did not anticipate Mister DuFour surrounding himself with so many guards during a charity event."

Connor scribbled *I don't believe him* on a note and slid it toward Kim.

Kim glanced at the message and then looked back at the screen. "I'm not sure I believe you, Mister Knox, but there's not much I can do about it now."

"Kim, do you have the books?" asked Hamilton, barely masking his anticipation.

"Yes, I do. I have them all. Yours and DuFour's."

"Excellent. Do you have the capability to scan DuFour's books?"

Connor looked inside one of Yuri's containers and nodded at Kim. "Yes, we do," she replied.

"Great. Could you please scan DuFour's books and forward that information to me as soon as possible?"

"We can," interjected Connor, "but why would we? I thought Kim's mission was to retrieve your stolen books and bring them home."

"Not true. I specifically said I want you to help protect Ms. Swiftwater while she steals Rosemary DuFour's books. That would include not just mine but the ones in Rene's possession."

Connor looked at Kim, who begrudgingly nodded her head. "Damn. I guess I'd best pay better attention to what you say from now on, Jason. But my question still stands: why should we scan the new documents when we could hand them over to you later today?"

"That, I will leave to Ms. Swiftwater to answer."

Connor didn't like where the conversation was going; everyone seemed to be hiding something. "Jason, I agreed to help protect Kim while she retrieved the books, so as far as I'm concerned, I've lived up to my part of the bargain."

"As I said, you may wish to discuss your situation before making any hasty decisions."

"Hasty! There's nothing hasty about them," Connor's voice grew loud. "Jason, you promised to finance an anti-poaching team in the Congo for the next ten years if I helped you. I hope you're not telling me that you bargained in bad faith because if you are, you won't be able to hire enough men to stop me from gutting you."

Knox interrupted. "Mister North, please relax. I have already transferred the funds required to keep your old team in the field. I can assure you that Mister Hamilton has kept his word."

"Then what the hell is going on?"

Kim placed a hand over Connor's. "Gentlemen, please let me speak to Connor before I scan the books. Okay?"

"That would be a wise idea," said Knox. "Please call me when you are ready to send the scanned files to us."

Kim nodded. "We'll speak to you soon."

The screen went dark.

"What gives, Kim?" asked Connor, mystified. "I need you to tell me what's really going on, or I'm out of here."

She faced him, took a breath, and looked him straight in the eyes. "Connor, I'm sorry if none of us have been totally forthright with you. You may have fulfilled your bargain with Mister Hamilton, but I still need your help."

Connor felt the muscles in the back of his neck tense. "Why do I get the feeling that I'm being played for a fool?"

"No. You're far from a fool. All I know for sure is this is just the beginning, and not the end, of the assignment."

Connor sat back and crossed his arms. "Kim, you're beginning to sound like Jason. What do you mean the mission's not over?"

"Mister Hamilton is looking for something. He wouldn't tell me what it is, but he thinks it's important."

Connor picked up one of the books and examined it. "And he thinks the answer lies in these books?"

"Maybe, maybe not. We won't know until he and Mister Knox have had a chance to read them."

"And then what?"

Kim shrugged. "I was promised a lot of money if I saw this assignment through to the end, and I need that money."

Connor furrowed his brow. "What for? You look like you're doing okay."

"Looks can be deceiving. I'm not as well-off as I'd like to be. Contrary to popular belief, a cat burglar doesn't make much money. Do you remember when I told you I had a sister?"

"Yes."

"Well, I didn't tell you everything."

Connor rolled his eyes. "What a surprise."

Kim glared at Connor. "Please don't be sarcastic. It's not helpful."

Connor knew he'd crossed a line and nodded. "Yeah, you're right. Jason's got me all worked up, and I'm sorry. Please continue."

"Three years ago, Kaya was arrested after killing her abusive husband for physically assaulting their four-year-old child and sentenced to ten years in jail. Her daughter, Tiva, was placed in a foster home with a pair of great people, but her injuries were so severe that she is blind in her left eye and has deep-seated mental health issues. So, Tiva needs a lot of attention and love. Not to mention money to look after her."

"I don't understand. If her husband was abusive, why did your sister get ten years in jail?"

Kim canted her head. "Connor, please. Courts all across North America aren't overly kind to First Nations people. Far too many of my people are incarcerated in the U.S. and Canada for crimes that would have netted much lesser sentences if they weren't from a reserve. Did you know that up to fifty percent of all women in prison in Canada are native? It didn't help my sister that the stats in Texas aren't much better."

"I'm sorry; I had no idea it was that bad."

"I'm not saying Kaya was a saint, but she didn't deserve to be put away for ten years. I only agreed to work with Knox and Hamilton if they hired her a good lawyer, who they promised would work tirelessly to get her case reviewed. They also said they would help Tiva stay in her foster home. For a man like Hamilton, that's spare change, but to me, it's a godsend. So, when he asked me to break into DuFour's house, who was I to say no?"

"Okay, so far, I'm on your side. But what did Jason tell you was going to happen next?"

"I wish I knew. I know Hamilton's been deliberately keeping me in the dark about something; what that is, is anyone's guess."

"Kim, when we first met, you said you'd already done a few jobs for Jason."

"That's right."

"What did you steal for him?"

"Nothing really of value. It was mainly private journals and diaries."

Connor leaned forward. "This is suddenly getting interesting."

"How so?"

"I'm not sure yet, but you're right; he's looking for something."

Kim picked up their portable scanner and smiled. "So, why don't we scan DuFour's books to try and shed some light on what's going on?"

Connor smiled. "Why don't we?"

Eight hours passed before the screen activated, and Hamilton and Knox's faces reappeared.

Hamilton started. "I'm not a fool, so I'm going to assume that you have read through the notebooks while you waited for me to call you back?"

Connor nodded. "And you'd be right. I can speak French far better than I can read it, but thankfully, you can find dozens of French-to-English translation Apps on the Internet."

"And what did you think?"

"Two-thirds of the books are written in a type of shorthand Kim, and I can't make heads nor tails of. As for the rest, I'm not an archeologist, but from what we read, it would appear that your ancestors may have stumbled across a tomb on the outskirts of Jerusalem that once housed the remains of a Templar Knight."

Hamilton toasted Connor with his coffee cup. "Correct."

"The knight, according to the inscriptions found in his tomb, took part in the First Crusade to liberate the Holy Land."

"Once again, you are one hundred percent correct. Unfortunately, I can't read the shorthand either and was hoping

DuFour's books contained a key to help me decode the writing, but as you can see, they did not."

"I bet DuFour was thinking the same thing when he arranged for the books in your house to be stolen," said Kim.

Hamilton nodded. "That would be the logical conclusion."

"And why is any of this important to you?" asked Connor.

"Let's call it unfinished family business."

Connor shook his head. "No way. That's not a good enough answer. Although you haven't said it yet, I know you want me to continue helping Ms. Swiftwater. If I'm right, which I know I am, I'm going to need a little more information than that."

Hamilton chewed on his lower lip for a moment. "Connor, for now, you're just going to have to trust me. I'll explain everything after you take those books to an old family friend who might be able to decode them for me."

Connor wanted to reach through the screen and throttle Hamilton, but his slowly budding respect for Kim made him sit back and keep his cool.

"Sir, who is this gentleman you want us to see?" asked Kim.

"The man's name is Professor Barry Keeley. He lives on Clare Island off the west coast of Ireland. His grandfather worked on the dig with my ancestors and should be able to translate the shorthand for us."

Kim narrowed her eyes. "How can you be so sure that he'll be able to read the documents?"

"I've spoken to him several times over the past year, and he agreed to help any way he could. So, before calling you, I sent him a few lines to read, and he translated it as if he were reading English," explained Hamilton.

Connor scratched the stubble on his chin. "If he can read the notes, why didn't you just send him the rest and be done with it?"

"Because he doesn't own an encrypted laptop. So, if you're willing, I'd like you two to fly to Ireland first thing in the morning to meet with Mister Keeley. I'd also feel better knowing the books are in your capable hands."

Connor easily saw through Hamilton's ploy to inflate his ego and let out an irritated sigh. "And what happens if we refuse to help?"

Knox smiled. "I don't believe you're in a position to turn down work. I've seen the balance in your chequing account. Or lack thereof, I should say. You're broke, aren't you?"

Connor resented the intrusion into his private affairs but didn't doubt Knox could easily access his bank account. "Yeah. The last time I checked, I had maybe forty bucks to my name. The Congolese government needed help stopping poachers but could only pay me a pittance of a salary, but I didn't mind. I needed the work and saw the value in it. So, whatever I made, I spread among my team, who got paid next to nothing for sticking their necks out, as well."

Hamilton said, "I'll pay you both one hundred thousand dollars if you see this through to the end."

"That's good enough for me," said Kim without hesitating. "I'm in."

Connor could see he was being painted into a corner. He thought about Kim's niece and knew Kim would do whatever it took to keep her safe. His gut told him that now was the time to walk away, but Connor couldn't. What would Rachel think if he abandoned a person in need? Connor shook his head. "Whatever. Okay, I'm in, too."

Hamilton beamed. "Mister Knox will make all the travel arrangements for you. I look forward to hearing from the two of you tomorrow."

"I'll call you back within the hour," said Knox, just before the screen went black.

Connor sat back in his chair and locked his fingers behind his head.

"Thanks, Connor," said Kim.

"What for?"

"For agreeing to come with me. If you hadn't been at the château, I'd be dead."

"Think nothing of it."

"That's easy for you to say. I'm a thief, not a soldier. I'm not used to people shooting at me."

"Marine," corrected Connor.

"Pardon?"

"The Army has soldiers; the Corps has Marines."

Kim rolled her eyes. "Whatever! You know what I mean."

Connor nodded. "I do. I was just being pedantic."

"Well, drop it, okay? I don't like people who talk that way."

Connor raised his hands in surrender. "Got it. Kim, do you ever get the feeling that Jason has gone fishing and that we're the bait for a much larger fish?"

Kim's lips quirked briefly. "I told you there was more to him than meets the eye."

"Yes, that's what I'm starting to become afraid of."

11.

Vallin tossed a manila file folder on his boss' desk and tapped his foot on the carpet while he waited for him to read what was inside.

DuFour stopped typing on his computer keyboard, flipped open the file, and skimmed over the report. He rubbed his tired eyes and glanced up at Vallin. "I take it you've double-checked your findings?"

"Yes, sir, I did. I ran the images taken by our surveillance cameras through the latest in facial recognition software and was able to identify the people who robbed you last night positively."

DuFour yawned loudly. "And who are they?"

Vallin didn't like his boss' dismissive attitude but continued. "The woman is Kim Swiftwater. I couldn't find much on her other than she's been the suspect in a string of high-profile robberies, but nothing has stuck to her to date. Of note, she's also been seen with Jason Hamilton several times over the past year."

"And the man?"

"Now, this is where things get interesting. The man's name is Connor North. He is a former Captain in the United States Marine Corps, and believe it or not, Jason Hamilton is his former father-in-law. According to reliable sources, North hates Hamilton with every fiber of his body and blames him for the death of his wife."

DuFour steepled his fingers and stared ahead. "Swiftwater, I understand. But North, that's an unexpected move. Maybe Jason is smarter than I thought. Or maybe not. Only time will tell."

"I've seen North's handiwork. He's one hell of a good shot and not someone we should take lightly."

A tired sigh escaped DuFour's lips. "I'll let you worry about North. I have bigger problems to deal with right now."

"Sir, shall I alert the gendarmes to have Swiftwater and North arrested before they can leave the country?"

DuFour wearily shook his head. "Dear God, no. That's the last thing I want. I have a good idea of where they're going next. But just in case they don't go there, please ask your friends in the underworld to keep an eye out for them and let them know that I'll pay top dollar for actionable information. Warn them that I don't want anyone wasting my precious time."

"Yes, sir. Will there be anything else?"

"No, Jean, I'm tired, and there's so much more that needs my attention before I can rest."

Vallin picked up his file and turned to leave.

"Jean."

Vallin hesitated. "Yes, sir."

"I never thanked you last night for your quick thinking. Setting off the fireworks early was a smart move. None of my guests had the slightest idea that something else was happening behind the château. Thank you."

Vallin nodded. "It was the only thing I could think of at the time."

"Keep it up. These next few days will require all the skill and intuitive improvisation we can come up with to help lead us to the greatest prize in all of history."

Vallin wasn't used to his boss speaking to him in such a serious manner. On any other day, it would have been one witticism after another until Vallin lost his temper and stormed out of DuFour's office. He preferred his boss' new demeanor but wished he would take him into his confidence. What did he mean by the greatest prize? Hyperbole or fact? Vallin had no idea, but if there was a threadbare chance that a fortune was waiting to be found, he wanted in on it. After all, retiring to a private island in French Polynesia wouldn't be cheap.

12.

Ireland.

Connor relaxed on a long wooden bench, looking out at the barren hills on Clare Island as their ferry crossed Clew Bay's dark, cold waters. The cold mist from the water splashed on his face, making him wrap a tartan-colored scarf around his neck to keep himself warm. A quick flight from Paris to Dublin, followed by a leisurely drive across Ireland to its west coast, had given Connor the time to unwind after his deadly run-in with DuFour's men.

"What do you think?" asked Kim, holding up a small leprechaun doll with wavy, green hair, wearing an oversized hat on its head.

Connor chuckled. "Where on earth did you get that?"

"While you stood in line to buy us some tea, I picked it up at the gift shop before boarding the ferry. Do you think my niece will like it?"

Connor smiled. "I've never met Tiva, but it looks comical enough. I'm sure she'll like it."

Kim opened a pocket on her dark-blue Gortex jacket and slid the creature inside. "I try to buy Tiva a souvenir each time I go somewhere. I think it helps brighten her world."

"That's a nice thought. You're better at this stuff than I am. I've never given my sister's boys a single thing from Africa. I'll have to do better next time."

"How old are your nephews?"

"Nolan is five, and his younger brother, Owen, is two."

Kim smiled warmly. "I hope they're good kids, not like my sister and I."

"What trouble can a five and two-year-old get up to?"

"You'd be amazed."

"Yes, probably." Connor sat forward and lowered his voice. "Kim, can I ask you a personal question?"

"Sure. What's on your mind?"

"Yesterday, when we spoke to Jason, you were very quick to accept his offer of one hundred K. I understand about your sister and her daughter, but I feel there's more you're holding back."

Kim paused and looked out over the water for a moment before answering. "Connor, have you ever been poor? And I don't mean not being able to afford the latest cellphone or a new, wide-screen TV, but dirt poor?"

Connor shook his head. "No, I can't say I was ever poor. My dad made a decent wage, and I worked every summer as soon as I turned thirteen until I joined the Marines. So, I've always had money."

"Well, I have been, and I hated it. I wasn't lying when I said that my grandparents never had enough money and scraped by living off their meager old-age pensions. My sister and I wore poorly fitting, second-hand clothes and lived in a house on a reserve that should have been condemned years ago. To save money, my grandparents wouldn't turn the furnace on in the middle of winter and only heated the room they were in at the time, so we were always cold. If it weren't for the charity of others, my sister and I wouldn't have had food for lunch at school. Connor, I hated my childhood and never want to live like that again. I don't want my niece to, either."

Connor heard the pain and sadness in Kim's voice and felt terrible for her. "I'm sorry that you had to grow up like that. It sounds awful."

Kim faintly smiled. "It was. But as you like to point out, it's in the past, so let's look to the future, shall we?"

"Agreed."

The ferry started to slow. A handful of people stood on the pier to welcome the boat's occupants. The ferry pilot smoothly docked his ship and switched off its engines as Connor and Kim gathered up their small packs and walked onto the pier.

"Good day, Darcy and Stephanie," called out a short man standing next to a rusty, 1980s, green Austin Mini Cooper. He wore thick glasses on his wrinkled face and had a mop of unkempt, white hair that made him look like Albert Einstein's double.

Connor waved back at the man. They walked over and shook their contact's hand.

"Oh my," said Keeley, with a thick, Irish accent, as he looked up at Kim. "I don't know how I'll ever get the two of you in my car."

Kim smiled. "Don't worry; I've been in tighter places before. I'll get in the back and hold my knees against my chest."

Keeley held open the door as Kim contorted her body onto the back seat. The room on the passenger side for Connor wasn't much better, but thankfully the drive was only three kilometers. Keeley parked next to a rustic-looking cottage with a thatched roof constructed in the seventeenth century. Connor helped Kim climb out of the back of the Mini and then grabbed their packs.

"Welcome to my humble home," said Keeley, unlocking his wooden front door. "Shall I put on a pot of tea?"

"Yes, please," responded Kim right away.

Connor stepped into Keeley's home and was instantly taken aback by the memorabilia adorning the walls. There were pictures of dig sites from all over the world, alongside dozens of small artifacts discovered at some of the locations. Keeley's home reminded Connor of a small but well-furnished museum. His eyes were drawn to a collection of medieval weapons hanging beside the fireplace.

"I see you like my toys," said Keeley.

"Are they real?" asked Connor, admiring an axe.

Keeley shook his head. "No, they're all replicas of some of the weapons I unearthed at a dig in Bannockburn, Scotland, when I was a wee lad in my late teens."

"They look real to me."

"They're supposed to. Now, let's all take a seat next to the fire and warm up after your ride over from the mainland."

Connor turned his attention back to their guest and noticed for a brief second a small, faded tattoo of a medieval-style red cross on the underside of Keeley's right wrist. He thought about asking him what it meant but decided to let it go for now.

Kim and Connor sat in a pair of old rocking chairs while Keeley filled the cups. To help everyone see better in the poorly lit home, Keeley lit an old-fashioned kerosene lamp and placed it on the mantle above the fireplace.

"Thanks," said Kim, sipping her black tea. "It's perfect."

"You're welcome. It's not often that I get a pretty lady for company these days," Keeley said, winking at Kim.

"Their loss," noted Kim with a captivating smile.

Connor opened his pack and hauled out the four journals. "Sir, we were asked to bring these books here to you in the hope you might be able to translate what's written inside of them."

"Yes, Mister Knox called yesterday to let me know you'd be coming, and please call me Barry. Sir sounds so old."

Connor handed over the journals. "We were told that if anyone can decipher these books, it's you."

Keeley opened one of the journals at random and started to read. He closed the book, opened another, and carried on reading. Smiling, Keeley said, "This shouldn't be a problem. It's the same shorthand my grandfather used to record his notes. I read in one of his dairies that years ago, in the Holy Land, he taught Rosemary DuFour how to use the code for her notes, too."

"If you ask me, this is an incredible stroke of good luck finding you," said Kim.

"No. Not really."

"Why not?"

"Because Jason Hamilton tracked me down about ten years ago and paid me to translate two of his books. It's these new ones I've never seen before today."

Kim and Connor exchanged a puzzled look.

Connor raised a hand. "Sir, I mean, Barry, I'm starting to get confused. Jason told us that he couldn't read any of his books because the notes had been recorded in a form of secret shorthand."

Keeley chuckled. "Well, my fine friends, that's because he lied to the two of you. Tell me, does he still introduce Henry Knox as his lawyer?"

"Yes, he does," said Kim.

Connor ground his teeth. How many layers of deceit were there to his ex-father-in-law and his friend?

Keeley shook his head. "Bah! Henry's no more a lawyer than I am a movie star. A better description for Mister Knox would be an obtainer of rare and priceless items for the rich and well-to-do."

"Well, that would explain a lot," observed Connor, wishing Hamilton and Knox were in the room so he could tell them what he thought of them. "An awful lot."

Keeley placed the journals on a small round table next to his feet. "By the looks on your faces, there's a lot you don't know about these two fine gentlemen."

"That's putting it mildly," agreed Connor.

"Let me see. To put things into perspective, Jason Hamilton believes he's descended from one of the founding members of the Knights Templar. This is why he has been after these other journals for nearly a decade. He's what we call a pseudo-archaeologist in my business. He's more interested in the legends surrounding ancient treasures than the actual historical facts."

"I'm starting to feel dirty," said Kim with a shudder. "I hope his money is at least real."

Keeley smiled. "Aye, that it is. He paid me ten thousand Euros in advance to translate these last two journals."

"Someone has a lot of explaining to do the next time we meet," stated Connor, frowning.

Kim placed a hand on her forehead. "Oh God, I think I need a drink."

"There's some whiskey on the dinner table. I think a glass or two may be in order."

"I'll get it," Kim said, getting to her feet.

As Kim walked by, Connor looked at her. "Remember when you told me that Jason Hamilton was nuanced? Oh, he's bloody nuanced, all right."

"Would you mind if I translated the books into Gaelic?" asked Keeley. "I find it helpful to keep the language alive."

"Not at all," replied Connor, turning on a small tape recorder and handing it to Keeley. "We can use an app and translate it back into English at the hotel. Just make sure you speak clearly into the mic."

An hour later, Keeley put down the last book, handed Kim the recorder, and shook his head.

"So, what can you tell us?" asked Kim, leaning expectantly forward in her chair.

Keeley downed his glass of whiskey and faced his guests. "Much of what's written in the journals relates to the day-to-day drudgery of working at a dig site. And that's to be expected, but I found a few tidbits of information I didn't know before tonight."

"Such as?"

Keeley cleared his throat. "How much do you two know about the First Crusade of 1099 that traveled from Europe to liberate the Holy Land?"

"We read what there was online before coming to Ireland," replied Connor. "To be honest, it's not an era I've read much about. I was, however, a little shocked to read about the massacre of Jewish and Muslim civilians after the Crusaders had taken Jerusalem. You won't see that in any of the old, classic, black-and-white movies about the Crusades."

"Sadly, the mass murder of innocent civilians, especially after a long and brutal siege, was common practice by all sides back then."

"Mister Hamilton mentioned something about finding a tomb, possibly related to a dead Templar Knight," said Kim. "Is that true?"

Keeley smiled and nodded. "Yes, it is. The tomb belonged to Sir Henry Wolfe, a devout Christian who left England in 1098 to participate in the First Crusade. He was wounded in battle and lived long enough to witness the founding of the Knights Templar in 1119 at the Temple Mount. Unfortunately, he died a year later and was entombed along with several religious artifacts."

Kim's eyes lit up. "Such as?"

Keeley picked up a book and adjusted his glasses. "Let's see. There's a portion of the true cross, a nail that had been driven through Jesus' feet, and a golden cup that Jesus had drunk from at his last supper."

"Good God, are you telling me they found the Holy Grail?"

Keeley shook his head. "No, not at all. Relics like the ones I've just described were a dime a dozen back then. Even my grandfather acknowledged that in one of his books."

"What was so important about this tomb?" asked Connor.

"Have either of you ever heard of Solomon's Copper Scrolls?"

Kim and Connor shook their heads.

"Between 1946 and 1956, a series of scrolls were discovered in a cave and were called the Dead Sea Scrolls because of where they were found. One of the scrolls was unique because it was written on copper, not papyrus. This scroll is essentially an inventory of gold and silver hidden throughout the Holy Land. To date, no one has found these mythical stashes of gold, and probably never will. However, according to legends dating back to the First Crusade, when Jerusalem was put to the sword, an English knight found a hidden chamber under the Temple Mount containing four copper scrolls. These scrolls allegedly describe in detail where King Solomon's vast riches were hidden before the Egyptians sacked his temple in 926 BCE."

Kim asked, "Are you talking about things like the Ark of the Covenant?"

"Most definitely. And not just the Ark. I'm talking about over two trillion Euros in gold. I'm also talking about religious relics dating back to the Garden of Eden if you believe such a place once existed."

"This is getting interesting," remarked Connor. "And by English knight, you mean Sir Henry Wolfe, don't you?"

Keeley nodded. "Yes, I do."

"So, did Rosemary DuFour find the scrolls when they excavated his tomb?" Kim asked.

"Unfortunately, not." Keeley stood and shuffled over to a wall covered in dusty bookshelves. "Unlike my grandfather, I'm not an expert on the Templars. I can't remember where he wrote it, but my grandfather strongly believed that the scrolls weren't actually scrolls but copper tablets about the size of a hardcover book. He also wrote that the scrolls were taken out of the Holy Land to a Templar castle on the island of Cyprus a few years after Wolfe died."

"And then what happened to them?"

Keeley shrugged. "No one knows for sure. Don't forget this is just a legend; the scrolls may have never existed."

Connor looked into the elderly scholar's pale blue eyes. "I was once told that all legends have a grain of truth in them. Do you believe the copper scrolls once existed?"

Keeley hemmed and hawed for a few seconds. "My grandfather did, so why not? But I can assure you that nothing in any of these journals could point you to the whereabouts of these missing scrolls. None whatsoever."

"So, we're at a dead end," said Kim.

Keeley raised a finger. "Maybe not. I know of a young lady in Germany who might be able to help you."

"Are you sure she's the right person for the job?" asked Connor.

"I don't go in for all these conspiracy theories, but one of my students did, and he couldn't help but go on about this woman morning, noon, and night. I think he said her name was Katarina or something like that. Patrick said she has the most comprehensive electronic library of legends and conspiracies in all of Europe. So, if the scrolls existed at one time, I suppose she'd be the person to ask. But I must warn you; I hear she's a tad bit paranoid of strangers, the government, dogs, chemtrails, well, just about everything."

"Great, a lunatic," said Connor under his breath.

"Professor, do you think she'd be willing to talk with us?" asked Kim.

"Yes. Maybe. I don't know. I'll need to chat with Patrick first."

"Can't we just call this Katarina person direct?" asked Connor.

Keeley shook his head. "Lord, no. These conspiracy people take their anonymity very seriously. Katarina will be the one to decide where and when the meeting will take place, if it does at all. I'll see if Patrick can help you meet her."

Connor got to his feet and stretched out his back. He looked out the window as the sun slowly began to dip below the horizon, painting the sky with pink and golden hues. With night approaching, Connor was happy they'd thought to call ahead and book a couple of rooms at a B&B overlooking the harbor. He was about to suggest they all head into town for a bite to eat when he heard a faint, familiar sound and froze. His breathing slowed as he concentrated on the noise, which grew closer by the second.

Connor spun on his heel and faced his companions. "Barry, what kind of helicopters does Ireland use for search and rescue work?"

"I don't know; they all look alike to me. But I think they're painted red and white. Why do you ask?"

"Barry, douse your lights. We've got company."

Fear filled Kim's eyes. "Connor, what's wrong?"

Connor pointed out the window. "A green BO-105 chopper is coming this way, and I doubt it's packed with tourists."

13.

Keeley hurriedly shuffled around his home, switching off the lights.

"Barry, is there another way out of here other than the back door?" asked Connor, apprehensively watching four men wearing dark combat-style clothing and balaclavas jump out of the helicopter hovering over an open field a hundred yards away. What troubled him more were the MP5 submachine guns the assassins were carrying.

"Yes, but I've never used it." replied the old scholar.

"Where is it?"

"This house used to belong to a smuggler in the 1800s. There's a tunnel that leads from my kitchen to one of the local houses. A pub, I think."

"Barry, listen to me. I want you and Kim to take that tunnel and get help!"

"And just what the hell are you going to do?" demanded Kim.

Connor grabbed a wooden bat with a metal ball covered in spikes from the wall. "My job. Now get going!"

Kim looked into Connor's eyes. She wanted to say something but turned, grabbed Keeley's hand, and ran into the kitchen. Keeley dragged his table aside and knelt to yank an old rug aside, exposing a trapdoor. Keeley struggled to lift the door, and Kim jumped in to help. She picked up an old silver flashlight and shone it down into the tunnel. Thankfully, there was a sturdy-looking ladder leading down into the darkened shaft. Kim gave Keeley a hand to steady himself as he climbed down the ladder. She turned and gave a quick wave at Connor before joining Keeley.

"Hey, you in the house," yelled a man with a Hispanic accent outside the cottage. "Come out with your hands on your heads, and no one will get harmed."

"How original," quipped Connor.

"Don't be stupid, man. Come on out!"

Connor crept to the front door and got down on one knee. He gripped his medieval weapon tight in his right hand. He had one chance to get out of the cottage alive, and he knew it. Connor held his breath as the doorknob inches from his face started to turn. The familiar mix of fear and adrenaline surged through his body. The door creaked as it was slowly pushed open. Connor saw the barrel of an MP5 appear and tensed.

"This is your last warning!" yelled the Latino team leader, activating a slender flashlight attached to his submachine gun. "Give yourselves up, or pay the consequences." The intruder stepped into the cottage and shone his light all around, trying to find his quarry.

Like a coiled viper, Connor struck. He brought his club down with all his might onto the man's right arm, easily shattering the bones in his forearm. The assassin cried out in pain and dropped his MP5. Connor pivoted and smashed his weapon into the wounded man's closest knee, crushing the bone and muscles to a pulp. A pained moan escaped the intruder's lips as he tumbled to the floor. In a flash, Connor dropped his club, scooped up the dropped SMG, and fired a burst out the door, hoping to wound or at least pin down the other assailants. Then, for good measure, he smashed an elbow into the injured man's face, knocking him out cold. Connor hurriedly helped himself to the man's extra ammunition and two stun grenades.

Crack!

Connor spun and saw shattered glass falling to the floor. He didn't have to be told what was about to happen next. He instantly threw himself flat on the floor and covered his ears. Two flash-bang grenades went off a split second later. A blinding light lit up the tiny hovel. The blast from the grenades knocked pictures and memorabilia from the walls. The lamp above the fireplace fell and shattered on the floor, leaking kerosene. A fire burst out in seconds and quickly spread to a packed bookshelf, setting it alight.

Intended to disorient a person, the grenades were wasted on a man as well-trained as North. He quickly rolled over, aimed his MP5 at the door, and waited. A heartbeat later, a man kicked in the door and went to rush inside, only to be cut down by a hail of bullets.

Connor jumped to his feet and ran for the smoke-filled kitchen. When Connor was mere feet from the trapdoor, he dropped down like a baseball player sliding into home and vanished into the darkness. Connor landed on the cold, rocky ground and was relieved to see that he'd made it this far in one piece. He turned around and yanked the ladder away, letting it fall. Above him, he could hear voices calling out and see the smoke and flames from the growing fire. Connor knew that it wouldn't take them long to figure out where he had gone. He moved his light up and down the tunnel, looking for something he could make into a bomb. Unfortunately, aside from a couple of dusty old wooden boxes, the passageway was empty.

From above came the sound of something rolling across the floor.

The hair on the back of Connor's neck shot straight up. He spun on his heel and sprinted down the tunnel just as a fragmentation grenade fell to the ground. In less than a heartbeat, the grenade exploded, sending thousands of razor-sharp metal shards hurtling through the air.

"What the hell was that?" asked Keeley, struggling to catch his breath.

"A grenade, I think," replied Kim, helping the aged scholar to remain on his feet.

"That doesn't sound good."

"No, it does not."

They turned a sharp corner and almost ran into a ladder leading up to another trapdoor.

"Catch your breath while I take a look," said Kim, shining her light up at the closed door. She passed the light to Keeley and climbed up the creaky wooden ladder. She heard music and laughter and took it as a good sign. At the top, Kim reached for an old padlock, barring their escape.

"Oh my," said Keeley, shining the flashlight on the lock. "I didn't expect that."

"Don't worry. I came prepared," Kim said, extracting her lock-picking tools from a pouch around her waist. She slipped the slender metal sticks inside the padlock and activated the tumbler, quickly opening the rusty lock. Kim tossed the padlock to the floor, climbed up the last rungs on the ladder, and pushed the trapdoor with her shoulder. With a loud creak, the door rose, and light from above flooded the tunnel.

"Oy, what the bloody hell is going on?" demanded a surprised bartender, looking at Kim's smudged face.

"Is that you, Liam?" called out Keeley.

"Barry?"

Keeley waved up at his friend. "'Tis I, as I live and breathe."

"What the heck are you doing down there?"

Kim climbed up into the pub and turned to help Keeley.

"It's a long story," said Keeley, slowly making his way up the rickety ladder. "But dial 9-9-9 and tell the Garda to go to my place ASAP."

Liam dug out his cell phone. "Why does the Garda need to go to your house?"

"Because there are four armed men there."

The ringing in Connor's ears wouldn't stop. He went to take in a deep breath to clear the fog in his mind and moaned. His chest felt as if a horse had kicked it. A dust cloud filled the air, making it hard for Connor to see.

A burst of automatic gunfire near his feet was all the incentive he needed to get to his feet. Disoriented, Connor looked like a drunk staggering home from the bar as he swayed back and forth down the passageway. He hadn't gone more than a few yards when he heard the sound of a man landing on the rocky ground. Connor looked back but couldn't see anything through the haze. Just to be careful, he emptied what was left in his MP5's magazine into the dust cloud and then switched magazines.

"Jesus, that sounded like gunfire," said Liam, staring into the tunnel.

"It was," replied Kim. "Please tell me you have a gun?"

"This isn't America, lass. Not everyone is armed in Ireland."

"I'm not American!" Kim's patience instantly evaporated. "*Do you, or don't you have a damned gun?*"

"Aye, I have a shotgun in the back but haven't used it in years."

"Get it! And be quick."

Liam nodded and hurried off to retrieve his shotgun, closely followed by Kim, leaving Keeley and a handful of interested pub onlookers staring at the open trapdoor.

Connor fought to catch his breath. Each breath he took felt like fire in his lungs. Connor was sure he'd bruised or broken a couple of ribs when the grenade had sent him flying. He glanced over his shoulder, half-expecting a man standing there, but so far, whoever was left was keeping their distance. Then, finally, Connor turned a corner and saw a ladder and light shining down from above like a welcoming beacon. In an instant, his spirits lifted, and he ignored the pain and started to jog for the ladder and safety.

"Stop where you are!" yelled a man from behind with a Scottish accent.

Connor swore and came to a halt.

"Drop your weapon and then turn around with your hands in the air. And don't try anything stupid. I couldn't possibly miss from here."

Connor let his MP5 drop to his feet and raised his arms. He gritted his teeth and begrudgingly turned to face his opponent. The gunman was slightly shorter but stockier than Connor. "Okay, you got me. Now what?"

"The book translations. I know you have them. Now, give them to me?"

Connor stalled, trying to buy time to think of a way out of his dilemma. "I have no idea what you're talking about. What translations?"

The man fired off a shot that echoed down the passageway. "Don't play dumb, Mister North. I know you came here with several books that didn't belong to you so you could get them translated. You've had plenty of time to get the job done. So, hand over the translated copies, or I'll be forced to kill you!"

"Oh, those translations," Connor replied theatrically. "I'm sorry, but you'll have to forgive me. I don't have them on me."

"Then who does?"

"No one. They're back in Professor Keeley's home on a table next to the fire. That's if they aren't incinerated along with the rest of his cottage by now."

The gunman raised his MP5 to his shoulder. "You're lying. You wouldn't leave them behind. Who has them? I'll give you a count of five before I shoot you in the right knee. Then, if you still won't tell me, it's on to your left knee and your groin. You'll soon be begging me to kill you, but I won't, at least not until I have the translations."

"No, wait!" called out Keeley from above. "I have what you're looking for. Give me a few seconds to climb down the ladder, as I'm not as young and spry as I used to be."

"Quit flapping yer lips and get down here, old man."

Connor heard Keeley slowly climbing down the creaky ladder until his feet touched the hard, rocky ground. "I'm here. Let the American lad go, and I'll give you what you want."

The assassin snorted. "I don't think so. Give me what I want, and I'll think about only kneecapping the bastard."

Keeley struggled to swallow and glanced apprehensively at Connor and then at the gunman. "There's only one slight problem. I lied. I don't have the translations. Ms. Swiftwater does."

"Who?"

"Me," said Kim, standing ten yards behind the shooter. "Now, it's your turn to drop your weapon."

The assassin snarled like a trapped animal, pivoted on his heels, and opened fire, as did Kim. Surprised by her opponent's sudden move, Kim fired both barrels of her shotgun. The first blast of buckshot flew right over the man's head. His luck ended when the second shot of fifty tiny balls struck him in the right shoulder, sending him flying onto his back.

Connor leaped at the gunman's weapons and tossed them aside before slamming his knee onto the assassin's neck. "Who sent you?" he growled.

"Screw you," the man defiantly replied.

Connor pressed harder. "A name. Give me a name, or I'll break your neck."

Surprisingly, the man smiled and then bit down on one of his back molars, releasing a deadly poison into his mouth.

Connor cursed and pulled his leg off the dying man's neck. White foam spilled out of the gunman's mouth for a few horrible seconds as his body convulsed violently. Connor got a whiff of almonds in the air and stepped back. "Cyanide! What would make someone take cyanide rather than be arrested by the Irish police?"

Kim tossed Liam's antiquated shotgun on the floor and slid to the ground. She pulled her knees to her chest and fought back the tears. "My God, who were these people?"

Connor walked over and sat beside Kim. "I have no idea. But I bet Jason and Knox do."

Kim held up a shaking hand. "Look at me. I'm a wreck. I've never had to shoot anyone in my life. Thankfully, the pub owner's gun was similar to my grandfather's one at home, or I would never have known one end from the other."

Connor took Kim's hand in his and gave it a gentle squeeze. "And speaking of that. Thanks for saving my life."

"I figured I owed it to you."

Connor looked back down the darkened tunnel and smelled smoke. "How the heck did you get in here?"

"I asked Barry to stall the gunman while I ran next door to an old church and got in the tunnel that way. It would appear that this place is absolutely riddled with tunnels."

Connor let go of Kim's hand. He shook his head at Kim's ingenuity and bravery. "Good thinking. Crazy, but good."

"Thanks, I think." Kim tilted her head. "Connor, how did you know to ask Professor Keeley if there was another way out of his house?"

Connor's lips quirked. "I knew running wasn't an option with Keeley. Besides, while I was waiting in line for our tea, I read a tourist brochure that said the island used to be a haven for smugglers and put two and two together."

"Thank God Keeley's home was connected to these tunnels, or we'd all be dead."

"Oy, Barry, the Garda's here," yelled Liam.

The elderly scholar placed a hand on Connor's shoulder. "These are my people, so let me do all the talking. All right?"

Connor was in no position to argue. "Feel free. Ms. Swiftwater and I will be in the pub. She can get plastered while I speak with a mutual acquaintance and try to get the truth out of him for once."

14.

It was more than an hour before Professor Keeley took a seat next to Kim and Connor at the back of the empty pub. The rest of the patrons had long since gone to spread gossip far and wide. Outside, the small local fire department was still sifting through the embers of Keeley's old home. Keeley said, "Sergeant Ryan says that a forensic team and a detective are on their way over from the mainland to take statements from the three of us."

Connor glanced at the white-haired police officer chatting with Liam, the pub owner. "Barry, are you telling us that there's just one policeman on the entire island?"

"Aye, that's right. Ryan's been here with us for about fifteen years now. He's plenty enough. After all, there are only one hundred and sixty people on the island. Until tonight, the worst crime ever committed on the island in the last fifty years involved a couple of drunken Norwegian students who came over here on Saint Patrick's Day and got absolutely sloshed. The fools ended up painting themselves green and ran around naked until poor old Ryan could catch them."

Kim smirked and shook her head. "That's quite some story."

"I know, but it's true."

"Barry, we're sorry about what happened to your house," said Connor. "You can replace a home, but you can never replace your memories."

"Don't worry about that. Last summer, Patrick, the boy I told you about, lived with me for a few weeks while he recorded all of my family's books and journals for his thesis. He even scanned my pictures, too. I may not have the originals, but my past isn't lost, either."

"That's a relief."

Kim leaned forward and said just above a whisper. "So, what did you tell Sergeant Ryan about us and what happened at your home tonight?"

"I told him your cover story that you're a couple of amateur archaeologists who were looking for information on a dig I did in Borneo in 2002."

"Amateur archaeologists, okay, but how are you going to explain away the dead bodies? I'm sure this will be all over the news in the morning."

"That's simple. I told Ryan the men were looking for an old conquistador map I found in the Andes back in the 1980s. And when I told them I didn't have it, they threatened to kill all of us. Luckily for me, Connor jumped into action and saved all our lives."

Kim shot back the rest of the Scotch in her glass and examined Keeley's face. The man looked like he was enjoying their predicament. "I'll give you this, professor; you're good at spinning tall tales."

"Not me. All the credit belongs to Knox. When he created your new aliases, he made sure that each of you had a believable backstory. As did I in case something happened like last night."

"Yes, I read our backstories coming over here on the ferry. I'm a professor of Native Studies, and Connor is a retired soldier, but I know the police; they're going to want answers. And the last thing I want is for them to see through our aliases and start digging into my past."

Connor's phone buzzed. He looked and saw there was a text from Knox. "Let's hope Henry and Jason have devised a workable plan."

"God, I hope so," said Kim, reaching for another glass of Scotch. She sat in silence while Connor spoke on the phone for a good five minutes.

"Okay," said Connor, laying his phone on the table. "Here's the skinny. Knox has hired a lawyer from Dublin who is already on her way here. He said we're to cooperate with the local police until our lawyer arrives. After that, Miss O'Donnell will become our point of contact with the police."

"That means she'll be here around nine forty-five tomorrow morning," said Keeley.

"I don't like this one bit," said Kim. "I'm used to working in the shadows. The last thing I need is for my picture to be plastered all over the newspapers. I'll never get another job after that."

"It may not have to come to that," replied Keeley cryptically.

Sergeant Ryan walked over and brought his right hand to the brim of his cap. "Evening, all. May I join the three of you at your table?"

Connor looked up and spotted a tattoo identical to Keeley's on the sergeant's wrist. He shook his head and pushed out a chair with his foot. "Please come join us, Sergeant."

Ryan sat and looked through his notes for a few seconds before placing his book on the table. "Mister and Ms. Wright, Barry tells me that you've had quite the evening."

"It's one I'll never forget," said Kim honestly.

"Nor I," added Connor.

"It may be a bit premature, but I'd like to thank you both on behalf of all the citizens of Clare Island for saving Barry's life and stopping four possible terrorists."

Connor cleared his throat. "I'm sorry, but did you say terrorists?"

"Aye. The word out of Dublin is that the crime scene has been declared level three, which means it's one of national interest. One of the dead men in Barry's home is from the FARC guerilla group."

"Who are they?" asked Kim.

"They're a Columbian anti-government faction who are also known for their narco-terrorism," explained Connor.

"Aye, that's right. But they've also branched off into looting antiquities, and it was Barry's map that made me suspicious," explained Ryan. "So, I took one of the dead man's prints and forwarded them to Dublin, and in less than a minute, they had a match. I'm still not sure who the other three are, but we'll figure out their identities soon enough."

"What does level three mean to my brother and me?" queried Kim.

"Because terrorists are involved, your identities will have to remain secret to protect you and Barry from retaliation."

Connor watched Kim suppress a smile. "Thank you, that's a load off our minds," he said.

Ryan's phone rang. He picked it up and got to his feet. A said a few words in Gaelic and then hung up. "It looks like the forensic team is about to land near what's left of Barry's home, so I'd best be off. And please don't leave the island until I've had the chance to get statements from the two of you."

"We wouldn't dream of it, Sergeant," said Connor.

Ryan ambled off to greet the incoming chopper, leaving the pub in silence.

"For the love of God," blurted out Kim. "Whoever that dead guerilla is, he's done us a bigger favor than he possibly could have imagined."

"The Lord moves in mysterious ways," observed Keeley.

Connor dug out his phone and dialed a number.

"Who are you calling?" Kim asked.

"Knox."

"Why?"

"Because he and Jason lied to us, and if they want us to continue with this assignment, it's going to cost them a lot more than 100K for our services. So, let's say 250K, a piece."

The next three days were mainly spent in Dublin in witness protection. At the same time, Miss O'Donnell did her best to keep the police from bothering Kim and Connor. Realizing that they knew next to nothing about the Crusades and the Templars, they searched the Internet for information. Most of their time was spent trying to separate fact from fiction.

Connor couldn't help but notice how focused Kim had become since they left the island. It was as if she was a new woman. Gone were her fears and apprehensions, replaced by a dogged determination to find the truth. He chalked it up to the rough life she had lived as a child. There was no room for pity, not in Kim's world. Connor's phone buzzed. He answered the call and reached for a pen and paper to jot down some notes.

"What gives?" Kim asked.

Connor slid his phone away. "That was Miss O'Donnell, and she said the Garda have all they need from us. They've closed the books and declared our actions to be self-defense. Oh, and we're free to go."

"Phew, that's good news. So, I take it we're off to Germany next?"

Connor looked into Kim's mahogany-brown eyes. "Yes, but it doesn't have to be. I'd understand if you've had enough and want to go home before anything else happens."

Kim shook her head. "No, not now. Not after what we've been through; I want to see where this is leading us. Don't you?"

"I'm here because I made a deal to look after you." Connor paused and then said. "Kim, there's no shame in admitting that we're in over our heads."

"But we're not. Besides, a quarter of a million dollars is quite the incentive."

Connor sat back in his chair. "Think back to the island. Didn't you think it a bit odd that Keeley had the perfect cover story or that Sergeant Ryan of the Garda was able to take the prints off a dead man whose body had been burnt to a crisp in the fire and then send those very same prints to his headquarters in Dublin? Because he'd have to be some kind of miracle worker to do that. Frankly, Ryan struck me as the kind of man who wouldn't have bothered to lift a finger before the forensic team arrived to take charge of the crime scene."

Kim furrowed her brow. "Well, when you put it like that, yes, it does seem a little too convenient. But didn't Keeley say Knox gave him a cover story in case anything happened?"

"Please, it's obvious that Knox and Keeley suspected someone would be coming."

"Then why didn't they warn us?"

"A good question. Also, did you happen to notice that Keeley and Ryan had the exact same tattoo on their wrists?"

Kim thought for a second and then shook her head. "Sorry. No, I didn't."

"Something stinks about this assignment. There are forces at work here that prefer to stay in the shadows like yourself. I have no idea who they are or whom they represent, but my gut tells me things can only get tougher from here on out, and I don't see any reason why you should get hurt."

Kim's eyes widened. "So, behind all of that macho posturing, there's a man who cares. That's nice to know."

"I've said it once, and I'll say it again, I'm here to protect you, but money isn't everything. You can't spend it on you or your niece if you're dead."

"Connor, this isn't about money anymore. It's about the truth, and I want to find out what that is. Don't you?"

Connor saw the determined look in Kim's eyes. With or without him, Kim was going to see this through to the end. He exhaled. "Germany it is, then."

"Excellent."

"But before we go, we need to get back in touch with Yuri."

"Why?"

"Because he's going to go shopping for us."

"Shopping?"

"Yeah, and whether he wants to or not, Jason's going to pay for everything."

15.

France

Rene DuFour returned from his early morning ride feeling refreshed. He strode up the stairs to his house, ready to start a new day, when the front doors opened, and DuFour's butler walked out, ramrod-straight, holding a silver tray in his right hand.

"Sir, a gentleman is waiting to speak to you in the drawing room," said the butler.

"Did he give you a name or a reason for his visit?" asked DuFour.

"No, sir. He only gave me his card."

DuFour picked up a business card from the tray and read it. There wasn't a name, only the word *Emissary* on the gold and red card. DuFour's guts instantly turned to water. He had never met the head of his order, but he was reaching out to DuFour through a messenger, which was never good news. Nevertheless, DuFour put on a good poker face to mask his true emotions and returned the card to the tray. "Phillippe, please have some coffee sent to the drawing room for my guest and me. And then ensure that we're not disturbed under any circumstances."

Phillipe nodded. "Very good, sir."

DuFour strode inside, dropping his riding crop and leather helmet in a basket. He checked himself out in a hall mirror, took a deep breath, and opened the doors to his drawing room. He spotted a short, slim man with his back to him, checking out the rows of books on a far wall. DuFour brought up a hand to his lips and pretended to cough. The man turned around and smiled.

"Please forgive me. I couldn't help; your bookcase is packed with such an exquisite collection of rare nineteenth and eighteenth-century literature," said the man.

"Thank you. My family has been collecting first editions for centuries. How may I help you, Monsieur—?"

"Sorensen, Peter Sorensen," said the man, extending his hand in greeting. Sorensen spoke French with just the hint of a Swedish accent.

"Rene DuFour," he said firmly, shaking the emissary's hand.

There was a knock at the door.

"Come," called out DuFour.

Phillipe walked inside and placed the coffee down on a side table. He bowed slightly before exiting the room.

DuFour picked up a silver pot and poured himself a coffee. He looked at Sorensen and said, "May I offer you a cup of coffee?"

Sorensen raised a hand. "No, thank you. I'm a busy man. Our discussion won't take long."

"Very well. Do you mind if I sit?"

Sorensen shook his head. "Not at all."

DuFour sat and sipped his coffee, waiting for his world to shatter.

Sorensen's voice turned ice cold. "Monsieur DuFour, the leader of our order has asked me to convey his deep displeasure at your recent failure in Ireland. An organization like ours can not afford to have such monumental failures in the future if we wish to remain anonymous. Would you not agree?"

"Yes. But I can explain."

Sorensen raised a hand. "There is nothing to explain. In the eyes of your leader, you have failed. No amount of backtracking will erase your fiasco."

Dufour meekly nodded. "Yes, I'm sorry. It won't happen again."

"It had better not. Remember, we chose you because we saw a spark of potential in you. Don't make The Order regret ever bringing you into their trust."

DuFour stood. "You won't. I promise."

Sorensen looked DuFour in the eyes. "We have kept the peace between ourselves and the other orders for centuries, but things are changing. The world is slowly shifting from one of order into anarchy, and we cannot allow that to happen, at least not without taking advantage of it."

"Yes, I agree wholeheartedly."

"You sold your plan to the council; now, make it happen, or be prepared to face the consequences."

A chill ran down DuFour's spine. He knew full well what failure meant: a slow and painful death as a warning to others that failure would not be tolerated. "I'll get things back on track."

"You had better. With Keeley laying low somewhere in the United States and his home a smoldering wreck, you had the best focus your efforts on locating Swiftwater and North before they succeed in making you look like a fool again."

"Please let our leader know that he has nothing to worry about. Everything that he has ever dreamed about will soon be his."

"I'll do no such thing. You can when you have succeeded in your mission. Or, you can explain to his face why you failed before a pack of starving dogs rips you apart."

DuFour's mouth went drier than the Sahara Desert. He couldn't speak, so he nodded and looked away.

"I'll see myself out," said Sorensen, leaving DuFour to crumble back into his chair.

For nearly a minute, Dufour didn't know whether to scream in anger or empty his stomach on the carpet in fear. Finally, his indecision ended when Vallin opened the doors and walked into the room.

"Who was that man?" demanded Vallin. "He wasn't on any of today's guest lists."

DuFour got to his feet and saw he was shaking. He strode to a liquor cabinet and poured himself a stiff drink of brandy. DuFour emptied the snifter in one gulp and savored the burn as the amber liquid slid down his throat. He quickly filled his snifter again.

"Sir, what's wrong? You look like hell."

"I'm sorry, Jean; I should have brought you into the picture long ago."

"Did that man threaten you?"

DuFour took another deep drink. "Yes and no."

"Does this have to do with the robbery?"

DuFour nodded. Wearily, he said, "That and so much more."

Vallin walked close. "Sir, no more games. No more riddles. If you don't tell me what you've gotten yourself into, I can't help."

"Jean, before I tell you, do you have contacts all across Europe that you can trust?"

"Yes, of course I do. Why?"

"Because I need to know Kim Swiftwater and Connor North's whereabouts, and I need to know now."

16.

Germany

Kim and Connor flew separately to avoid drawing attention to themselves and checked into a hotel Keeley had recommended. They ordered some room service and waited in Connor's room for Yuri to appear. They didn't have to wait long when a knock came on the door thirty minutes later. Connor warily checked who was there before opening the locks. The black-market dealer Yuri walked in carrying a suitcase, looking like he'd been on the go for a week.

"You two do get around," observed Yuri, tossing the suitcase on Connor's bed. He undid the lock and flipped it open. "Voilà, I managed to obtain everything—and then some—from your shopping list."

Connor grinned as he examined the merchandise. Everything he'd requested was all there. From the latest GPS watches to radio earpieces and contact lenses with a camera built into them, along with slender, liquid, body-armor vests, ceramic blades, and thermal cameras.

"How does this watch work?" asked Kim, examining a timepiece.

"Whatever you do, don't press the large, black button on the side of the watch, or you'll activate a GPS tracking device," explained Connor. "Should we ever get separated and run into trouble, all we have to do is activate the GPS tracking device, and the other person will know where they are anywhere in the world."

"That's handy."

Connor winked. "I know. That's why I asked for them."

Kim turned the utilitarian-looking watch over in her hand. "It looks like a man's watch. I don't suppose there are ones designed for women?"

"Sorry," said Yuri. "I'm sure there are, but this shopping trip was kind of short notice, so one size fits all today."

"It'll have to do," she said, slipping it over her hand and onto her wrist. "You never know. I might get used to it."

Yuri popped open a small, black container and held it in his hand. "The camera in this contact lens is the best on the market and has a range of five kilometers. It's been made to look like one of Ms. Swiftwater's dark brown eyes. So, Mister North will be able to see everything you see on the tablet I provided you."

Connor picked up the tablet and turned it on. He chuckled when he saw his face on the screen. "Neat trick."

"*Da.* As all of these toys cost a lot of money, would you happen to know if any of the equipment I gave you back in Paris is still there?"

"Yes, it's in the second safe house," replied Kim. "We didn't use much, so most of it should still be there."

"Good, I hate throwing money away."

"Yes," said Connor. "I've noticed that."

"Look, I don't know what you two are up to here in Germany, but be careful. I've seen some stuff about you on the Dark Web that makes my skin crawl. You should be aware that there's a price on your heads, so be wary, as I can't have two of my best new clients dropping dead on me."

"Swell," huffed Connor. "Do you know who's looking for us?"

Yuri shook his head. "Not by name; most of the business done on the Dark Web is anonymous, but if I were you, I'd put my money on Rene DuFour."

"Great," Connor muttered.

"If there's nothing else left to discuss, I must be on my way, as I have a lady friend waiting for me back at my hotel."

"Thanks for sharing," quipped Kim. "But you still haven't told us when or where we're going to meet Keeley's contact."

"Sorry about that," he responded, handing Kim a note. "Mister Keeley called yesterday and said you're to go downstairs to the hotel restaurant at precisely 0815 tomorrow morning, where you will be met by some of Katarina's people."

"Is that it?" Connor asked.

"It is. If that's all there is to discuss, all I can say is good luck," said Yuri, exiting the room.

Connor picked up a ceramic knife and ran his thumb lightly over its razor-sharp edge. "So, Kim, I know I ask this twice a day, but are you sure you still want to go on with this?"

Kim let out an exasperated sigh. "Quit asking, and that's an order, Captain. There's no way in hell that I'm turning back now. These thugs don't scare me."

"They should." Connor tossed the blade aside and examined a subcompact stun gun. "I'd feel better if I had the real thing."

"Like the French, I doubt the German authorities would be too pleased if you ran around the countryside, armed to the teeth."

"To hell with them. The deeper we go into this mystery, the more I wish I was armed."

The following day, Kim and Connor woke early and met outside the elevator.

"You're early; it's only 0812," said Connor, showing Kim his watch.

"Stop it," she scolded. "As a former Marine, I thought punctuality was a must for you."

Connor pressed the call button. "There are only retired Marines. No one is ever a former Marine."

Kim shook her head. "If you keep that up, it's going to be a really long day."

The elevator chimed, and the doors slid open. Kim and Connor walked inside and pressed the button for the lobby.

"I don't know about you, but I'm getting nervous," said Kim.

"I'm more curious than nervous," replied Connor, waiting for the elevator to stop. But it didn't. Instead of landing on the ground floor, it continued into the basement. Instantly, the hair on the back of Connor's neck stood straight up.

"What the hell?" said Kim, frantically pressing the open-door button.

"Get behind me," warned Connor, drawing the ceramic knife from behind his back.

The elevator slowed and came to a stop. A second later, the doors slid open, and Connor found himself confronted by three men armed with pistols and wearing dark face masks.

"Drop the knife, or you're a dead man," warned one of the black-clad men in German-accented English.

Connor clenched his hand tight around his blade. If Kim hadn't been with him, he might have tried to fight his way out, but that wasn't an option today. He swore and tossed the knife on the ground.

"Hands up and walk out slowly!" ordered the team leader.

Connor warily walked out with Kim right behind him.

"Over to the van."

Connor glanced over at a battered Volkswagen van with its side door wide open.

"Nice trick with the elevator," said Connor, playing for time.

"It was quite easy to do. Now shut up and get in the van."

Connor and Kim climbed into the back of the vehicle and sat down. "Now what?" asked Connor.

"This," said the man, holding a pair of dark hoods.

"No way!" objected Connor. "This wasn't part of the deal."

The man shrugged. "Suit yourself. No mask, no Katarina. Those are the rules."

"Let's do as he says," urged Kim. "I mean, after all, we've come this far. So, why turn back now?"

"How do you know we can trust them?"

"If we had wanted you dead, your bodies would be on the floor of the elevator, Mister North," said the leader.

Connor hesitated. The thought of wearing a bag over his head like a hostage went against all of his training and instincts.

"Please," said Kim, reaching for one of the hoods.

Connor let out his breath through his teeth and reluctantly took one. He was far from claustrophobic but didn't enjoy not being able to see. He heard the vehicle start and then begin to move. Connor pressed his back against the side of the van and wondered where their contacts were taking them. He felt Kim move beside him and was surprised when she took his right hand in hers. Maybe she wasn't as tough as she pretended to be. He squeezed her hand and prayed that they hadn't just made the worst decision of their lives.

Connor had no way to be sure, but it seemed they had been driving for an hour when the van stopped, and the driver switched off the engine. The side door slid open, and fresh air wafted inside the vehicle.

"Please let me help you out," said a woman, offering a hand to help Kim and Connor get out of the van and onto their feet. "Ms. Swiftwater, please hold my hand, and I will guide you. Mister North, place your hand on your partner's shoulder, and you won't get lost."

Connor gently reached out, touched Kim's shoulder, and rested his hand.

"Let's go," ordered the woman.

As infuriating as it was, Connor kept his mouth shut and trailed behind Kim. He heard a meal door swinging open and suspected they were going underground.

A split second later, their guide said, "We're approaching a staircase. We will go slowly; please be careful."

It didn't take long for them to reach the landing. They walked for about a minute more before stopping. There was the sound of another heavy door opening.

"Please step inside," said the woman.

They took a few more paces and stopped. Behind them, the door swung closed with a metallic clang. The guards yanked off their hoods and tossed them to one side.

Connor blinked to adjust his eyes to the bright surroundings. They were inside a vast, concrete room packed with dozens of computers and television screens. Four black-clad young people sat behind computers; the rest seemed to be running automatically.

A chair swung around, and a slim woman in her late thirties with short, curly, blonde hair, silver-rimmed glasses, and a black-leather outfit smiled at Kim and Connor. "Good morning, Ms. Swiftwater and Mister North. Please let me introduce myself. My name is Katarina Shulman, but you can call me Kat. What do you think of my fortress of solitude?"

"It's something else, that's for sure," said Kim.

Connor raised an eyebrow at their host's obvious theatrics.

Kat got to her feet and unhurriedly walked toward her guests. "Professor Keeley, through Patrick Moran, told me you're seeking information. Is this correct?"

"Yes," said Connor, with an abrupt nod.

"And what kind of information might that be?"

"Our situation is quite complicated," explained Kim.

"That's all right. I like complicated."

"Okay, here goes. We're seeking information on four copper scrolls allegedly found under the Temple Mount during the First Crusade. We believe they may have been moved out of the Holy

Land for safekeeping sometime after the founding of the Templar Knights but have never been seen again."

Instead of offering her hands in greeting, Kat steepled them. "That's almost word for word what Professor Keeley said you would say. So, I must ask you this: why do you seek this information? Is it for glory, riches, or some other pursuit?"

Kim held her head up high. "For the truth. We're searching for the truth."

"The truth. How noble of you. Now, Ms. Swiftwater, what would you and your partner do if the scrolls were real?"

Kim looked over at Connor and then back at Kat. "I don't know. I haven't really thought that far ahead yet."

Kat laughed. "The precious few people I have allowed in here have all tried to BS their way past me, and all of them left without getting any information whatsoever. But you, you're different, Ms. Swiftwater. I admire your honesty."

"Kim, please call me Kim."

"As for you, Mister North, I would appreciate it if you gave one of my colleagues the weapon you have hidden under the sleeve of your right arm. I dislike violence."

Connor slowly withdrew a small Taser. "Sorry, you never can be too cautious."

"I agree."

Connor handed the Taser to the closest black-clad person and faced this host. "What sharp eyes you have, Kat."

"Not at all. I watched you on our CCTVs, noticed you fidgeting, and deduced you had a concealed weapon."

"Good for you, Sherlock," Connor muttered.

"Oh, by the way, please say hello to Patrick Moran."

The young man holding Connor's Taser waved. "*Guten tag*," said the man with a German accent.

Connor narrowed his gaze. "You're not Irish, are you?"

The man laughed. "Not one bit. Professor Keeley knew that when we met. But I needed an airtight story to explain why I was at his house, so we concocted Patrick Moran, a student from the University of Galway. It worked so well that I became Karl Gustav in Sweden and Keanu Williams in California."

"So, Keeley's one of you?" Kim asked Kat.

"Not really," said Kat. "He's more like an ally."

"It seems there's more to the eye about Professor Keeley than I had imagined," said Connor. "Then again. I've yet to meet someone who's told me the whole truth since I left Africa."

Kat smiled. "Welcome to my world, Mister North."

"Secrets and lies," said Connor, glancing back at the dozens of screens and shaking his head. "I should have anticipated a person like you would surround himself with the latest surveillance technology."

Kat raised an eyebrow. "What do you mean when you say a person like me?"

Connor was about to call Kat paranoid when Kim slid in front of him. "Connor didn't mean anything. It was just a slip of the tongue. My friend's tired from all the traveling we've been doing."

Kat shrugged. "Whatever. You, I like. Him not so much."

Kim shot Connor a disapproving look and turned to face their host. "Kat, can you help us?"

Kat tapped her right foot on the floor for a few seconds and then snapped her fingers. "Heike, be a dear and show our guests what you have found about the Templars and the four copper scrolls."

A young woman sitting behind a computer screen with a dozen earrings in each ear gave Kat a thumbs-up and started typing on her keyboard.

"Kat, while we wait for an answer, would you mind if I asked you a personal question?" Kim asked.

"That depends on the question."

"What are you doing down here, and why all the secrecy?"

Kat grinned. "Aside from researching esoteric material for a fee, my fellow cyberwarriors and I try to level an increasingly unlevel playing field. You may think I'm mentally unbalanced, maybe even a little psychotic, but the world isn't truly run by governments these days. Anonymous actors and corporations using the Dark Web have made it hard for people who genuinely care for their people to succeed anymore. Take the recent invasion of Georgia, for example. The people there did nothing to provoke an attack, but the recent discovery of billions of dollars of natural gas stirred their neighbor into action. So, my friends and I ensured the attacking force's computers and communications gear failed on the second day of the war and were spectacularly defeated. This is what we do, Kim."

Kim shook her head. "That's amazing."

"And that is why secrecy must be maintained at all times. If word ever got out where we were, a kill team would descend upon this site and murder every last one of us."

"Kat, you mentioned a fee. I don't remember Professor Keeley saying we'd have to pay for information."

"An operation like ours needs money, a lot of money, to survive. A question like yours usually costs upwards of one hundred thousand Euros, but because Keeley practically begged me to help you, I'll waive the fees. This time."

"You're far too kind," Connor said dryly. "Forgive me, Kat, but your team's goth persona is slightly clichéd. Wouldn't you agree?"

Kat shrugged. "The university students I take into my confidence decide how we look. Like most things, fads and clothing styles change. Over the years, we've worn punk, cyberpunk, cosplay, you name it. I don't care. It keeps my people happy. And a happy workforce is a productive workforce."

"Kat, I've retrieved the information they're looking for," announced Heike.

"On the main screen, please. Heike has been working diligently on this little mystery of yours for the past two days, so I'll let her show you what she's uncovered."

A crudely drawn map showing what looked like the coastline of Baffin Island, Newfoundland, and the eastern coast of the United States from Maine to the bottom tip of Florida appeared.

"My friends, this is the only known reproduction of the so-called Green map, drawn by Captain William Moore on his deathbed," explained Heike. "According to Captain Moore, an English sea captain hired to discover the fabled northwest passage in 1510, his expedition ventured too far north. It became trapped in the ice, and they were forced to spend the winter huddled inside their ship. One day, a hunting party brought back a young Inuit boy and his elderly grandmother. The young boy explained that they were all that was left of their family, and what Moore found truly amazing was that they could speak understandable French. When he questioned them, he said his name was Phillip Grenier, and his ancestors had fled France two centuries earlier to avoid persecution, only to be shipwrecked. Phillip claimed that their ship, crushed by the ice, was damaged beyond repair, so the survivors tried to make the best of things. They found an abandoned settlement and used the wood from their boat to build a place to live. Unfortunately, the first winter nearly wiped out the original crew. Nearly starving to death, they met some local Inuit who saved their lives. Over time, they married into the local Inuit community, eventually becoming one."

"The thirteen hundreds," mused Kim. "That's before Columbus, but after the Vikings. Right?"

"Bingo," said Kat.

Heike continued. "At first, Moore was skeptical and surmised that a French ship had beaten them to the New World and taught a pair of locals to speak French. However, when the boy produced a cloth map which he claimed had been in his family for generations, along with several ancient gold coins, the likes of which Moore had never seen before, he became very interested. According to the boy's family's oral history, he claimed that a vast fortune in gold was buried on a nearby island, but he wasn't sure which one it was."

"What happened to the boy and his grandmother?" Kim asked.

"The old woman died a week later in her sleep. When spring came, and the ice broke up, Moore scoured the area for this mysterious island but found nothing. So, he eventually gave up and sailed for home. Unfortunately, the boy died from a fever on the return trip to England and was buried at sea. When his ship arrived in Plymouth, Moore's story about meeting French-speaking Inuit and hidden treasure was ridiculed. Because he had failed to find the Northwest Passage, Moore's creditors thought him a poor sailor and never gave him command of another ship. He died a penniless drunk in London five years later."

"Did Moore's journal say what happened to the map?" asked Connor.

"Unfortunately, no," replied Heike. "But I may have found evidence to corroborate the young boy's story."

"Please, go on," said Kim, genuinely interested.

"I found a small entry in a diary written by a French knight in 1309. In it, Robert Junot, a former Templar Knight, describes the night the King of France dispatched him and dozens more like him to rid the country of the Templars. He, however, arrived too late to stop an old friend, Marc Grenier, and his family from fleeing by boat. Junot had known Grenier for decades, and with a heavy heart, he had pledged allegiance to the king and turned his sword on his old order. He suspected that Grenier had been hiding a small fortune in gold in his old home, and part of the treasure allegedly included four copper scrolls taken from the Holy Land."

"Wait a second," said Kim. "Grenier and Green, what are the odds they're the same last name?"

"Pretty good," responded Connor. "Knowing the English, Moore's sailors probably anglicized the boy's name, and Grenier became Green."

"Just as it was getting good, we seemed to have hit a brick wall," said Kim. "I'd love to know what happened to that map."

"I may have a couple of leads I can look into for you if you have a few minutes to wait?" announced Heike.

"We're not going anywhere," replied Kim. "This is amazing. I'm getting goosebumps just thinking about the copper scrolls buried somewhere waiting to be found."

"Don't get ahead of yourself, my dear," cautioned Kat. "The coastline of North America is enormous, and just because we have found two entries in a pair of centuries-old books that seem to support one another doesn't mean they are true. For example, suppose Heike was to spend a few days more looking for references on four copper scrolls. In that case, there's a good chance we'd find people claiming they were buried somewhere in Brazil, France, Italy, or even hidden away in a safe in the Titanic at the bottom of the ocean."

"But if we could find the map, it would go a long way to verifying Moore's and Junot's stories."

"That's a big if."

"If you can stop a war, you should be able to find a little old map," murmured Connor.

"An opponent's computer systems are easy to hack, Mister North," Kat shot back. "Finding a map that hasn't been seen in over five centuries is something else altogether."

"Kat, I think I may have something," said Heike.

"What is it?"

"Just before Moore's death, a man called James Reynolds heard about the missing treasure and claimed to have bought the map from Moore. That spring, he hired a ship and went in search of the fabled treasure. Unfortunately, like Moore, he became trapped in the ice for a long and miserably cold winter. The next spring, his crew had had enough and mutinied. They set Reynolds and four loyal officers adrift with enough provisions to last them a month. They, regrettably, were never seen or heard from again. The mutineers then sailed South to the Caribbean to try their hand as pirates."

"And then what happened?" asked Kim, excited to hear more.

"Apparently, they weren't very good at being outlaws because their ship, *Electra*, was captured by a passing Spanish warship. The crew was taken to Havana, where they all died in prison from disease. The Spanish man-o'-war's captain, Luis Carrero Blanco, took whatever he wanted from the *Electra* and sailed home to Spain. Amazingly, Blanco's ship's manifest included a threadbare cloth map of the New World. Since Spain already knew about the Americas, the map was considered a novelty, so it was locked away in Blanco's family home in Coruna. And that's the last reference I've found regarding the map."

"Thank you, Heike," said Kat. "As always, you've surpassed my expectations."

"Heike, are there any living descendants of Captain Blanco?" asked Kim.

Heike's fingers danced across the keyboard. A minute later, the image of an older woman flashed up on the screen. "This is a picture of Sofia Meyer, the only living relative of Captain Blanco. She is eighty-one years old, unmarried, and lives in Neuchatel, Switzerland."

Kim looked at Connor and smiled. "Fancy a trip to the Alps?"

"I wouldn't pack your hiking boots if I were you, at least not yet," said Heike.

"Why, what's wrong?" asked Connor.

"I'm sorry, but I've found a more up-to-date newspaper article that says she died in her sleep five days ago."

"Damn," uttered Kim, dropping her shoulders.

"Her estate, does it say what happened to her belongings?" asked Connor.

Heike scanned several other papers and shook her head. "Yes. Since she has no living heirs, her estate will be auctioned off at the Gerhardt Auction House in Neuchatel three days from now."

"That gives us plenty of time to get there," said Kim.

"Whoa, let's not get ahead of ourselves," said Connor. "We have no idea if the map still exists or if Ms. Meyer still owned it at the time of her passing."

"I know it's slim, but it's our only lead, and I say it's worth following."

Connor shook his head. "I don't know."

Kim hit Connor on the arm. "Come on. Where's your spirit of adventure? There's no turning back, now."

"A second ago, you looked like someone had stolen your favorite stuffed animal. And now you're ready to take on the whole world?"

Kim's eyes lit up. "We can do this."

"I hope you're right."

"I know I am," replied Kim firmly.

"If, and that's a big if, if the map is part of her estate, I doubt it will be sold separately."

"Then we'll go there and bid on behalf of Mister Hamilton until we've bought the entire lot."

Connor chuckled. "I hope Jason has deep pockets because, depending on the size of her estate, this could be a pricey venture."

"He'll pay. I know he will."

"I take it we are done?" asked Kat matter-of-factly.

"Yes, and thank you," replied Kim. "We're in your debt."

"Remember, my dear. If we could track down the last family to see Green's map, others could also. We're good at what we do, but we're not the only people out there who can access this information. I give you, at best, twenty-four to thirty-six hours before someone else figures out what is going on and comes after you. So, please be careful out there."

"We will," interjected Connor.

Kat grinned and snapped her fingers loudly. "Gerhardt, our guests are leaving. Their hoods, please."

17.

L'Aubier Café-Hotel

Neuchatel, Switzerland

Kim sat at a table in the hotel's dining room, sipping her coffee and reading an English-language edition of the local paper on her tablet. She glanced over at the empty chair across from her. Connor was late for breakfast, and that was odd. Kim had just reached for her phone to call him when Connor walked in, pulled out a chair, and sat down. Right away, she noticed his red eyes and disheveled appearance. "Rough night?" she asked.

Connor poured himself a cup of coffee, emptying the carafe on the table, and sat back in his chair. "Pardon?"

"I asked if you'd had a rough night last night. You look exhausted."

Connor cracked his neck. "I couldn't sleep."

"Why not?"

"I've got a million questions swirling around in my mind and not many answers to go with them."

"Like?" Kim popped a grape in her mouth.

A waiter approached the table and went to hand Connor a menu. Connor looked over at Kim. "Have you already ordered?"

"Yes," she replied.

"What are you having?"

"I'm having a fully loaded omelet with brown toast and fried potatoes."

"Sounds good. I'll have the same, please," said Connor to the waiter. "Oh, and some more coffee when you get the chance."

"Excellent choice, monsieur," said the waiter, hurrying back to the kitchen to place the order.

"Now, where were we?" asked Connor.

"Your mind, and why it wouldn't let you sleep last night," responded Kim.

"Oh yeah. In my opinion, there are two major hurdles we need to overcome before we can even start to begin believing that we're on the right track."

"And those are?"

"Geography and the map."

Kim sat back. "What about them?"

"When I couldn't sleep, I opened my tablet and learned that Baffin Island is enormous."

"I know. It's the fifth largest island in the world," added Kim.

Connor narrowed his eyes. "Yeah. How did you know that?"

"I did the same thing last night but was smart enough to call it quits at midnight so that I could get some sleep."

"Well, you're smarter than me because I couldn't let things go. I had no idea that Baffin Island is over fifteen hundred kilometers long, and if you add in the rest of the east coast of Canada and the States, that's a lot of ground to search."

"That's a compelling reason to get our hands on the map."

Connor nodded and stared pensively into his now-empty coffee cup.

The waiter returned and placed their scrumptious-looking meals on the table.

"I'll be right back with the coffee," said the waiter as he turned and walked away. He returned a few moments later with a full carafe and refilled their cups.

Connor waited until the man was out of earshot before continuing. "Kim, I've been doing the math. Let's say there were three to four generations born into the Blanco family every one hundred years since the map was discovered. So, there could have been at least twenty-four or more descendants who also had families kicking around Europe or elsewhere. Which means the map could be anywhere by now."

Kim understood her partner's logic but countered with some of her own. "But it's not, or Katarina's people would have found a reference to it in a book or some other document to it, which they didn't."

Connor raised his right eyebrow. "Okay, I'll give you that. But, even if we manage to get our hands on the map, you know it could be fake. Have you checked out maps from that period? I wouldn't be surprised if a couple of sea monsters were drawn on it."

"I know what you're getting at, but why would DuFour send people after us if he didn't think it was real?"

"Because, like you, he wants to believe it's real."

Kim placed her knife and fork down and leveled her gaze straight at Connor. "That's not fair. I'm nothing like DuFour. He wants the scrolls to enrich himself, whereas I want the truth to come out."

There was a slightly uncomfortable pause. Then, Connor raised a hand and said, "You're right. I'm sorry; I shouldn't have said it that way. Unfortunately, after a few months of hunting poachers in the jungles of Africa, I seem to have forgotten how to watch what comes out of my mouth. It's just that I don't have your unwavering belief that the map will be of any use in finding the scrolls if they still exist and aren't at the bottom of the North Atlantic."

"It's all right. I have enough faith for the two of us."

"Yes, I see that." Connor took a long sip of his coffee. "I know I'm starting to sound like I don't have faith in what we're doing, but they didn't have sextants back then to help them find their latitude and longitude. Most navigation in the 1300s was done using the sun, the stars, and very crude compasses. So, the map, if it does exist, may be useless to us."

Kim smiled. "Connor, you're overthinking things. Let's worry about one thing at a time. First, let's eat our breakfast before it gets cold, and then visit the auction house to see if they have an itinerary ready for tomorrow night's auction."

"I can't help overthinking things," replied Connor with a wry chuckle. "My brain's hardwired that way."

"Well, switch it off, and let's try to have a relaxing meal."

At the bar, the waiter opened his phone and checked the image provided by a friend with connections to the black market. The more he studied the picture, the more he knew it had to be them. The waiter surreptitiously took a quick photo of Kim and Connor and forwarded it to an associate. Ten seconds later, his phone chimed. The waiter read the text message and smiled. All he had to do was feed his contact the whereabouts of the two foreigners for the next two days, and ten thousand Euros would be his. It would be the easiest payday he'd made since leaving prison.

Connor parked their rented Kia Rio across from the auction house, switched off the engine, and applied the hand brake to ensure the car didn't roll down the steep cobblestone roadway. He'd wanted a larger car with more horsepower, but Kim had insisted they'd blend in better if they rented a smaller, more fuel-economical vehicle. Connor opened the door and got out, checking their surroundings to see if anyone was watching them.

Kim joined Connor and stared at a sign on the building's front door. She furrowed her brow and cursed their luck.

"What's wrong?" Connor asked.

"It's closed," she responded. "See, it says *fermé* on the door."

They hurried across the busy street, nearly being hit by a pair of teens on a scooter.

Kim read the sign and then looked over at her partner. "If we didn't have bad luck, we'd have no luck at all."

"What do you mean?"

"The sign says that until further notice, the auction house is closed for business."

"Are you sure?"

Kim pursed her lips. "Yes, I'm sure. I may not have a university education like yourself, but I can read enough French to get by, and it says the place is closed."

"Okay, sorry." Connor tapped his foot on the pavement for a few seconds and then pressed a buzzer on the wall.

A few seconds later, a small, bookish-looking man with a round face and balding head opened the door. He looked suspiciously over at Kim and Connor. "*Guten tag.*"

"*Guten tag,*" replied Kim. "Sir, My German is awful. Do you speak English?"

The man smiled and nodded. "Yes, of course I do. How may I help you?"

"My associate and I have come all the way from the United States on behalf of an anonymous buyer to bid on Madame Meyer's estate, but I see that your doors are regrettably closed."

"I'm sorry. It's most unfortunate that you've traveled so far for nothing, but her entire estate has been impounded."

"What do you mean impounded?" Connor blurted out.

"Sir, we were contacted by the Ministry of Justice earlier this morning and told to impound Madame Meyer's estate until an antiquities agent arrives from Bern to inspect all of her belongings."

"Did they say why?"

"It would appear that several rare artifacts in her estate allegedly belong to the people of Peru. Their embassy got wind of some cultural items that are part of the estate and contacted our government to stop the sale."

"What kind of items?" asked Kim.

"I'm sorry, but I'm not at liberty to discuss that."

Connor decided to push their luck. "Sir, my colleague and I don't wish to return home empty-handed. Could you please tell us if there was a map from the 1300s as part of the auction? It would mean a lot to us if you could confirm this so we could bid on it after your government releases the remainder of Madame Meyer's estate for sale."

The man let out an exasperated sigh before flipping through several pages of notes on his clipboard. "Four maps are listed in my notes, all of which are part of lot number twelve. By the looks of things, the Peruvians are after some of the more expensive items in her estate. So, you should be able to bid on the lot when it comes back on the market."

"And when might that be?" Kim asked.

The owner shrugged and went to close the door to the auction house.

Connor stopped the door with his hand and stared down at the balding man. "Sir, the lady asked you a question. When do you think we'll be able to bid on lot twelve?"

"I'm not sure," stammered the man. "Something like this has never happened to me. But if I know our government's bureaucracy, I'd say check back in with me in about three months from today."

"That long?" asked Kim, looking past the man at the motion sensors and cameras on the walls covering the entrance to the facility.

"I'm only trying to be realistic, Miss. When it comes to illegally obtained antiquities, my government moves at a snail's pace to ensure that the rightful owners get their possessions back."

Connor let go of the door and smiled. "*Danke*, for your time."

"*Auf Wiedersehen*," responded the man, quickly closing and locking the door.

The two of them headed back to the car. Once inside, Connor turned to face Kim. "Well, that didn't go as well as I'd hoped it would. Did you see everything you needed to, too?"

Kim nodded. "Yeah. For a small business, the owner has got the place wired. Going in through the front door looks tricky. So, I'll check the back, and if that's no good, I guess I'll go in through the roof."

18.

Connor chose a darkened spot in the alley behind the auction house and parked their car. He switched off the vehicle's lights and turned in his seat. He tapped his fingers on the steering wheel, his nerves slowly growing taut.

"Before you say a word," said Kim, slipping an earpiece in place. "I know what I'm doing."

"You said that in France, and look what happened."

Kim scrunched up her face. "Really? Are you going to keep bringing France up? Trust me; this auction house will be a walk in the park compared with DuFour's home."

Connor was growing to trust Kim's instincts, but he was used to leading, not sitting on the sidelines as an observer, and it bothered him to no end. However, rather than waste time talking, he reached for a tablet on the seat behind him and turned it on.

"Let's do one last check of the equipment before I get to work," Kim said, pulling a black balaclava over her head.

"So far, so good," Connor said, looking at the crystal-clear image on his tablet from the tiny camera in Kim's contact lens.

"Comms check."

Connor heard her loud and clear in his earpiece and gave Kim a thumbs-up.

Kim returned the thumbs-up and went to open her door.

"Good luck," said Connor, silently praying everything would turn out okay.

"There's luck, and luck you make yourself," Kim held up her utility belt, winked, and stepped outside. She made sure her belt was on tight, and then, as graceful as a cat, Kim slipped into the shadows, creeping along a tall stone wall until she reached the back of the auction house. There, she removed a small thermal camera from a pouch on her belt and affixed it to the wall so that Connor could get a good view of the establishment. Kim's gut warned her to be wary when she saw a white van parked behind the building. It appeared empty, but its presence was a red flag in her book. She decided to be wary but not overly so for now.

"*I've got a great view of the back door,*" said Connor in her earpiece. "*What do you make of the van?*"

"I don't see anyone. Maybe it belongs to the auction house?"

"*I dunno. I don't like it. Maybe we should call it quits for tonight and come back tomorrow.*"

"Let's not be too hasty. Let me take a quick look around, and then ask me again in thirty seconds."

Kim heard Connor sigh. "*It's your call. Whatever you do, please be careful.*"

"Always. I'm going in."

"*Watch out for surveillance cameras.*"

Kim bit her lip and reminded herself she was used to working alone. Connor's concerns for her well-being were new and honestly not unwanted. Kim tiptoed out from behind the wall with a small laser in her hand. She bought the laser up and activated it. In less than a heartbeat, the laser fired, crippling the camera covering the back of the auction house. Kim slid the laser back into its pouch and took a quick peek in the front of the van. She was relieved to see it was empty and hurried to the back door. Kim dropped down on one knee and went for her skeleton keys when she noticed the door was open. Her stomach instantly knotted.

"Connor, we're not alone."

"I see that. Kim, abort the mission and get back here before something goes wrong."

Kim hesitated. She was torn between her desire to know what was happening and her self-preservation instincts. Then, suddenly, a set of car lights coming down the alley toward the back of the house from the opposite direction changed everything. Kim had nowhere to go but inside if she didn't want to be seen. With her heart pounding, she pushed the door slightly ajar and slid inside the dark warehouse.

"Thermal," whispered Connor. *"Go thermal."*

Kim moved behind a tall crate and slid a set of lightweight thermal glasses over her eyes. Her world turned into different hues of green. "How's that?" she whispered back.

"Perfect. But we've got trouble. That car stopped right behind the auction house, and four armed men got out. They're checking out the van. Kim, I have a bad feeling about this. You need to find another way out and fast."

"Got it. Have they spotted you?" Kim asked, looking around, desperate to spot an exit nearby.

"Not yet. I think I'm out of their line of sight."

"Thank God for that."

Somewhere nearby in the dark, a man cursed in an Asian language Kim didn't recognize. She froze and held her breath. It sounded as if the man was on the other side of the crate she was hiding behind.

Connor had seen and heard enough. He tossed his tablet aside, popped open the glove compartment, and retrieved a pistol-shaped Taser. Connor armed the weapon and carefully opened his door, trying not to make a sound. He crept out into the night, the Taser at the ready. There was no way in hell Connor was going to allow any harm to come to Kim. He hugged the wall and moved along until he could see the back of the auction house. Connor eyed the four gunmen and ground his teeth when he recognized one of them as the bald, intimidating man he had seen at DuFour's home. Connor watched helplessly as the men quietly opened the van's back doors, revealing several crates. The gunmen said something in French he couldn't catch, made their way to the back door, and prepared to go inside. Seconds later, three men with their SMGs tight against their shoulders entered the building, ready for action, while a bull of a man stayed behind to guard the door. Connor's mind spun, creating and discarding ideas at light speed.

Kim could hear men arguing as they strained to carry something. She dropped down and slowly inched along the side of the crate until she could see what was going on. Any chance of sneaking past the thieves evaporated when she counted eight men. Four struggled to carry a heavy crate while the others, carrying wicked-looking machine pistols, urged them on.

Suddenly, a blinding light filled the room.

Kim ripped off her thermal glasses and blinked her eyes to get rid of the spots that filled her vision.

"What the hell do you think you're doing?" yelled a man in English with a strong French accent.

How could anything get any worse? thought Kim the instant she identified the man speaking as one from DuFour's estate aiming a weapon at the thieves.

The robbers carefully set the crate down and scooped up their Skorpions.

Tension filled the room as three men faced off against eight.

One of the Asian men stepped forward. In English, he said, "I think it is I who should be asking the questions, Frenchman? *N'est pas?*"

"Where are North and Swiftwater?" demanded DuFour's bodyguard.

The Asian man scrunched his brow. "Who?"

Kim flinched at hearing their names.

There was an awkward pause as both sides eyed each other. Then, the big Frenchman with dragon tattoos on his bulging neck looked at his compatriots and back at the opposition. "What about Hamilton? Surely, you're working for him?"

The lead thief shook his head and let out an exasperated sigh. "Look you, big ape. I haven't a clue who you're talking about. Drop your weapons and then kick them over to my feet!"

"That's not going to happen," said DuFour's man. "Step away from the crate, and no one has to die."

A chuckle escaped from the mercenaries' throats.

"I don't think so," said the Asian leader. "I'll give you five seconds to drop your weapons or face the consequences."

Kim felt her muscles tighten. All it would take was the slightest spark to ignite the powder keg, and all hell would break out.

Connor warily crept forward with his Taser tight in his hand. He slipped behind the van and took in a deep breath. He could hear the man guarding the back door pacing back and forth while he smoked a noxious-smelling cigarette and waited for his comrades.

Connor took a breath as he stepped out from behind the van and walked purposefully toward his target. At the last second, the man spotted Connor approaching. Without hesitating, Connor fired his Taser.

Before his target could react, a pair of barbed darts struck the man in the chest. In the blink of an eye, fifty thousand volts surged through wires attached to the barbs and into his body, causing him to spasm in agony.

Connor dropped his Taser and ran to grab the guard's weapon. Only he was a fraction of a second too late. The guard's trigger finger slid over the trigger and involuntarily tightened, firing a burst of 9mm rounds into the pavement. Connor came to a sliding halt and looked up at the back door.

To Kim, what happened next seemed to happen in slow motion. One of the French robbers heard the shots outside and went to fire his weapon.

Two Asian mercenaries saw him raise his weapon and opened fire, hitting the man in the chest and head.

The two surviving Frenchmen took to their heels and sprinted for the door. The leader was faster and quickly disappeared from view while his partner fell to the floor with his back riddled with bullets.

The lead Asian mercenary yelled at his men and ran for the exit, closely followed by three of his assassins.

Kim watched the remaining four men grab the heavy crate and haul it off the floor. She spotted the number twelve painted on the side of the box and silently swore at their bad luck.

The back door burst open, and DuFour's man ran out, nearly knocking over his tased comrade. He sprinted past the van, ignoring Connor altogether, jumped into his car's driver's seat, and started the ignition.

Connor instantly stepped back from the doorway. He had barely moved when the door burst wide open, and four armed men spilled out. The lead gunman never hesitated and fired two shots at the stunned guard, killing him. Every nerve and fiber in Connor's body told him to run. He spun on his heel and dove behind the van just as a hail of 9mm bullets flew through the air.

Kim heard the gunfire and instantly feared the worst.

She tapped her earpiece. "Connor, can you hear me?"

"*Don't come out the back*," he replied quickly.

Kim heard more shots and gnashed her teeth. "Screw this."

She glanced over her shoulder at the front entrance and took off running. "Meet me out front."

"Roger," replied Connor, watching DuFour's man drive straight backward under fire. Dozens of bullets struck the hood and blasted holes in the front windshield, but that didn't stop the killer, who kept going and rapidly vanished down the alleyway.

Connor knew his window of opportunity to escape was fading fast. He pumped his legs and sprinted out from behind the van, running as fast as his legs could carry him. He heard the crack of bullets as they flew past his head. Adrenaline filled his veins, allowing him to dig deeper for every ounce of strength he had in his body to escape. At the last second, he dove over a pair of garbage cans, landed on his shoulder, and rolled onto his feet. Amazed that he hadn't been hit, Connor ran for his car like a madman. He yanked open the door, jumped in, and started the vehicle. Connor ducked below the dash, threw the car in reverse, and jammed his foot on the accelerator. Unable to see where he was going, Connor heard a loud crunch of crumpling metal as he bounced off the stone wall, running down the alley, ripping his driver's side mirror off the side of the car, and cutting deep streaks into his door.

"*Where are you?*" asked Kim.

"I'm almost at the end of the alley, I think," he replied, popping his head up just as a man fired at his escaping vehicle, riddling the front grill with bullets.

"*I've unlocked the front doors. The second I see you, I'm coming out.*"

Connor looked over his shoulder at the end of the alley. He sat up, pulled up the emergency brake, and swung the steering wheel around in his hand. The car spun around, leaving smoke and black tire marks behind it. Connor released the brake and pressed hard on the gas pedal. In seconds, he was out front of the auction house. He brought his rental car to a screeching halt and reached over to open Kim's door. Then, like an athlete hearing the starter's pistol fire, she sprinted for the open door and dove inside.

"Drive!" she said, slamming her door behind her.

Connor placed the Kia in gear and drove off. "Are you all right?"

"I'm fine, but they've got the map."

"Are you sure?"

"Yes. The number twelve was stenciled on the crate they were carrying out."

"Damn," replied Connor, turning the steering wheel sharply to head back toward the alleyway. He barely had time to slam his foot on the brakes as the van sped past him, going in the opposite direction.

Kim snapped her seatbelt in place and pointed at the escaping vehicle. "Follow that van."

Connor spun the wheel over and pressed down on the gas pedal, praying their car could catch up with the fleeing van.Luckily for them, there was almost no traffic on the narrow, winding streets at three in the morning. However, the rows of cars parked beside the tall, dense buildings that snaked alongside the winding road considerably narrowed the lane.

"Can we catch them?" Kim asked as Connor sped around a yellow delivery truck barely going the speed limit.

"Maybe," he replied. "The problem is, what do we do then? In case you've forgotten, we're slightly outnumbered."

"I hadn't thought of that."

"It's all right. We'll figure something out."

Connor clenched the wheel until his knuckles blanched. He was doing his best on the curved road but took one corner too fast and slid into the front end of a parked car, crushing one of its headlights and triggering its alarm. Connor ignored the damage and kept going. He glanced back to see their car's bumper rolling end over end down the road.

"Thank God we got insurance," Connor said dryly.

"Seriously, you're worried about that at a time like this?" retorted Kim.

Up ahead, the road turned straight and ran alongside the dark waters of the Aare River. The van with its larger motor started to pull away.

Kim saw they were falling back and dug out her phone. "The cops, should I call them?"

Connor couldn't see any other way to stop the thieves and nodded. "Don't tell them who you are; just tell them you saw them rob a store, the make of the vehicle, and where the crooks are heading."

"Right." Kim dialed 1-1-2, and waited for someone to answer.

All Kim heard was *guten nacht* before she cut off the operator. "Hello, I've just witnessed a bank robbery. The thieves are in a white Ford van and are heading north on—just a second." Kim looked for a street sign and read it aloud, "Engehaldenstrasse, I think that's how you say it. But, whatever you do, be careful because I think they're armed."

"Did you say Engehaldenstrasse?" asked the police operator.

"Yes, that's it."

"Can I have your name, please?"

Kim instantly hung up.

Connor sped up to pass an eighteen-wheeler hauling lumber. He was almost beside the vehicle's cab when Kim suddenly shot back in her seat and pointed at the windshield, screaming, "Car!"

An unexpected vehicle had just turned a bend and came speeding out of the dark toward them, flashing its high beans and blaring its horn. Connor swore. His stomach leaped into his throat. He had a split-second to decide what to do. Connor knew he had only one chance and turned his wheel hard to the left, steering his car onto the narrow shoulder on the other side of the road, barely missing the other vehicle by a hair's breadth. The other car, a BMW, raced past with a window down, and the driver giving Connor a rude hand gesture.

"Damn, that was a bit too close," Kim said, holding onto the dash for dear life.

Connor steered back onto the road and got in front of the semi. "Yeah, let's not do that again."

The familiar and welcoming sound of police sirens coming from behind instantly changed the mood. Their luck might have turned.

A minute later, a pair of blue-and-yellow police Volvo V90s, with their sirens blaring and blue-and-white lights flashing, flew past Connor's Kia and took up the chase.

"I never thought I'd like to hear that sound," said Kim. "Let's pray the police get them."

"Amen to that."

Connor joined the police cruisers in pursuit of the van. Like a snake slithering through the underbrush, the three cars wound their way through the traffic, flashing their lights and honking their horns to warn people to get out of their way.

"It looks like the police are catching up," observed Kim when the gap between the van and the police cars dropped to less than fifty meters.

Connor nodded. "I hope they know the opposition is armed and isn't afraid to use force."

Prophetically, the van's rear doors swung open at that moment, and a pair of men opened fire, spraying the lead police cruiser's windshield with a deadly hail of gunfire. The driver and his partner never stood a chance as the thieves' armor-piercing rounds easily shattered the front windshield. Broken glass and 9mm bullets flew inside, striking the doomed men trapped inside the car.

Anger surged through Connor when the lead cruiser slid off the road and flew into the air, landing with a massive splash in the cold waters of the Aare River. Neither man could have survived.

"No," whispered Kim as the mercenaries turned their attention to the second car and let loose a deadly volley. Bullets tore into the vehicle's hood and then its windshield. With smoke billowing from its engine, the second car's driver, unable to see the oncoming traffic, smashed headlong into a heavy-duty truck and compacted beneath its weight.

Connor saw what had happened but couldn't believe that four men were dead. He dodged around a piece of burning debris and again took up the chase. He said darkly, "Kim, get a hold of the police and let them know what's happened."

"Right," Kim replied numbly, going for her phone. She was about to redial the emergency number but stopped. Three police motorbikes flew past like the wind at that moment in pursuit of the mercenaries. In the sky above them, a police helicopter joined the hunt, shining its light on the white van.

"All right, that's more like it," said Connor, backing off slightly to let the police do their jobs. "If they're smart, the Swiss will put up a roadblock a few kilometers down the road to stop them."

Kim crossed her fingers. "Here's hoping."

The flashing lights from the police pursuit shone off the river, glinting like some sort of giant strobe light. Connor was happy to see that the Swiss seemed to know what they were doing. The motorbikes were keeping safely back and herding the van down the road. However, everything changed instantly when a 4x4 pickup truck roared from a side street onto the road just behind the white van.

"What the heck?" said Kim at the sight of two men in the back of the pickup truck aiming a ground-to-air missile at the helicopter. A bright flash preceded the launch of the heat-seeking warhead. The police helicopter pilot saw the launch and banked over to avoid the incoming missile. But it was pointless. In seconds the warhead hit home and exploded, creating a brilliant red fireball that brightened the heavens as the crippled helicopter fell from the sky and landed in the river.

Connor swore and smashed his right hand hard on the steering wheel. His blood was up. All he wanted to do was get revenge.

The missile team in the pickup discarded their launcher and picked up AK-74s to fire on the Swiss police. The motorbike riders saw what was about to happen and swerved from side to side on the road, trying to throw off their assailants' aim. Unfortunately, it only worked for a very short while before the mercenaries cut the riders down one by one, leaving their bodies and bikes to slide down the darkened highway.

It was over. Connor lifted his foot off the gas and watched the two vehicles speed off into the night.

"What are you doing?" demanded Kim. "They're getting away."

"I know," he replied resignedly.

"Damn it, Connor, why are you letting them get away?"

Connor stopped next to a bike and its rider lying on the road. "Because our car is on its last legs, and we can't do anything for the wounded police officers if we're dead."

"But they'll get away."

Connor looked Kim in the eyes. "Let them get away. This isn't over. But for now, it's people first, treasure second, yes?"

Kim exhaled and nodded. "You're right. I'm sure the authorities already know, but I'll call for additional ambulances and tell them we need help immediately."

Connor got out of the car and watched one of the police officers try to roll over. He dashed over and got on one knee. Connor gently slipped his hand under the officer's neck and looked into a woman's bright blue eyes. "I don't know if you can understand me, but you've got to hang on. Help is on the way."

19.

Chateau Sainte Croix, France

The sound of his phone buzzing woke Rene DuFour, and he sat up in bed.

"Who's calling?" a red-haired, young woman wrapped in the black silk sheets asked groggily. She had the slightest hint of an Irish accent.

DuFour saw Vallin's number on the screen and leaped out of bed. "It's no one, Demi. Go back to sleep."

"Okay," she replied, rolling over and hugging a pillow tight to her naked chest.

DuFour answered the call succinctly, "One second." Then, DuFour wrapped a robe around his naked body and walked out onto a balcony overlooking his estate. It was chilly in the gray light of dawn, but DuFour liked the freshness of an early morning. He inhaled deeply through his nose; it smelled of opportunities. He desperately wanted to hear good news, but the early hour of the call could only mean that something had gone wrong.

DuFour brought up his phone to his ear. "Okay, Jean, I'm listening."

"Sir, I'll be brief. This morning's activities were an unmitigated disaster from the word go."

DuFour's gut churned. "I take it that means you don't have the map?"

"Correct. Someone beat us to it."

DuFour closed his eyes. His order would not be very pleased with him once they discovered what had happened. "Let me guess, North and Swiftwater?"

"No, sir, it was someone else."

"I don't understand. Who else is involved?"

"Koreans. North Koreans, to be specific."

DuFour's head was spinning. Why would anyone from North Korea want a map from the fourteenth century? "Are you sure they were North Koreans?"

"Sir, I've worked with Koreans before, so I know their language when I hear it."

"What made you think they were from the North and not the South?"

"These men were professional mercenaries. I've seen their type before. Trust me, sir; they were North Korean agents."

DuFour took a seat and shook his head to clear it. "Okay, Jean, you win. If you say they were North Koreans, then they were North Koreans. So where is the map now?"

"I'm not sure. But I have a good idea where it may be headed."

Vallin's words felt like a knife to the guts. Ideas didn't always become action, and that's precisely what he needed right now. DuFour's hand started to shake; his life was hanging by a thread. Finally, he paused to compose himself. "Jean, what do you need to get your hands on my map?"

"First off, from here on out, you've got to trust me to do things my way. You kept me out of the picture in Ireland when you used hired thugs instead of professionals to do the job, and that didn't turn out so well. Neither did things in Switzerland. The men you sent to work with me were worse than useless. They panicked at the first sight of trouble and are all dead."

"All of them?"

"Yes. From here on out, I want to use my people."

DuFour knew he'd messed up and relented. "If that's what it will take."

"I'm not finished. I also want ten million dollars deposited in a Swiss bank account by noon today so I can start hiring men I trust to get the job done."

Dufour felt as if he had slipped into a dream. Nothing seemed real anymore. "Ten million, yes, of course. I'll take care of it right away."

"Good. I'll call you once I know where the map is." With that, Vallin hung up.

DuFour dropped his phone and struggled to stand. It wasn't supposed to be like this. His throat was parched, and his stomach ached. Everything was spinning out of control. In an instant, his stomach turned, and DuFour emptied his stomach over the side of his balcony until only bile slipped from his quivering lips. He looked up at the sky.

"God, if you can hear me, please help me. After all, I'm doing your work."

"I wouldn't go that far," said Demi, stepping out to join DuFour on his balcony. She handed DuFour a handkerchief to wipe the drool from his chin,

"How much did you hear?" he asked, cleaning his face.

The redheaded woman chuckled. "All of it. Do you honestly think a woman as good-looking as me would sleep with you for no reason?"

DuFour's eyes widened. He stammered, "You're with The Order, aren't you?"

"Yes, I am. It's nice to see you're not the complete fool they make you out to be."

"I'm not sure how to take that?"

"As it was meant, as a compliment."

"So, what are you doing here?"

"Isn't it obvious?"

DuFour felt a chill creep down his spine. "You've been sent to keep a close eye on me, haven't you?"

"I'm impressed, Rene. That's two for two. You have to understand that we want the map just as much as you do, and so far, in my boss' eyes, you haven't done a good job getting your hands on it."

"Demi, if you heard the conversation, you'll know how much more is going on than was originally anticipated."

Demi shrugged. "True, but The Order doesn't care, and if they don't care, I really don't give a damn about your problems. You said you could do this job, and that's all that matters."

DuFour licked his dry lips. "I know. Vallin won't let me down. I promise."

Demi lightly patted DuFour on the cheek. "Your childlike promises don't mean a thing to me. You know, you weren't half bad in bed, so do you know what I'm going to do?"

"No, what?" moaned DuFour.

"First, I'm going to assign one of my better people to make sure your man doesn't mess things up in the future, and then I think I'll give you one more chance."

DuFour stood, speechless, as Demi slipped back inside. He was wrong. His world wasn't a dream; it was a nightmare.

20.

Neuchatel, Switzerland

"You're full of crap!" bellowed a stocky police sergeant with a thick black beard and a sagging roll around his waist. "You both know more than you're telling me."

Connor sat back in his uncomfortable metal chair in the police interrogation room and exchanged a tired look with Kim. He shook his head, picked up a cold Styrofoam cup of coffee, and emptied it in one gulp. Connor tossed the empty cup into a wastepaper basket as if he were an NBA pro and rubbed his red eyes.

The sergeant jumped out of his chair and loomed over Connor. "Hey, you! Didn't you hear a word that I said?"

Connor checked the time and then looked up at the sergeant. "I did. I heard every word. Look, we've been here for hours, and I don't know how many times Kim and I can tell you the exact same story."

"Let's try again from the top, shall we?"

"No," said Connor defiantly. "I'm tired of your games, Sergeant. Two of your officers would be dead if we hadn't stopped to help them. Have you ever thought of that?"

The sergeant stepped back, pulled his chair, and sat. His demeanor calmed slightly. "Yes, and I can't thank you enough for helping Bruno and Isabel, but you've got to see things from my point of view. Just what the hell were the two of you doing on that road chasing after a van packed with stolen artifacts? And please don't tell me that you didn't know about the artifacts, as the auction house owner has positively identified the two of you, and he says that you were asking a lot of questions about Madame Meyer's estate earlier in the day."

"That's all true," replied Kim. "We're not hiding anything. Our employer, Jason Hamilton, is quite keen to get his hands on antique maps from all over the world and sent us to act on his behalf at an estate sale. Unfortunately, when we arrived in Bern, we discovered that Madame Meyer's estate had been impounded. You can check with him if you want."

"I already did, and he corroborates your story. Yet that doesn't explain why you were chasing a van packed with stolen goods."

Connor let out an anguished cry. "For the love of God, we've already told you five times before."

"Well, tell me again."

"We couldn't sleep, so we went for a drive around the city and saw a van racing away from the auction house and knew something was wrong," explained Connor. "I guess we just got caught up in the moment and took off after the thieves, hoping to stop them."

"With what?"

"As I said, we weren't thinking straight."

"Sergeant, we did the best we could and even called 1-1-2 to report the crime," said Kim.

"I know, I've listened to the recording. So why did you hang up and not identify yourselves?"

Kim let out a tired sigh. "I must have dropped the phone by accident."

The sergeant snorted. "Not bloody likely."

Kim's stomach growled loudly. She raised a hand. "Sergeant, the gurgling in my stomach's telling me that besides coffee and a dry pastry, I haven't had a decent meal in over twelve hours. Also, my clothes still have blood on them from the accident. I desperately want to get out of them and then have a nice long, hot shower."

146

"So, what's your point?" said the sergeant bluntly, returning to form.

"My point is, how long can we be held in Switzerland before you have to charge us with a crime or let us go? Because you're starting to try my patience."

The sergeant sighed and ran a hand through his unruly black hair. "Madame—"

"It's Ms. Wright," corrected Kim.

The sergeant took a deep breath and continued, "Ms. Wright, according to Section 219 of the Swiss Criminal Procedure Code, you can only be detained for twenty-four hours. That is unless the prosecutor's office wishes you held for an additional twenty-four hours while they build their case."

"And would you happen to know if the prosecutor requires an additional day?"

"No, she does not," said a woman over the intercom. The interrogation room door opened, and a tall woman in her mid-forties, wearing a dark gray suit, walked in, holding a brown leather briefcase in her right hand.

The sergeant respectfully got to his feet. "Frau Wild, I wasn't expecting you for another hour."

"I didn't need it," responded Wild. "I take it that you have their signed witness statements?"

"Yes, ma'am."

"Then your job is done, Sergeant. Please release our guests with the thanks of Bern's mayor for their heroic, lifesaving measures."

The sergeant paused. "But, Frau Wild, I'm not sure they're as innocent as they appear."

"The chief of police and the mayor are, so let them go."

Connor stood and shook Frau Wild's hand. "Thanks."

"My pleasure," she replied, looking Connor over.

"Yeah, thanks," said Kim, an eyebrow raised.

"This way, please," said the sergeant gruffly, "I'll see you out."

"That won't be necessary," said Wild, dismissing the police officer. "I'll see them out."

The sergeant shook his head and left the room, mumbling to himself.

"Follow me," said Wild, guiding Kim and Connor to the police station's front doors. Along the way, a couple of the on-duty officers stood and shook their hands, thanking them for stopping to help their friends.

At the exit, Wild gave a small, sad smile. "You'll have to forgive Sergeant Bulow's behavior; he was close to three of the officers killed during the chase last night."

"It's all right," replied Kim. "I'm sure I would have felt the same way had I been in his shoes. I'm just glad to be free."

Wild looked at Kim and Connor. Her voice turned sober. "Just to let you know, I agree with Sergeant Bulow; there's something you're not telling us. But you're considered heroes in the eyes of many people, and it would be foolish to detain you longer than necessary. So, all I ask is that you remain in the city until tomorrow morning, just in case the mayor or chief of police wishes to speak with you. After that, you're free to go anywhere you would like."

"We can do that," said Connor.

"Have a good day, Mister and Ms. Wright," said Wild, with not a small amount of sarcasm, before walking to her car and driving away.

"That was close," said Kim. "You know, at some point, someone is going to see through our aliases and nail us."

"Who says Wild hasn't already pegged us?" replied Connor. "She could be acting on orders."

"But whose? The mayor's or someone else's?"

"That, Kim, is the question of the day."

"Whatever the answer is, it can go on hold for now. I want—in this order—a shower, a change of clothes, and a heaping plate of wiener schnitzel."

Connor sipped his Coke and marveled at his friend's never-ending appetite. He'd watched Kim eat escargot and a green salad before moving on to her schnitzel and now a slice of apple strudel with ice cream for dessert.

"Where the heck do you put all that food?" Connor asked.

"When I'm stressed, I eat," Kim replied.

"It's a good thing you're in phenomenal shape, or you'd be packing on the pounds."

Kim placed her fork down. "And what's the problem with that? Don't you like dating women with a little meat on their bones?"

Connor shook his head. In his mind, he envisioned he was stepping into a minefield. "I never said that. I was just making an observation. That's all."

Kim leaned forward and smiled. "I'm just teasing you. You need to learn to lighten up."

Connor glanced at Kim's half-empty wine glass, trying to remember how many drinks she'd had with her supper. He didn't want to be that friend who lectured others about their drinking, but it was clear that Kim had consumed a little too much red wine tonight. Then, as if to reinforce Connor's thoughts, Kim finished her glass of wine and looked sad when she picked up the empty bottle.

Connor was reaching for his Coke when a young woman dressed in black walked past their table. She deftly placed a cell phone next to Connor and kept walking. He instantly dropped his napkin over the phone, slid the phone closer to him, and looked straight ahead as if nothing had happened. The woman never looked back and walked out of the hotel restaurant into the night. Connor raised his hand and asked their server for two to-go coffees and the bill. Supper was over.

As casually as possible, they paid the bill, made their way back to Kim's room, and locked the door behind them.

"Did you recognize the woman who dropped off the phone?" asked Connor.

Kim furrowed her brow. "Yes, I think. Wasn't she the one working the computers in Katarina's lair?"

"Yes, she was."

Kim sipped her black coffee. "If I remember right, her name is Heike."

Connor smiled. Kim might have had a little too much wine tonight, but her memory was as sharp as ever. "Correct."

"I doubt Heike wants to speak with us. It must be Katarina."

Connor held out the phone and started to scrutinize the device.

Kim placed her hand over her mouth to suppress a tired yawn. "What are you looking for?"

Connor intently studied the phone, looking for anything that might appear to be out of place. "Phones have been used as bombs before. Press the wrong button, and the phone goes off, taking most of your head with it."

Kim's eyes shot wide open. "Katarina wouldn't kill us…would she?"

"Who knows, but people like her will do anything to preserve their anonymity."

"What a way to die. Death by telephone."

Connor stopped his inspection and offered Kim the phone. "It looks clean to me."

She shook her head. "Maybe you should make the call. I think she has a thing for you."

"Talk about selective memory. I'm fairly certain that it was you, not me, who caught Katarina's eye, but if you'd prefer me to make the call, I will."

Kim took a step back and gave Connor a thumbs up. "Yeah, let's do that."

Connor switched the phone on and scrolled through the contact list; as he suspected, there was a single number listed. "Here goes nothing," he said, pressing the number.

A phone began to ring.

Connor placed the phone on speaker mode and put it on a nearby table.

"*Guten abend*," said Katarina.

"Good evening to you, Katarina," said Kim. "I hope you are well."

"I am, and you?"

"We are. How are things going?"

"Not great. I'd complain, but who would listen?"

"I hear what you're saying," Kim replied with a shrug.

"Before we begin, may I give you two a helpful word of advice?"

"Yes, of course."

"It would help if you two were more covert in the future. Your exploits from last night are all over the news and the web. Especially the Dark Web, it's the last place you want your faces to be shown."

"Is that why you called?" asked Connor. "To warn us to lay low?"

"Yes, and a whole lot more."

Kim and Connor glanced at each other.

"We're listening," said Kim apprehensively.

"Honestly, I'm amazed you survived last night's gunbattle. I was sure I'd be reading your obituaries today, but somehow you managed to survive, and that's quite the accomplishment when you consider who you were up against."

Connor's eyes narrowed. "And who's that?"

"Have you ever heard of Office 39?"

Connor shook his head. "No, I don't think so."

"Me neither," added Kim. "Is it some kind of government office?"

Katarina snickered. "It is, but it's a secret North Korean organization that uses the black market to enrich the leader of North Korea and his family. It is estimated that their clandestine activities brought in over one billion dollars in hard currency last year alone. I personally think it's closer to two billion, but who's counting?"

"Are you telling us that the men who stole from Madame Meyer's estate were North Korean agents?" said Kim.

"Yes. It would appear that Office 39 has branched out from selling illegal drugs into the world of black-market antiquities to raise money for their Dear Leader's expensive habits. Madame Meyer's wasn't the only estate they hit. According to Interpol, it looks like they've hit over a dozen auction houses and private estates over the last month alone."

Connor sat down near the phone. He had a million questions to ask, but he knew their time with Katarina was limited, so he got straight to the point. "If you know who stole Madame Meyer's artifacts, you must know where they are."

"I may," teased Katarina.

Connor leaned closer. "Then where are they?"

"It would be no fun telling you everything, Captain. I'm here to level the playing field, not to give you everything you want. What fun would that be?"

Connor frowned. He opened his mouth to speak when Kim picked up the phone and stepped back from the table.

"Could you at least give us a clue?" asked Kim. "After all, what harm would that cause?"

"Okay, and it's only because you're asking. If I were you, I'd fly to Thailand and then make your way to Ta Phraya, where General Kirdpan will be hosting a, shall we say, less-than-legal get-together at one of his secret air bases near the border with Cambodia."

"And when will this meeting take place?" asked Connor.

"My sources say it will be held five days from today."

Kim narrowed her eyes. "Katarina, what exactly does this have to do with the North Koreans?"

"Let's just say General Kirdpan isn't among the most honest generals in the Thai Armed Forces. Good night and good luck." The line went dead.

Kim tossed the phone onto her bed and sat next to Connor. "Please tell me that made some sense to you?"

"Some of it was clear, the rest not so much," he replied. "From what she said, aside from DuFour, the North Koreans are now in the game. And from what I know about Thailand's Armed Forces, it wouldn't surprise me if this general was somehow mixed up with North Korean agents."

"Didn't Yuri also warn us that our names were all over the Dark Web?"

Connor instantly knew what Kim was thinking. "Yes, he did."

"We're going to need new identities and fast. Do you still have his number?"

"I do, but before I call him, are you sure this is what you want to do? I feel like we've been groping around in the dark so far. We're not government agents with the resources of a nation to back them up. It's just you and me out there. And Katarina was right; we're lucky to be alive after last night."

Kim smiled. "I'm not a fool, Connor. I know that compared to some of the people we may encounter, we're a pair of amateurs. But we've done okay so far, and Grenier's treasure is still waiting out there to be found. I know you're just being protective, but I'm not going home without knowing the truth."

Connor got to his feet. He was quick to learn that a decision made by his colleague rarely ever changed. "Well, I think that ends this discussion. So, from here on out, we're not doing things on the fly. Nor are we going to keep Jason and Mister Knox in the loop. They can sweat it out while they pay the bills. It's time we got ahead of the game." He picked up his phone and dialed Yuri's number from memory.

"Mister North, what can I do for you?" said Yuri, sounding as if he had been woken from a deep sleep.

"Yuri, my man, how would you like an all-expenses paid trip to Bangkok, Thailand?"

21.

Thailand

After an exhausting, fifteen-hour flight from Bern, Switzerland, to Bangkok, Thailand's capital, Kim and Connor picked up their luggage and made their way through customs. As they weren't planning on staying any longer than needed, they didn't need to purchase an entry visa to enter the country and were greeted warmly by the customs agents. Before leaving the busy airport, they decided to stop and pick up a few things at a kiosk run by a teenage boy with an infectious smile who loved to haggle with foreigners.

Kim was sure they'd paid too much for their provisions but didn't care as it was her first time in Thailand, and she expected to be slightly taken advantage of by the merchants. As soon as they stepped outside, the humidity struck them like a wet cloth. Even though it was overcast, the air was still very damp. They did their best to politely ignore the swarm of pushy street merchants and taxi drivers waiting for the tourists as they left the terminal and made their way to a waiting shuttle bus to their hotel. Kim and Connor took seats at the back, so they could speak in private. They watched while the shuttle's driver deftly negotiated the multitude of cars and taxis driving on both sides of the road as if they didn't care for their lives until they hit the highway and then sped up.

Kim finally broke the silence. "Connor, about last night. I'm sorry. I think I may have had one too many drinks with my supper and then said some stupid things."

Connor chuckled. "Don't worry about it. It's already in the past."

"Not for me, it isn't. I want to talk about what happened."

Connor could sense there was something more going on. "Sure, but if only if you want to."

"I do."

"Okay, I'm listening."

Kim cleared her throat. "I don't want you to feel uncomfortable, but I've had trouble with my relationships ever since I was a teen. You have to understand that I have deep-seated trust issues and tend to keep most men at bay so I won't get taken advantage of or get my heart broken. It's been a long time since I've been able to trust or feel comfortable around anyone. I must have drunk too much and dropped my guard."

Connor smiled grimly. "If it makes you feel any better, I'm not that much different from you. After Rachel died, I descended into the deepest and darkest part of my soul. I drank way too much and cut off everyone I had ever loved. Would you believe that I haven't spoken to my parents in over two years?"

Kim shook her head and tutted. "Connor, that's awful."

Connor looked out the window at the traffic swarming all around the bus and then back at Kim. "I often wonder if they know I'm alive or not. If I hadn't ended up in Africa, I'm sure I'd be dead by now. By the bottle or by a bullet to my brain."

Kim placed a hand on Connor's arm. "Connor, I'm heartbroken to hear that. It took me a long time to realize it, but a person's family is important to them. Even if you don't get along with them all the time, they're still your family. You should call your parents the minute we arrive at our hotel."

Connor drummed his fingers on his leg and went quiet for a few seconds. "I don't know. I don't even know what to say after all these years."

Kim mimed a phone in her hand. "How about, hello, it's your son here, and no, I'm not dead."

"Just a second, when did this conversation become all about me? I thought we were talking about you and your trust issues."

Kim raised her eyebrows. "We were, but now we're talking about you. Did you see how I did that?"

"Yes, so cut it out."

"Seriously though, you should call your parents. Two years is a long time."

"Yeah, yeah. Maybe when the mission is over."

"I'm not going to push you, but I really am. I want you to call them the instant we find the scrolls."

Connor raised a hand. "Okay, you win. I'll call them."

Kim sat back with a quiet smile.

Their bus parked in front of the Mandarin Oriental Hotel in downtown Bangkok. Right away, half a dozen young men in white uniforms, wearing traditional, black, pith-style helmets, ran over and grabbed hold of everyone's luggage.

"My God, can we afford this place?" gasped Kim, looking around the grand, glass-covered entrance to the hotel.

"I think we've got adjoining rooms at around one thousand U.S. a night," said Connor.

Kim turned on her heels, admiring their hotel. "A grand? My God. That's insane."

"I know. But we're not paying; Jason is," said Connor with a grin.

"This place is amazing. How did you hear about it?"

"Yuri recommended we stay here."

"For a man who wears dirty Hawaiian shirts, he has expensive tastes."

"I agree, but again, we're not paying for it. Come on, let's check in and see if Yuri's in town."

Connor tipped the luggage handlers well, knowing a new set of young men would be waiting in the lobby to take their bags to their room. The air in the hotel's interior was cool and refreshing compared to the stifling humidity outside. The mix of modern and old-fashioned architecture mirrored the nation—a people with a rich cultural heritage and an eye on the stars. Connor checked them in and waited patiently as his fake credit card was scanned. He let out a held breath when the desk attendant removed the card and handed him some complimentary chips for the casino.

"Please enjoy your stay," said the desk attendant, sliding over a packet with the electronic keys to their room.

"*Khob Khun*," replied Connor, thanking the attendant.

"I didn't know you could speak Thai," remarked Kim.

"I can't, really. I only know a few phrases I picked up during a two-day stopover in Bangkok when I was just getting started in the Marines."

Kim raised an eyebrow. "You'll have to tell me about your adventures here one day."

Connor shook his head. "Oh, no. I don't think so. What happens when you're young and stupid in Bangkok stays in Bangkok."

"But we are in Bangkok," teased Kim.

"Don't use logic. It's wasted on me."

They rode the elevator to the sixth floor and walked down a lush, green-carpeted floor to their adjoining rooms. Connor tipped the teenage boys and waited for them to close to Kim's door behind them.

Kim stepped onto her balcony and looked down at the hotel's pools and cabanas. "This place is unbelievable. I can't wait to go for a dip in the pool."

Connor joined her and felt the sun on his face. "Those pools do look inviting, but I don't remember packing any swimming trunks when I left the States."

"Neither did I. But that's not going to stop me from going swimming. We'll have to add your trunks and a couple of bikinis for me to Jason's bill." Kim turned and looked back into her room. "This is nice."

Connor's phone buzzed. "Good afternoon, Yuri. Where are you?"

"I'm downstairs, in the hotel restaurant," the black marketeer replied.

"Which one? There are at least ten different ones at this hotel."

"It's called the Riverside Terrace, I think. You can't miss it. It has a great view of the Chao Phraya River."

"Yeah, I know the one you're talking about. We're on our way down."

"Give me a minute," said Kim as she tossed her suitcase on a bed and opened it. She dug through her clothes until she found a clean shirt. "There's no point looking like we just stepped off a plane."

Connor knew it was time to leave Kim alone. "I'll, uh, meet you in the hallway."

"With a new shirt on," replied Kim, with a smirk.

Connor shrugged in defeat and went to check his luggage. They found Yuri sitting at a table a few meters away from the river, sipping a strawberry daiquiri. Kim and Connor sat across from him and ordered a couple of glasses of Perrier to drink.

"I can see why you picked this spot," Kim observed dryly when two young women wearing revealing bikinis walked by.

Their waiter returned and placed the cold drinks on the table. Connor tipped the young man and asked for some privacy.

"So, Yuri, please tell me you have friends here in Thailand who can help us?" asked Connor.

Yuri feigned being insulted. "Come on; this is Yuri you're talking about. What's not to love? But to answer your question, yes, I have friends here in Bangkok who owe me a favor or two, so getting your gear won't be hard at all."

"That's a relief."

"I know you've only been here a few hours longer than us," said Kim, "but have you been able to learn anything about Ta Phraya and where General Kirdpan?"

Yuri shook his head. "No, not yet. I have feelers out, but it's too early. Give me two days; I should have something for you by then."

"That sounds fair."

"I hope so because Thailand may look like a pleasant country to visit, pretty lady, but its police can be very unforgiving if you know what I mean."

"I think I do."

Yuri's voice became agitated, but he kept it low. "Good, because I'm not being paranoid when I say Thailand has almost become a police state these past few years. So, we would all be wise to keep off the government's radar. People like me don't go to jail. If I can't pay off whoever has arrested me, I'll disappear and become just another tourist who died of an overdose while on vacation in Thailand."

"We hear what you're saying," said Connor, hearing the fear in Yuri's voice. "And we'll keep as low as possible."

"So, when should we plan to meet next?" asked Kim.

Yuri ran a hand over the stubble on his chin. "Why don't we meet here for breakfast on Thursday morning and go over what I've learned?"

"Okay, until then," said Connor.

"So, what are you two *siblings* going to do for the next two days?" said Yuri, smirking as he handed two new passports to Connor under the table.

Kim smiled. "We're going swimming, and then I'm going to eat until I fall asleep."

Yuri arrived a little after eight, looking like he hadn't gone to bed once in the interim. His eyes were bloodshot, and his clothes wrinkled.

"Well, look what the cat dragged in," quipped Kim.

Yuri collapsed into his seat and reached for a silver carafe to pour himself a coffee. "Don't say a word. It took me until fifteen minutes ago to get everything I was after."

"Here, let me," said Kim, pouring Yuri some coffee.

Connor smiled and shook his head as Yuri held his cup in his hands as if it were some kind of lifesaving elixir. "Would you like some breakfast?"

Yuri shook his head. "Oh, God, no. Just coffee this morning."

"Do you mind if we eat?"

"No, not at all."

Connor waved over their server and ordered two continental breakfasts. Thankfully, it didn't take long for the plates to arrive. Their waiter nodded politely and left them in peace to eat.

Kim casually looked around the restaurant to ensure no one was listening to their conversation and then took a bite from her blueberry muffin. In a quiet tone, she asked, "So what can you tell us, Yuri?"

"Do you want the good news first or the bad news?"

Connor shrugged indifferently.

"I always like getting the bad news upfront. That way, the good news always sounds so much better," said Kim.

"Okay. The bad news is there is no way in hell I can get you a pass to the base in Ta Phraya."

"Why not?" asked Connor.

"Because, according to the Royal Thai Air Force, the base doesn't exist."

"And the good news?" asked Kim.

Yuri smiled roguishly. "I know where you can get a pass."

Kim sighed. "To me, the balance sheet seems even right now. So, Yuri, where can we get our hands on a pass?"

Yuri downed his coffee and poured another cup. "The pass you're looking for is in a room safe at the nearby Millennium Hilton."

Kim's eyes narrowed. "Who's the target?"

"The man's name is Joseph Quinn. He's a loudmouthed Englishman who likes to throw his money around. A friend of mine gave me a heads-up that this gentleman was going through ten-thousand-dollar business ladies two, sometimes three, a day." Yuri made air quotations around *business ladies*.

"And he has a pass?"

Yuri nodded. "*Da*. The more he drinks, the looser his tongue becomes, and he couldn't help but brag about it to one of my friend's business associates."

"What does he look like?"

"I'll send you a picture later today."

"Thanks."

"So, what's the plan?" asked Connor.

"This evening around 2300 hours, while he's busy at the bar, you're going to break into his room and steal his pass."

"And if he notices it missing, then what?"

"He won't, at least not until it's too late. I've arranged for Mister Quinn to be given a sedative that will keep him in a state of near unconsciousness for two days. So, by the time he finally comes to and realizes that he's been robbed, you two should be long gone."

"I like it," said Kim. "Simple and effective."

Connor raised a hand. "Being the non-criminal here, it all sounds a bit too simple to me."

"The best robberies usually are," remarked Kim. "I honestly like Yuri's plan."

"You're the thief. If you like it, I guess so do I."

Kim smiled. "Thanks."

"Yuri, the question that's been bugging me ever since we arrived in Thailand is, why here? Why would North Korean agents hold a secret antiquities auction on a base run by the Royal Thai Air Force? After all, they're not exactly the best of friends."

Yuri held up three fingers and then lowered one. "For two really good reasons. First, General Kirdpan is as corrupt as they come.

His base in Ta Phraya is used for what we in the business would call black ops. My contact told me the installation is home to a squadron of drones. But instead of using them to patrol the borders, General Kirdpan uses them to fly illegal shipments of heroin from a village just across the border in Cambodia into Thailand."

"And the other good reason?" asked Kim.

"He gets a healthy cut of the profits from every auction held on the base. See, I told you he was corrupt."

"Okay, but wouldn't the sudden arrival of North Korean agents at one of Kirdpan's bases tip off the authorities that something was up?" asked Connor.

Yuri gulped down his coffee and reached for more. "Why would it? I already told you the base doesn't exist. So, you can't get suspicious if there's nothing there to begin with."

"True."

"I've learned the whole process, from beginning to end, is quite impressive. The stolen antiquities are shipped out of Cyprus onboard Liberian-registered ships until they reach Pakistan. After that, they are flown to Thailand. Once they arrive here, they are picked up by some of General Kirdpan's people and flown straight to his black ops base. I'm not even sure if anyone in Kirdpan's chain of command has the slightest clue about what's going on. And if they do, he's paying them good money to be quiet and look the other way."

"Good lord," said Connor. "Who says crime doesn't pay?"

Kim leaned forward. "Yuri, do you know when the auction is taking place?"

"Tomorrow evening. Mister Quinn's invitation is also his identity card for the event. Luckily, his card allows him to bring another person with him, or Mister North would be going on his own."

"If this base doesn't exist, how are we supposed to get there?" Kim asked.

"My informant wasn't one hundred percent sure, but he thinks that info is on the back of the ID card. Follow it to the *T*, and you should be okay. When you arrive at the base, your card will be scanned, and you'll be escorted to a hangar where the auction will take place sometime after 2000 hours."

"So far, so good. But what if we want to take a better look at the items for sale? After all, I wouldn't want to bid millions of dollars on the word of a North Korean agent."

"I've been told the bids are not binding. The highest bidder will get a chance to inspect the artifact, and if they're not happy, they can withdraw their bid, and the next highest bidder will get the chance to buy it."

"And you got all this from your friend?" Connor asked suspiciously.

"Yes."

"For a man in your shape, that's quite the accomplishment."

Yuri winked. "Don't worry. I have friends in low places and do some of my best work half-drunk."

Kim waved a hand in front of her face. "Half! I can smell you from here."

"The gear I asked for; did you manage to get that as well?" Connor asked.

"I sure did. I'll drop it all off tomorrow morning before you begin your day." Yuri blinked his eyes to focus them. "Please don't tell me you brought a tuxedo to go to the auction in?"

"No, but I was hoping to rent one from the hotel."

Yuri muttered something undistinguishable under his breath. "Don't even think about wearing a tux. You'd stick out like a sore thumb if you did that. Please dress casually and do your best to look like you belong at the auction. You're my best clients right now, and I would hate to lose you."

"Or the money?" said Connor bluntly.

"Yeah, there's that, too."

"Thanks, Yuri," said Kim. "You're the best."

"Whatever you do tomorrow evening, don't get caught. General Kirdpan won't care if you're from the West or a man or a woman. He'll torture you to get whatever information he wants from you and then dispose of your bodies in the closest river."

"Swell," said Connor.

"Until later," said Yuri, staggering to his feet.

"He's thorough. I'll give him that," said Kim, watching Yuri try not to trip over his feet as he passed a table with two scantily dressed women sitting there.

"Please, Kim, it's an act," countered Connor. "No one that drunk would be that lucid. Yuri barely slurred his words. He probably poured half a bottle of rum on his clothes and made sure he looked like hell in case the police were watching him."

"Why?"

"So, they'd think he's just another drunken ex-patriot fool and not waste their time on him. Yuri's information was too precise to have come second-hand from one of his business associates. He's got a contact working inside the base, and he's covering for them."

"Okay, he's thorough, smart, and a good actor." Kim was silent momentarily, and then she glanced suspiciously around the restaurant. "Do you think we're being watched?"

Connor shook his head. "I doubt it. We're nobodies. However, someone like our target for tonight is most likely on the police's watch list. We'll have to be extra careful tonight."

Kim leaned close. "Connor, you don't think Yuri would sell us out, do you?"

"As long as Jason keeps paying the bills, I think we're safe. However, the instant the money stops flowing, we're going to be truly on our own."

22.

Kim and Connor strolled into the bar at the Millennium Hilton wearing clothes they had bought only hours ago from a high-end store near their hotel. Connor wore pressed, white trousers, with a white, open-necked shirt under a light beige jacket, while Kim sported a cream-colored outfit with a matching leather purse. A young lady in a white tuxedo escorted them to a table near the back of the circular lounge. Not only did it give them a great view of the city at night, but it also allowed them to see many of the other patrons. The mood in the bar was captivating. Tunes played by a small jazz band filled the air as elegantly dressed people from all over the world mingled, laughed, and drank.

"I'd love to be a fly on the wall when Jason gets the bill for these clothes," said Connor, imagining his former father-in-law reading the bill and having a fatal heart attack.

"I call it the cost of doing business," said Kim, looking around the room for Joseph Quinn. She soon spotted him sitting at a table with three women, barely out of their teens. The women wore far-too-revealing tops and laughed at every word Quinn said. Kim also noticed three half-empty bottles of champagne on their table. She thought of her sister and felt a flush of anger at the life she had once lived.

"Have you got eyes on?" asked Connor, bringing her back.

Kim nodded. "Yeah, he's that fat loudmouth over by the band."

Connor moved in his seat and saw Quinn. He shook his head at the thought of Quinn with the three young prostitutes.

A smiling waiter took their order before moving to the following table.

Kim placed her purse on the table and pretended to look for something while she double-checked its contents. "I guess it's time to get to work."

Connor nodded and carefully slipped his earpiece into place. He checked the feed coming from Kim's contact lens on his cellphone and smiled at his partner. "I think we're in business. Good luck and good hunting."

Kim went to get to her feet. "Quit worrying. It'll be a walk in the park."

"That would be refreshing," Connor quipped.

"You know, before we met, everything used to go so smoothly; you must be some kind of jinx, Connor North."

"That's one way of looking at it."

Kim stood and walked out of the bar, heading for the nearest elevator. From the information provided by Yuri, Kim knew Quinn was staying on the eighth floor, in room 811. She glanced at her watch and saw it was precisely 2300 hours. It was time to get to work. Kim boarded an elevator and lowered her head, feigning to look at her nails to avoid having her face recorded by a surveillance camera.

The elevator began to slow.

Kim took a deep breath through her nostrils and cleared her mind. All that mattered was getting in and out of Quinn's room without being caught. The elevator doors opened, and Kim stepped out. She knew the hotel's cameras would record everything she did, so Kim pretended she was applying lipstick, which blocked most of her face from view, and strode toward Quinn's room. At the door, she opened her purse, extracted a fake room card, and ran it over the door's card reader. Kim's card, programmed to override more than ninety percent of the world's passcodes, effortlessly opened Quinn's door. She opened the door, flipped on the lights, and stepped inside.

"Oh God," she muttered. The unmade bed and the filthy carpet were a mess. At least a dozen empty champagne bottles lay beside the bed: uneaten room service meals and women's underclothes added to the clutter. Kim gagged at the smell of stale cigars floating in half-finished glasses of Scotch.

"*Someone's having a good time,*" said Connor in Kim's ear.

"If you say so. This place looks and smells worse than a pigsty."

"*Don't touch anything you don't have to.*"

"Trust me; I won't."

Kim slid on a pair of thin rubber gloves as she studied the room. She walked over to a cupboard with slightly ajar doors and gently pushed the doors open. Kim smiled. The hotel may have been expensive to stay in, but the safe in Quinn's room was run-of-the-mill. The safe had a universal numbered keypad for a lock. Kim thought about using her thermal scanner, but knowing nothing about Quinn, she opted for something else and dug out a small can of breath freshener. Kim held it about six inches from the keypad and depressed the actuator valve. Instead of breath freshener, liquid nitrogen shot out, instantly freezing the thin metal around the lock.

"That should do," said Kim, sliding the empty spray can back into her purse.

"*Uh, Kim, how are you doing?*" asked Connor. He sounded on edge.

"I'm almost done. Why?"

"*Because that goon we saw at DuFour's and again in Switzerland is here.*"

Kim's nerves heightened. "Has he seen you?"

"*Not yet; he seems to be looking for someone in the bar.*" There was a slight pause. "*But I don't think it's me.*"

Kim didn't like what she was hearing. DuFour's man seemed to be a like a shadow. Wherever they went, he was there too. "Head back to the lobby. I'll be down shortly."

"Got it. I'm on the move."

Kim looked around and picked up a heavy glass ashtray. She brought it up over her head and then slammed it down hard on the keypad. The metal all around it shattered like glass, exposing the contents of the safe.

"Yes," said Kim, pumping her fist in the air. She peered inside and saw several bags of cocaine, Quinn's passport, a laminated pass, and several stacks of U.S. one-hundred-dollar bills. The thief in her wanted to help herself to the money, but she fought the urge and only grabbed the pass.

"I've got the pass, and I'm on my way down," she reported.

"Great news. I'm waiting for you by the elevators."

Kim slipped the pass into her purse, removed her gloves, and calmly exited the room. She again lowered her head just enough that it would be hard for the hallway cameras to catch a good look at her face and made her way to the elevator. Kim pressed the down button and started to tap her foot on the carpet. Finally, the doors slid open, and Kim walked inside, relieved to find she was the only passenger. Her nervous tension faded as the floors counted down. All they had to do was walk out of the hotel, and they were free.

"Evening," said Connor as the doors parted and Kim joined her colleague.

"Time to go," remarked Kim with one eye on the bar, hoping DuFour's man was still inside.

They walked calmly through the lobby and stepped outside into the refreshing night air. The city streets seemed alive, with dozens of cars and taxis jostling for the right of way. At the same time, a multitude of street vendors vied for their attention.

"What do you want to do?" asked Connor. "Walk or take a cab?"

Kim bit her lip. "I think I'd prefer if we took a cab."

Connor nodded, turned to a white-jacketed hotel employee, slipped him a gratuitous tip, and asked him to hail them a cab.

"Going somewhere?" said a man behind Kim and Connor with a strong French accent.

Kim and Connor turned simultaneously and looked into the cold eyes of DuFour's bodyguard.

"You again," muttered Connor darkly.

"I thought it was you in the bar," said the man to Connor. "Please let me introduce myself. My name is Jean Vallin, and you two have proven to be quite the challenge to find."

"I'm sorry if you've had such a difficult time finding us, but you'll have to excuse us. We have a cab to catch."

"I have a better idea. Why don't we go back inside and talk for a while?"

Connor's eyes narrowed when he spotted the small pistol in Vallin's hand. "And if we don't want to?"

Vallin's voice turned threatening. "Let's not play dumb, Captain. Inside, now!"

In a move neither man saw coming, Kim pretended to trip and fall into Vallin's arm. Then, as fast as a cobra striking its prey, she jammed a mini-Taser in the form of a stun ring against Vallin's neck and activated it, shocking the unsuspecting killer. In the blink of an eye, Vallin's knees buckled, and his body shook from the powerful surge of electricity. The second Kim was satisfied Vallin was no longer a threat, she deactivated her Taser and stepped aside as Connor grabbed the Frenchman and lowered him to the ground.

Connor feigned concern and yelled, "Help, this man needs a doctor!"

An Asian gentleman with salt-and-pepper hair pushed his way through the crowd. "I'm a doctor," he said. "What appears to be the problem?"

"I don't know," replied Connor. "I think this man's having a stroke."

"Let me take a look," said the doctor, kneeling to examine Vallin.

Kim and Connor saw their chance and smoothly faded into the crowd. They jumped into the first cab they saw, and both started to chuckle.

"Where the heck did you get that ring?" asked Connor.

"Switzerland," replied Kim. "It was in the box Yuri gave us. I wasn't sure if I'd ever use it, but here we are."

"Well, I'm glad you brought it with you tonight. Things were about to turn ugly back there."

"That man gives me the creeps. I don't think he's the kind of man to give up and walk away."

Connor nodded. "I know. I'll call Yuri. For starters, we're going to need a new hotel."

"And after that?"

"I don't know, but we'd best be ready for anything tomorrow. And I do mean anything."

23.

"What a night," griped Connor, getting to his feet. He slowly rotated his aching neck, listening to the vertebrae pop.

Kim opened her tired eyes and leaned forward in her wobbly plastic chair. "This is not what I had expected when Yuri said he had a safe house in Bangkok, but as they say, any port in a storm will do."

Connor looked around their tiny, one-room apartment and shook his head. "The only saving grace is that this place has a working toilet."

"Well, it's better than being dead," observed Kim, heading for the bathroom.

Connor's stomach growled as he checked the time. It was nearing six in the morning.

Knock-knock-knock.

Connor edged to the door and knocked twice in response.

"Good morning," said Yuri cheerfully from behind the closed door.

"I hope you brought some food," said Connor, unlocking the door. "I'm starving."

Yuri entered the apartment, carrying two paper bags and three cups of coffee in a cardboard tray. On his back was a small canvas pack. "I stopped by McDonalds on the way here. I got us something called the big breakfast. It has eggs and something that looks like a sausage patty."

"Right about now, that sounds like five-star dining."

"Is that coffee I smell?" said Kim, joining her partners.

"*Da*, it is, pretty lady," replied Yuri, handing her a cup.

"Thanks," said Kim, flipping off the lid so she could hold the cup under her nose and smell the aroma. "Thank God for coffee."

"Come, let's eat. We have a lot to talk about," suggested Yuri.

They sat at a small plastic table and helped themselves to breakfast.

"Okay, first things first," said Yuri. "My contact tells me that the bulk of the people attending the auction later today are middlemen and women bidding on behalf of their clients, so you two should fit in just nicely."

"That's a relief," said Connor.

Yuri looked at his accomplices. "Have either of you ever bid at an auction before?"

"No," said Kim.

"Me neither, but we were prepared to in Switzerland," replied Connor.

Yuri tutted. "My friends, Switzerland is not the same as a secret base on the Cambodian border. You're dealing with powerful and paranoid people who won't think twice about killing either of you should they suspect anything wrong. So, I called Mister Knox late last night and arranged for a Swiss bank account to be opened. Upon arrival, Kirdpan's people will undoubtedly ask for this information to prove you're genuine bidders."

"Thanks," said Kim. "You're a lifesaver."

"Don't relax just yet. If you could get a pass to tonight's auction, so could that man you tased last night. So be careful. General Kirdpan's base is well over three hundred kilometers from Bangkok. If anything goes wrong, there's precious little that I'll be able to do to help you."

"Yuri, let's suppose something does go wrong," mused Kim. "Can't your contact help us?"

"Nope," said Yuri, firmly shaking his head. "When you leave here today, you're on your own. I can't risk exposing my network by giving you my contact's name."

"Fair enough," noted Connor. "But I'm with Kim; if we have to make a quick exit, is there somewhere we can go to ground until you reach us?"

Deep in thought, Yuri chewed on his lower lip. "If you have to make a run for it, head south into Cambodia. It may take me a few days, but I promise I'll find you."

"Are you sure?" asked Kim.

"Of course. I'm not just a man who can obtain the obtainable; I'm also a damned good pilot. Trust me, I'll find you."

Connor sipped his coffee and eyed Yuri's pack. "What's in the bag?"

Yuri dragged the sack closer and opened the cover. "You're lucky that Mister Hamilton is paying me a lot of money to keep you two supplied in the field."

Connor chuckled. "Yuri, this isn't like the movies. Kim and I can't fly from country to country carrying Tasers, bear spray, and ceramic knives without getting caught. Comms gear is easy to explain, the rest not so much."

"I know, but it sure would be a lot less expensive if you could."

Connor tapped his hand on the table. "Quit being cheap, and show us what you've brought."

"Yeah, let's see what you've got," added Kim.

"Because you're heading into the unknown, I have resupplied you with daggers and knives you can easily conceal on your bodies, along with some t-shirts made with liquid body armor."

"What about the pistol I asked for?" asked Connor.

"Mister North, are you sure you want to bring a pistol into Kirdpan's base?"

"After what happened in Switzerland, yes, I am."

Yuri reluctantly placed a micro 9mm Sig Sauer pistol and an ankle holster beside Connor. "It's your head if anything should go wrong."

"I know; that's why I want to be armed," responded Connor, picking up the pistol and inspecting it. It was lightweight and fit in the palm of his hand. It wasn't something Connor was used to operating, but it would have to do.

Kim placed Joseph Quinn's stolen pass on the table. "Yuri, the information on the back of the card says that we're to be at the Hotel Peninsula's helipad at 1500 hours to be picked up by a chopper and flown to Ta Phraya. Is this information still up to date?"

Yuri nodded. "As far as I know, nothing has changed."

Kim sat back and let out a deep breath. "Well, unless something drastically changes, I guess we're off to Ta Phraya."

"All I can say is good luck," said Yuri, offering his hand to Kim to shake.

"Let's hope we won't need it," she replied, shaking Yuri's hand.

"Knowing us, we're going to need all the good luck we can muster," said Connor, sliding his pistol into his ankle holster.

"Ready?" Connor asked Kim as their elevator began to slow.

"Quit asking; I'm nervous enough without you constantly asking how I'm doing," replied Kim, needling her friend on the ribs with her elbow.

"You know it's not too late to call the whole thing off."

For his suggestion, Connor received an even harder shot in his ribs.

The doors parted. A young woman in a white uniform, holding a scanner in her hand, greeted them. "Good afternoon, and welcome to the Hotel Peninsula's helipad reception area. May I please see your pass?"

"Of course," responded Connor, handing over Quinn's card.

The woman scanned the pass and smiled. "Welcome, Mister Quinn. May I have the name of your guest for the flight manifest?"

"Kim White," he replied without hesitation.

"Thank you," said the receptionist, logging in Kim.

The room was more spacious than Connor had expected. It had a comfortable lounge and a small museum's worth of displays on the walls, covering the history of aviation in Bangkok. There were four other people in the reception area. Luckily, Vallin wasn't among them. Connor and Kim decided to join the other passengers. They strolled over and pretended to be interested in the model of an old seaplane. No sooner had they stopped when a young waiter walked over and offered them a flute of champagne.

"None for me," said Connor.

"Nor me," said Kim. "Do you have any Perrier?"

The waiter nodded and called one of his colleagues over.

As soon as they were alone, Kim protested. "Kim White! Seriously? Is that the best you could come with?"

"I never picked it. It's the name on the new passport Yuri gave us."

"Sorry, I forgot to check mine. I take it you're Connor White?"

"Yep. It's not very original, but easy to remember. But let's not forget that my alias for tonight is Quinn, not White."

"It's a good thing I have a good memory," quipped Kim. "Or this would get confusing real fast."

Behind them, the elevator chimed. In an instant, the hair on Connor's neck stood up. He looked over his shoulder and clenched his jaw at the sight of Vallin, accompanied by an athletic-looking Asian woman, walking out of the elevator. He nudged Kim to get her attention.

"What?" asked Kim irritably.

"We've got company," said Connor, turning to face Vallin.

"Oh crap," said Kim as Vallin nodded at them and walked over with his guest on his arm.

"Good afternoon, Mister-?" said Vallin.

"Quinn, Joseph Quinn," replied Connor, faking a smile. "And who might you be, Monsieur?"

"Emil Jacobin," said Vallin, offering his calloused hand.

Connor took a step and took Vallin's hand.

Vallin lowered his voice and squeezed his hand as tight as a vise. "So, Mister Quinn, how did you get your pass?"

Connor had never wanted to smash his fist into another man's face before as much as he did Vallin's. He pushed back, tightening his grip until his hand hurt. If anyone was going to give in, it wasn't going to be Connor. "My man's drugged up. And yours?"

"In a dumpster somewhere," replied Vallin, grimacing in pain.

"Really, Jean?" moaned the woman by his side. "These kinds of macho BS games are for adolescent boys and men with low self-esteem issues. Let go of his hand right now, or I'll make you!"

Vallin and Connor released each other from their grips and shook their hands to get the blood flowing again. Both men breathed deeply and glared at one another.

"I'm sorry," said the woman to Kim, stepping between the two antagonists. "But I doubt Jean will ever introduce me. My name is Rin."

Kim didn't know if she should trust the woman but guessed that Rin already knew who she was, so there was no point in playing dumb. "Hi, I'm Kim."

"It's a pleasure to meet you. Jean told me that you're quite the thief. Is that true?"

Kim ran her finger around the rim of her glass. "I try my best."

Rin eyed Kim over from her feet to the top of her head. "If you're good at it, I suggest you stick to it and leave the rough stuff to Jean and me. Okay?"

Kim felt the tension in the air between them. But, like her partner, she had no plan to back down. Kim narrowed her eyes. "Sure, Rin. Whatever makes you happy."

Rin sighed loudly and gave a dismissive hand gesture inches from her face. "Come, Jean or Emil, or whatever you want to be called, these people bore me, and I want a glass or two of champagne before we leave."

Kim and Connor watched their adversaries walk away in search of a drink.

"Jesus, what a pair," said Kim, shaking her head. "That woman sure is full of herself."

"Yeah, it's as if they were made for each other," observed Connor.

Kim crossed her arms. "I don't like this."

"Nor do I, but when you think about it the odds are still even."

Kim scrunched her brow. "How so?"

"Vallin, like us, is using a stolen pass. He can't out us to Kirdpan without outing himself, and I doubt he wants to do that."

Kim grinned. "I like that. I guess tonight will come down to who has the larger bank account, DuFour or Hamilton."

24.

Connor glanced out the window of their helicopter as it landed inside a sprawling base cut out of the jungle. It reminded him of an operation in the Philippines that had ended badly, with one of his men dangerously wounded and five Filipino Marines dead. That day's information had been wrong, and he never forgot the value of good intelligence before launching an operation.

The pilot switched off the engines as a squad of heavily armed soldiers ran out from behind a camouflaged trailer and smartly formed a cordon around the chopper.

"Game on," murmured Kim, holding her purse tight in her hands.

"Yeah, let's do this," said Connor, trying to sound confident. He knew the odds were stacked against them, but Connor banished such thoughts from his mind. He had a job to do.

A side door opened, and a young Thai lieutenant boarded the helicopter.

"Good day, ladies and gentlemen," he said in English. "It's a great honor to have you here today. Unfortunately, General Kirdpan is quite busy, but he sends his warmest greetings. If you would please exit the helicopter and follow me to the reception center?"

A flash of white-hot anger surged through Connor's body, watching Vallin and Rin make small talk with the lieutenant as they left the chopper. Kim gently placed a hand on Connor's right arm. "Easy does it, Marine. I need you to wipe that angry look from your face right away. I know it's hard, but you've got to learn to mask your feelings, or they'll be your undoing."

Connor took a deep breath and nodded at his comrade. He walked past the junior officer and stepped onto the black ops base. The facility was a hive of activity. Groups of soldiers moved quickly about the installation with a purpose. Kim and Connor fell in and strolled with another couple, trying to blend in as best they could. Then, out of the corner of his eye, Connor spotted a crew of technicians in coveralls working on a drone inside a hangar. A neat pile of heroin rested on a table next to the UAV.

"This way, please," said the officer, waving for the bidders to stay close. "We're almost there."

"Oh, crap," said Kim under her breath.

"What's wrong?" asked Connor.

"That," she replied as a man with a camera waved at the new arrivals.

"Well, that changes everything."

"Yeah, for the worse. I really don't want them taking my picture."

"There's not a lot we can do about it. If our cover gets blown, so will Vallin's. We can always say Quinn gave us the card as he's too sick to attend the auction. Besides, Knox's bank account gives us some credibility."

"I hope so."

Connor leaned close. "Do you still think the hunt for the truth is worth this?"

"God, you're annoying. Yeah, I do. But I wish it wasn't so stressful."

At the reception center, a Thai sergeant smiled at Connor and scanned his ID. "Good day, Mister Quinn."

"Good day," replied Connor.

The sergeant faced Kim. "And your name, please."

"Kim, Ms. Kim White."

The NCO checked the flight manifest and nodded. "Welcome, Ms. White. Please step aside and allow Corporal Lee to take your picture."

Kim and Connor went along with the charade and stood side by side as Lee took their pictures.

"If you don't mind me asking, what are the pictures for?" Connor asked Lee.

Lee shrugged and said, "Sorry, I no speak English."

"Thank you anyway," responded Connor, suspecting Lee knew far more English than he let on.

A man in pressed combat fatigues walked into the room accompanied by a couple of alluring women carrying trays of champagne. "Hello, everyone. My name is Major Chakrii, and I will be your host for the evening. As you're the last group to arrive and have made good time, we can commence the auction a little earlier than planned tonight so you can all return to your hotels at a decent hour and celebrate your good luck at the auction. Once you have helped yourselves to a glass of the finest champagne in all of Thailand, please follow me to the hangar, where the auction will take place."

Kim and Connor each took a flute but never brought it to their lips.

"What's wrong, friend?" asked a swarthy-looking man with curly, salt-and-pepper hair and a gold-capped front tooth, smiling at Connor. "Don't you like champagne?"

Connor shook his head. "Not really. I prefer bourbon. Would you like mine?"

"Hell, yes. This stuff is great."

Connor handed the man his drink. "Is this your first auction, Mister—?"

The man toasted Connor. "Makris, Spiros Makris at your service."

"Joseph Quinn. Mister Makris, you wouldn't happen to be from Greece, would you?"

"Yes. Let me guess, the name gave me away," he jested.

Connor pretended to chuckle. "A little."

"And yes, this is my first auction." Then Makris unexpectedly turned and playfully poked Connor with his elbow. "At least one like this, if you know what I mean?"

"Oh, yes, I do."

"Is this your first as well, Joseph?"

Connor nodded. "What are you bidding on tonight?"

"There are some exquisite stone sculptures from the time of Alexander the Great on the block tonight. My boss is absolutely fascinated with that period of Greek history and is willing to pay a ton of money to get his hands on these items."

"So he can put them in a museum for all to see?"

Makris paused and looked at Connor as if he had just insulted him.

"I'm sorry, Mister Makris, but you'll have to excuse my friend's sense of humor," said Kim. "As you can see, he has none."

Makris smiled and broke out laughing. "Good one. And you, what are you after?"

"The man we're bidding for has an eye for Pre-Columbian artifacts," replied Connor. "The older, the better."

Makris mimed, wiping sweat from his brow with the back of his hand. "That's a relief. The fewer people interested in the sculptures I'm after, the easier the bidding will go."

"Let's hope so," said Connor, thinking not of Makris' items but Grenier's map.

As they approached the auction hangar, Connor noticed the heightened security and a small line of people waiting to go inside.

Major Chakrii snapped his fingers in the air. "As you enter the hangar, please enter your client's banking information into Staff-Sergeant Chen's encrypted computer to speed things up once you have won your bids. Also, you don't need to worry about cellphone coverage here on the base. I can assure you that you can reach anywhere on the planet other than the South Pole. But who lives there anyway, am I right?"

A few people laughed at Chakrii's attempt at humor, but Kim and Connor did not.

"Thank God for Yuri and Knox," said Kim quietly.

Connor stepped up in line and typed in Knox's banking information, silently praying nothing went wrong. When a green light appeared on the computer, the staff sergeant indicated with his hand for Kim and Connor to proceed. "Wow," uttered Connor, looking around the spacious hangar. Two bars were open for business, and a long buffet table was topped with tasty-looking finger foods.

"Let me guess, it was like this every day when you were in the Marines?" teased Kim.

"Good lord, no. For the Air Force, maybe, but never the Marines." Connor slowly turned on his heel, checking out the rest of the tent. A dozen uninterested-looking soldiers were on duty, with their rifles slung over their shoulders, pacing back and forth. Connor noted where the six exits were if they needed to leave quickly.

"Damn, our friends made it in," observed Kim.

Connor frowned, his shoulders tensing.

"Hey, what did I say about body language?" said Kim, gently nudging her partner. "Calm yourself and mask your feelings."

Connor took a couple of deep breaths and turned his back on Vallin and his associate. For now, he decided that he'd have to pretend that the two assassins weren't in the room with them.

"Let's grab a program," suggested Kim. She flagged down a young soldier carrying a listing of the items on the block tonight. Kim hurriedly scanned the document, looking for their lot.

"Have you found what we're looking for?" asked Connor.

Kim nodded. "Yes, it's second from last; it's in lot fourteen. My goodness, Madame Meyer's family was quite naughty. Aside from the maps, there are priceless antiquities from the Mayans and the Incas in the lot. No wonder the government of Peru wanted these items back."

Connor tried looking over her shoulder to see how much Madame Meyer's estate was going for. "Is there a starting price listed?"

Kim chuckled and tried to hide the page with her right hand. "Take a guess."

Connor paused and then shrugged his shoulders. "I dunno. Ten million?"

Kim lifted her hand. "Yeah, it's ten million dollars. But, it's got to be worth at least ten times that amount."

"Be happy; it's not our money."

"Speaking of that. When you called Knox this afternoon, how high did he say Mister Hamilton would be willing to go?"

"Somewhere around twenty million."

Kim tutted. "There's no way he's going to win."

Major Chakrii moved to the front of the hangar. "Ladies and gentlemen, we are ready to begin the auction, so if you wouldn't mind, please take a seat."

Kim and Connor sat near the back, in a spot with a clear view of the auction table and the closest exits.

A man with snow-white hair, dressed in a tuxedo, walked to a podium and loudly banged a gavel. Then, with a hint of an Italian accent, he said, "Ladies and gentlemen, let the bidding begin."

The first item on the block was a pair of large tablets inscribed with pre-cuneiform Sumerian script from around 3400 BCE that allegedly were the keys to finding a fortune in gold looted during a raid on a city-state on the Tigris River. The bidding started at five million but was soon over twelve million dollars, with no sign that the bids would slow down.

"Hey, this is kinda exciting," said Kim, moving in her seat to get a better look at the two bidders locked in verbal combat for the tablets. The lot eventually sold for eighteen million, making Kim wonder how much Madame Meyer's antiquities would fetch. Unfortunately, it was evident to her that twenty million dollars would not suffice.

Time seemed to fly by as priceless antiquity after antiquity was sold at outrageous prices. Before they knew it, Kim and Connor's lot was brought out and reverently placed on a long wooden table for everyone to admire.

The auctioneer took a sip of water and smiled at the crowd. "Ladies and gentlemen, I present to you lot fourteen. In it, you will find some of the most exquisite examples of pre-Columbian artifacts found outside of a museum. And, as an added bonus, there are four maps, two of which allegedly claim to show where Montezuma hid his vast treasure. Shall we begin the bidding at ten million dollars?"

Right away, Vallin raised his hand.

"I have ten million," announced the auctioneer. "Do I hear eleven?"

"Eleven," said Kim, smiling.

A split-second later, Vallin said, "Fifteen."

The auctioneer looked at Kim. "Madam, your bid?"

"Eighteen."

A man in a white suit with a dark beard entered the bidding. He held his hand high and announced, "Nineteen!"

Connor could see the lot was going to go for an astronomical sum. So, he stood, dug out his phone, and moved away from the other bidders.

Knox answered on the second ring. "Good day, Connor; how are things going?"

"Is Jason with you?"

"Yes."

"Good. Put him on the phone."

"I'm putting my phone on speaker mode."

"Hello, Connor," said Hamilton. "How are you today?"

"Stuff the pleasantries," responded Connor gruffly. "The bidding is already near twenty million for the estate. How high are you prepared to go?"

"It's that high already?" Hamilton's voice sounded dejected.

"Yep. The map is worthless. It's all of the other antiquities that are driving up the cost. I'm willing to bet the lot will go for at least fifty million. Do you have that kind of petty cash?"

There was a pause, and then Hamilton spoke. "I had no idea the bidding would go this high. I can go to twenty-five, and then that's it."

"Okay, got it." Connor abruptly ended the call and slid his phone away. He sat down and saw Kim wide-eyed, staring at the lot as if transfixed. He gently nudged her arm.

"Sorry," said Kim. "I got distracted. What did Mister Hamilton say?"

"Twenty-five million, and then we're done."

"We're out of time, then. Vallin just bid twenty, and our mystery bidder with the beard is sure to go past twenty-five."

Connor bit his lip as the bid reached twenty-three million dollars. Suddenly, an idea flashed in his mind. He looked at Kim and said, "How light are your fingers?"

Kim grinned. "The lightest. Why?"

"It's time to earn our money." Connor stood and brought up a hand.

"A new bidder. Are you bidding, sir?' asked the auctioneer dryly.

"No, sir, I am not. However, my client back in the United States would like my partner and me to examine the artifacts before the bids go any higher."

The auctioneer placed his gavel down. "You may approach."

Kim and Connor were aware that everyone in the room was watching them as they made their way to the front of the room. They stepped apart and pretended to examine the unbelievably rare artifacts. There were two golden Mayan death masks inlaid with jade and other precious stones lying on the table. Next to them were at least a dozen statues, necklaces, Incan headdresses, earrings, and even more necklaces made from gold. And then, by themselves, at the end of the exhibit were the maps. It was a sight to behold.

Kim looked over the Incan artifacts while Connor made a pretense of examining the death masks. Behind them, the crowd grew bored and began to talk among themselves.

It was time to strike.

Kim eyed the maps at the end of the table and strolled toward them. At the last second, she faked tripping over her own feet. Kim brushed her hand against the maps, knocking them off the table. She instantly dropped to one knee and caught the maps before they could touch the floor. "I'm sorry," said Kim, getting up and gently placing the maps back on the table. "I get nervous sometimes around such precious items."

"It's all right," said the auctioneer. "Have you seen what you needed to?"

Kim smiled. "Yes, thank you, sir."

Connor addressed the auctioneer. "Unfortunately, my client can not afford these items, so we will have to withdraw from the auction."

"As you wish," replied the auctioneer.

Kim and Connor casually made their way back to their seats.

"Do you have it?" whispered Connor.

"Uh-huh," she replied.

"Where? I didn't even see you take it?"

"It's in my shirt. See, I told you I was good."

Connor looked over his shoulder at the exits. "Now all we have to do is get out of here before anyone notices the map is missing."

"I doubt the bearded man will care, but Vallin and Rin sure as hell will."

"I think it's time we got some fresh air," suggested Connor.

Kim stood. "Yes, let's."

Behind them, the auctioneer rang his gavel, recommencing the auction. "Please, let us continue. I had a bid of twenty-three million dollars. Do I hear twenty-five?"

"Twenty-five," said the bearded bidder.

Kim and Connor were almost at the door when Vallin stood. "Sir, I just spoke with my client, and he also wants me to examine the lot before the bids go any higher."

The auctioneer placed his gavel down. "Please approach."

Connor swore under his breath. "Time to go."

They hurried outside and stopped in their tracks, desperately looking for a way out. Luckily, there were only a handful of soldiers hanging around their vehicles. The rest were off-duty or asleep already.

"That'll do," said Connor, taking Kim by the hand toward a soldier cleaning the windshield on his parked Humvee. Connor looked around to ensure no one was following them and clenched his right fist. The unsuspecting private turned and smiled at Kim, only for Connor to cold-cock him. The soldier dropped to the ground like a sack of potatoes.

"Is he okay?" asked Kim.

"He'll be fine in a few minutes," said Connor, helping himself to the soldier's keys.

They had just opened the Humvee's doors when an alarm rang through the air.

"Get in," said Connor firmly as he jumped in and started the engine.

Kim slid onto her seat and slammed the door shut.

Connor placed the vehicle in gear and slammed his foot on the gas pedal. Mud and rocks flew into the air behind the Humvee as it sped off. Kim quickly buckled her seatbelt.

"Where are we going?" asked Kim.

"Cambodia," replied Connor, skirting a fuel truck. Then, with his hands clenched tight on the wheel, he aimed their Humvee straight at the front gate like a battering ram.

A soldier on guard duty saw them coming and fumbled for his pistol. In mere seconds, the Humvee was only meters from running the guard over. In an act of self-preservation, he panicked and dove to one side, landing facefirst into the mud. Then, with a curse on his lips, he got to his knees and opened fire wildly at the Humvee as it smashed through the wooden main gate. One of the guard's poorly aimed rounds struck the bulletproof glass at the back of the vehicle, chipping a small hole.

Kim cried out and ducked at the noise.

"It's okay," reassured Connor. "We're in an up-armored Humvee. It's going to take a hell of a lot more than a pistol to stop us."

Kim slowly sat back up. "Thanks for the warning."

"Sorry, I didn't have time to explain why we stole this vehicle. Now, help me find a trail heading south-south-east toward Cambodia before they send an angel of death to stop us."

25.

"Are you sure?" demanded Major Chakrii, dropping his cigar into a full glass of champagne.

"Yes," said Vallin, standing next to the auctioneer. "There are supposed to be four, not three maps. Those people must have stolen one when they examined the lot."

"He's right," said the auctioneer. "One of the maps is missing. Why they took that one is beyond me. In my opinion, it was the least useful of the four maps."

Chakrii swore in Thai and ripped a Motorola radio from his belt. "Stand to. I say again, stand to. This is not a drill. On my orders, the base is sealed until further notice. No vehicles get in or out."

A duty officer reported. "*Sir, it's too late. Someone stole a Humvee and crashed it through the front gate.*"

"Where is it now?"

"*I don't know, sir.*"

Chakrii could see his career ending before his eyes. His mouth turned dry. General Kirdpan was not the kind of man who forgave and forgot. He had to do something. Chakrii brought his Motorola to his lips. "Operations, this is the XO, I want an armed drone in the air in the next five minutes, or you'll have to answer to me."

"*But sir, only the general can order the launch of an armed drone,*" objected the duty officer.

Chakrii had had enough. "Do it, or you're dead!"

"*Yes, sir. Right away*," replied the panic-stricken officer.

"Five minutes," grumbled Vallin. "They'll be in Cambodia by then."

"What the hell do I care about a line drawn on a map?" said Chakrii. "They're not going to get away. Not on my watch."

"Major, I used to be a soldier. Would you mind if I watched the hunt from your operations room?"

Chakrii spat on the ground. "Sure, why not? Let's go."

"Don't forget me," said Rin, walking close behind.

"I can't see a thing," said Kim, staring out the reinforced front windshield of their stolen Humvee as they barreled through a dark jungle trail.

Connor had switched off the vehicle's lights the instant they left the main road to help make it harder for anyone to spot them from the air. He knew it was, at best, a stopgap measure, as any UAV sent to find them would most certainly have a thermal camera on it. But he reasoned every little bit helped.

Tree branches whipped the side of the vehicle, making it sound as if something horrible outside was trying to claw its way inside.

"How far do you think it is to the border?" asked Kim.

Connor shrugged. "We could be in Cambodia now, for all I know."

Kim gnashed her teeth together and stared out into the night, desperate for a sign, any sign, that they were safe.

Major Chakrii paced the operations room, talking to himself. Then, finally, he stopped to butt out a cigarette in a half-empty coffee cup and light another.

"Sir, I've got something," announced the drone operator.

"What is it, Sergeant?"

"It looks like a Humvee heading southwest on a jungle trail."

Chakrii looked up at the screen. His eyes lit up. "It has to be them. Lock a missile onto the target, and then fire."

The sergeant looked over his shoulder. "Sir, they're in Cambodia. We don't have that kind of authority."

Chakrii drew his pistol and aimed it at the operator. "I don't care. I'm ordering you to blow them to pieces!"

"Yes, sir," the sergeant stammered as he tagged the speeding Humvee with a laser and activated one of the drone's missiles. "Firing in three-two-one."

The air in the operations room grew still as everyone held their breath and watched the missile race toward its target. Three seconds later, a bright white flash filled the ops room's screen. The mood instantly turned euphoric. Men cheered and clapped each other on the back in celebration. They'd done it.

Chakrii let out a loud whoop and slid his pistol back into its holster. "Quiet down, everyone! It's not over yet. Launch the QRF. I want their bodies returned here to the base, along with the map, if it survived the explosion."

"Yes, sir," said a junior officer, picking up a phone to dispatch the quick reaction force.

Major Chakrii collapsed onto a chair. His hands shook uncontrollably. He lit another cigarette and inhaled deeply, trying to calm his shattered nerves. Because of his quick thinking, for now, at least, his life wasn't in danger. He sat back, closed his eyes, and listened as the QRF boarded a helicopter and prepared to fly into the night.

Kim slowly opened her eyes and looked up at the stars through the jungle canopy. Wet and confused, she couldn't understand why she was lying on her back in the middle of a stream in a jungle. She went to roll over and sit up, but her stomach had other ideas. In a flash, her innards turned, and Kim moaned as she emptied her stomach onto the dirt. Waves of nausea wracked her body until she painfully arched her back and drained the last of the bile from her guts.

"Oh, God, what have I done?" said Kim, resting on her knees and wiping the drool from her face. Aside from the ringing in her ears and the feeling that she'd been in a fight that she'd lost, Kim didn't think she had broken any bones or suffered any internal injuries. Kim fought to remember what had happened. In her mind, she could see Connor driving, and then the sound of something like a jet engine speeding right at them, and then nothing.

She splashed some cold water on her face and blinked her eyes. Slowly, a large, dark object came into view. Instantly, Kim knew where she was and what had happened. There had been an explosion that must have thrown her from the Humvee onto the soft mud. But where was Connor? Kim's heart began to race. "Connor, where are you?" called Kim, getting slowly to her feet. Her head began to spin. Kim held her hands out to steady herself. She breathed in deeply and warily walked to the Humvee. "Connor, are you all right?"

The Humvee lay on its side, with a plume of steam hissing as it escaped from the destroyed engine. Kim walked to the overturned vehicle and bashed her hand on the side of the Humvee, trying to get Connor's attention. When she didn't hear a response, Kim climbed up onto the side of the vehicle. She was relieved and horrified at the same time to see the blast had taken off the driver's side door. She looked into the darkness and called out, "Connor, are you in there?"

There was no reply.

With her heart rapidly sinking into despair, Kim grabbed her cell phone and switched on a light. There, just out of reach, lay Connor dangling off to one side, still strapped into his seat. Kim could see blood trickling down from a cut on his forehead. But, apart from that, he looked in one piece. A pained moan escaped Connor's lips, telling Kim he was still alive. She could have leaped for joy but kept her mind fixed on the problem of how to get Connor safely out of the vehicle without hurting him. Kim crawled closer and reached down to unbuckle Connor's seatbelt. No matter how hard she pushed on the buckle, the belt wouldn't budge.

"Come on, come on," willed Kim, tugging at the belt. It was pointless; the seatbelt was jammed. Kim paused momentarily and recalled that Connor had hidden two ceramic knives in his belt. If she could reach them, she might be able to cut him free. Then, all of a sudden, a new noise caught Kim's ear—the rhythmic beating of a helicopter's rotors growing closer by the second.

"No, no, no," she said at the realization that a helicopter from the base was on its way. Panic filled her heart. Kim took a deep breath, grabbed Connor's seatbelt, and gave it one last tug with all she had left. It was hopeless; it never budged an inch. There was only one last thing she could do. Kim took hold of Connor's right arm and brought it up until she could see his watch.

A searchlight suddenly shone down from above, lighting up the jungle.

Kim had seconds. She depressed the GPS tracking button on Connor's watch, slid off the Humvee, and hobbled into the jungle. Kim didn't stop until her aching and battered body begged her to stop. She dropped onto all fours, taking deep breaths to fill her lungs. In the distance, Kim could hear men calling out to one another as they searched the area around the Humvee. Exhausted, Kim dropped back and rested against a tree. She patted her pants, relieved she hadn't lost her phone running through the jungle. Without it, she would be in far deeper trouble than she already was.

"Here goes nothing," Kim said, activating her watch's GPS tracker. Hopefully, Yuri would get their signals and come to help rescue them. No matter how slim, there was still some hope. Kim sat there for a few minutes, listening to the buzzing insects and the howls of the animals calling to each other. Finally, she let out a tired sigh and shook her head. Maybe Connor was right. Perhaps they had pushed things a bit too far. For the first time since they'd met, Kim figured that they'd bitten off more than they could chew.

"For the love of God, no," Kim uttered, moving her hand under her shirt. Her hand began to tremble. She looked up at the stars and then let out an anguished cry. The map was gone. Kim had never felt so alone and lost in her life.

"Roger that," said Major Chakrii into a radio handset.

"What's up?" asked Vallin.

"The QRF has found the Humvee and is on its way back."

"Survivors?"

"One."

"Which one?" Vallin shook with rage. Why couldn't the major be more specific?

"They report they have a man with them."

"And the woman?"

Chakrii shrugged. "Dead, I expect."

"Major, I wouldn't make that mistake if I were in your shoes."

Chakrii narrowed his eyes. "For a simple soldier, you seem to know quite a lot about my job."

Vallin raised his hands. "No offense intended, Major. I was just caught up in the excitement of everything." He lowered his voice and indicated at an exit with his head. "Why don't we step outside for a second, Major? I have a business proposition that you're going to like."

Chakrii followed Vallin out into the brisk night air. He lit another cigarette and faced Vallin. "So, what's this business proposition of yours?"

Vallin got straight to the point. "How much?"

Chakrii shook his head. "How much for what?"

"The man."

"Why do you want him?"

"Why do you care?" Rin asked, joining the conversation.

"I don't, really." Chakrii licked his lips. "Okay, if you want him, you can have him, but it's going to cost you."

"How much are we talking about?" asked Vallin.

"One hundred thousand dollars in cash."

"It's a deal," said Rin instantly.

"But not here. If you're going to interrogate him, you can't do it here."

"Not a problem." Vallin glanced over at a neat line of military vehicles. "Say, could I borrow one of your trucks for a few hours?"

26.

How did my life come to this? Kim thought darkly, staring at a muddy track in the middle of nowhere. She was tired, miserable, and soaked to the bone. She'd spent hours on her hands and knees in the muck, searching for the map to no avail. It was well and truly lost. It had rained on and off all morning, and no matter how hard she tried, Kim couldn't find enough cover under the leaves of a tall Chankiki tree to keep her dry.

Her stomach gurgled, reminding her it had been hours and hours since her last meal. Kim glanced around at her surroundings but couldn't identify anything edible. And she certainly wasn't going to take the risk, either. Kim didn't want to venture far, either, knowing that there could be soldiers looking for her, but food would become a high priority very soon. She glanced skyward at the cloudy sky and grimaced; the last thing she wanted was to sit through another torrential downpour.

The sound of a vehicle's engine caught her ear. Faint at first but growing with each passing second. A pair of trucks had passed Kim's hiding spot first thing in the morning, but it had been quiet ever since. She edged forward slightly until she could get a better view of the road. A blue and red minivan was slowly making its way down the path. She crossed her fingers for luck.

Unexpectedly, the van slowed and then stopped. A door opened, and Yuri stepped out, holding a tablet in his hand.

Kim's heart soared like an eagle into the sky. "Yuri!" she yelled, leaping onto the path and running toward Yuri, her arms open wide.

Yuri turned and was almost tackled by Kim, who enthusiastically embraced him.

"Pretty lady, you look like hell," said Yuri, looking down at Kim's torn and mud-splattered clothes. "Luckily, I thought ahead and brought some coveralls for you to change into."

Kim let go of Yuri and smiled. "Was it hard to find me?"

Yuri chuckled. "Yes and no. The signal in your watch was easy to track, but the roads in this part of Cambodia are nothing more than muddy trails hacked from the jungle. Come get inside; we have a long drive ahead of us."

Yuri slid open the door on the side of the minivan, and Kim climbed inside. She picked up a blanket and wrapped it around herself to warm up.

"Good morning, miss," said the driver, startling Kim.

"Sorry," said Yuri. "Kim, meet Lek. Lek, meet Kim. He's here because I needed someone who could drive while I tracked your signal."

Lek smiled, exposing his yellow tobacco-stained teeth.

"Okay," replied Kim, guzzling a bottle of orange juice before ripping open a bag of freshly cut carrots and devouring them as if they were the best meal she had ever eaten.

Yuri climbed back into the passenger's seat and did up his seatbelt. He looked over his shoulder at Kim. "You might as well get changed out of those wet clothes and then get comfortable back there. It's a long ride back to Bangkok."

Kim instantly straightened. "Why Bangkok?"

"Because that's where Mister North's signal is coming from."

"Are you sure? I thought he'd be back at that secret drone base."

Yuri shook his head and held up his tablet for Kim to see. "No. It's definitely coming from Bangkok."

Kim couldn't see what Yuri was pointing at, but all of her aches, pains, and negative emotions evaporated in an instant. "Then why are we talking? Let's get moving."

"You heard the lady, Lek, get moving."

"Okay, boss," replied Lek, placing the van in gear.

Kim looked around the back of the minivan and went to reach for a set of clean blue coveralls when she suddenly remembered something. "Yuri, do you have something, anything, I could draw on?"

"I don't. Lek, do you have something Kim can use?" Yuri asked in Thai.

"Yes," replied Lek. "In the back, you'll find a pad of paper and some colored pencils my kid left in here last night. Lucky for you, she didn't listen to me when I told her to grab her school bag."

Yuri passed the message. Instantly, Kim rummaged around until she found a small pink knapsack. Kim opened the bag and smiled with relief. There was a large pad of paper and more than enough pencils for what she had in mind. Kim sat with her back resting on the side wall of the van, closed her eyes, and collected her thoughts. Then, she opened her eyes and started to draw.

"What are you doing?" queried Yuri.

"I lost the map sometime last night during my escape, but it's still in my mind."

"You lost it?" gasped Yuri.

"Yes, but don't worry, I still have it stored upstairs."

"Kim, please don't take this the wrong way, but how much time did you have with the map to memorize it?"

Kim looked up from her work. "Let me think. It was no more than a second or two, but that was more than enough time for me."

"Less than a second?" repeated Yuri disbelievingly.

Kim recommenced drawing the map. "Plenty of time."

27.

So, this is where it all ends—not with a bang but a whimper, thought Connor, twisting his wrists, trying to loosen the rope tying him to a reclining lawn chair. No matter how hard he tried, it was no good. Whoever had tied him up had, unfortunately, done an excellent job. Apart from a sliver of light seeping in under a far door, Connor found himself in near-total darkness. He had no idea where he was or how he got there. All he knew for sure was that his body ached everywhere and that he was famished.

The sound of a key turning in a lock made Connor sit up as best he could in his chair. He held his head high and vowed not to give his captors the satisfaction of seeing him in pain.

A man stepped inside and flipped the light switch. Dozens of fluorescent bulbs hummed and sputtered as they came to life, flooding the warehouse with light. The light bothered Connor's eyes. He looked away for a second and blinked his eyes to get them used to the brightness.

"Ah, Mister North, it's good to see you awake," said Vallin, striding toward Connor. "You were out so long; I was honestly beginning to wonder if you'd ever come to."

Connor cleared his parched throat and asked, "Where am I?"

"Bangkok," replied Vallin, unscrewing the lid from a water bottle and helping Connor take a sip. "Easy does it. If you drink too much, you'll be sick."

"Thanks," said Connor, licking the moisture from his lips.

Vallin made his way to a small table and picked up Connor's mini-Sig Sauer pistol. "You had such interesting toys on you when you were captured, Mister North. I'll have to get your supplier's name when this is all said and done." Vallin placed the gun down and examined Connor's watch, careful not to turn the emergency button off. "I particularly like your watch. I had one just like it a couple of years back."

"Is he awake, Jean?" asked a woman standing in the doorway.

"Yes, he is," replied Vallin, laying the watch on the table.

It took a moment for Connor to recognize the voice and the woman's face.

"Aside from smelling to high heaven, he doesn't look too bad," noted Rin, walking around Connor's lawn chair.

Vallin nodded and helped Connor drink some more water.

"So, Mister North, where is the map?" asked Rin, standing over him.

Connor took a deep breath through his nostrils and closed his eyes. "The last time I remember seeing it was at the auction when Kim stole it. After that, who knows? For all I know, it could be in New York by now."

Rin slapped Connor hard across his face. The sound of her hand hitting his skin echoed through the vast warehouse. "You're lying!" she snarled.

Connor could taste the coppery tang of blood in his mouth. He defiantly looked up at his tormentor and smiled. "I have no reason to lie. I have no idea what happened to Kim after the missile struck our vehicle. Conceivably, she could be dead or partying it up in Hong Kong. So, there's no need to hit me again, as I honestly couldn't tell you where Kim or the map is right now."

Rin raised her hand to strike Connor again when Vallin grabbed her arm. "I believe him. If we're going to stand a chance at getting our hands on the map, we're going to need him alive. At least for now."

"You don't really believe she'll come for him, do you?" Rin asked contemptuously.

"Yes, I do. I've seen these two in action. She'll come for him, and when she does, we'll grab her and the map."

Rin cursed and shook her head. "This is on your head, Jean. If she fails to show, I'll be forced to tell The Order that you've failed, and they may order me to take your life as punishment."

God, how Vallin hated being supervised by a killer from The Order. Even the name, The Order, made him want to scream in anger. Instead, he looked at Rin and smirked smugly. "Rest easy, woman; it's just a matter of time until I get everything that I want."

Connor didn't like what he was hearing. They were using him as bait. He coughed to get their attention. "If I were you, Vallin, I'd be filling out my will right now."

Vallin smirked again. "And why would I do that?"

Connor decided to do some fishing. "Because, for all we know, Kim could be lost somewhere in the jungles of Cambodia."

Vallin wagged a finger in Connor's face. "I don't think so. When the rescue team found you strapped into the Humvee, they couldn't find Ms. Swiftwater's body. No, she's alive and will be coming for you."

Connor suppressed a sigh of relief. If Vallin was telling the truth, Kim was alive, and, like his captor, Connor was optimistic she'd come for him. It was now a waiting game.

Kim looked over at a darkened warehouse next to the black water of the Chao Phraya River through her NVGs and counted four armed men standing about talking next to a closed door. She slowly moved her head, checking to see if anyone else was guarding the building. To her relief, the four men seemed to be the only obstacles between her and Connor.

"Are you sure you want to do this?" asked Yuri. "We could call the Thai police and let them handle this situation."

"Yuri, you sound just like Connor," she retorted. "Do you honestly trust the local police to do their jobs? Because I sure as hell don't."

"No, I guess not."

"Yuri, don't worry. I'll be fine. Your plan is sound."

Yuri opened the glove compartment of their clandestinely-borrowed truck and retrieved a pistol. "Here, take this. It'll make me feel a hell of a lot better knowing you're armed."

Kim shook her head. "I'd probably hurt myself if I tried to use it. You keep it. I'm as well-armed as I need to be."

"It's your call," said Yuri reluctantly.

Kim lifted the NVGs from her eyes, opened the door, and stepped out into the night. She lowered the rusting truck's tailgate and slung a coil of rope over her shoulder. She ensured it was snug before slipping a tactical canvas belt covered in pouches around her waist.

"Good luck," Yuri murmured.

"Thanks. Just remember to give me ten minutes to get into position and then cut the power."

"Will do, pretty lady."

Kim, dressed from head to toe in dark clothes, winked and jogged toward a darkened stretch of road. She stopped beside a wire chain-link fence and opened a pouch on her belt. Kim paused for a few seconds to ensure she was alone and then sprayed liquid nitrogen in a wide circle on the fence. The metal hissed and cracked as it froze. Kim grabbed hold of the loosened fence, pulled it toward her, and gently laid it on the ground. She slid the spray can back into its pouch and slipped through the hole onto the warehouse grounds.

In her mind, she knew she had already used up one precious minute and wanted to get going. However, Kim didn't want to make any mistakes and brought down her NVGs. Then, she picked a spot at the back of the warehouse to gain entrance and sprinted toward it. Kim's heart raced as she closed in on the building. She came to a sliding halt and instantly grabbed hold of a drainpipe running along the side of the warehouse all the way to the roof. Kim tugged it. The pipe was solidly nailed in place.

"Okay, I'm in," Kim reported.

"*I can see you,*" replied Yuri in her earpiece.

"The guards?"

"*They're still at the front of the building.*"

"All right. I'm heading up top. See you soon."

"*Right, I'll be there.*"

Kim took hold of the pipe with both hands and started to climb. She used her feet as anchor points and calmly scaled the warehouse. In under a minute, Kim was on top of the building. She hunched over and carefully tiptoed across the roof until she reached a skylight and got down on one knee. As expected, the glass was covered in muck, so Kim gently wiped it with her gloved hand and looked down. She gave a nod of satisfaction when she spotted Connor on a lawn chair. Kim couldn't tell from this vantage point if he was just asleep or unconscious. She studied the rest of the space that she could see and spotted a lone guard sitting on a chair, watching something on his phone. Kim unwound her rope and tied one end off to a sturdy pipe. Next, she jimmied the window and ever-so-slowly opened it all the way.

"Okay, Yuri, I'm ready to go," she whispered, attaching a carabiner to her skin-tight belt and feeding the rope through it.

"*Give me thirty seconds,*" he replied.

"Got it."

Kim's stomach tightened. She tried to decide if she was more nervous than scared and concluded it was a little of both.

Back at the car, Yuri brought up a rifle with a silencer on the barrel to his shoulder. He aimed at a transformer on a telephone pole that supplied power to the warehouse and pulled the trigger. A split second later, the transformer exploded, plunging the block into darkness.

Kim instantly sprang into action, tossing her rope inside the pitch-black building. She never hesitated, dropping through the open skylight and smoothly rappelling to the cement floor. Kim's first target was an armed guard. She quickly pulled what little rope there was left through her carabiner to free herself and rushed the man.

In the dark, the guard had no idea he was about to be attacked.

Kim tensed and balled up her right fist. She lashed out and smashed her fist hard onto the guard's nose, shattering it. The man cried out in pain and reached for his broken nose, leaving the rest of his body exposed. Instinctively, Kim dropped slightly and thrust both fists several times like jackhammers into the guard's sides, painfully bruising his kidneys. The man moaned and dropped to his knees just as Kim brought her right leg back and kicked him squarely on the side of his head, knocking him out cold.

"Kim, is that you?" asked Connor.

Kim stepped back from the unconscious guard to catch her breath. "Yes, it is. Are you all right?"

"Yes, but I can't see you."

Kim raised her NVGs and switched on a small, red-filtered flashlight. "Voila!" she said, shining it on her face.

Connor smiled. "Thank God. I thought I'd never see you again."

Kim flipped open a razor-sharp knife and dashed over to cut Connor's bindings. "Tell me you're happy to see me."

"I will once we're out of here."

Kim cut through the ropes and helped Connor to his feet.

"Now what?" he asked, rubbing his aching wrists. "What's your plan of escape?"

Crunch!

Kim and Connor spun around and looked in amazement as the far wall exploded inwards. Chunks of wood and debris flew everywhere as Yuri plowed his truck through the wall and drove into the warehouse. He brought his vehicle to a screeching halt and threw open the passenger side door. "Get in!" he screamed.

They started to run when a side door flew open, and four guards rushed inside, yelling and brandishing their firearms. Kim pivoted on her heels to run, but to her dismay, Connor ran in the opposite direction. She could hear Yuri yelling and waving to her, but her eyes were fixed on Connor. She watched as Connor snatched something from a nearby table and dove for the floor. He landed with his arms outstretched, holding a pistol. The onrushing guards saw him but reacted too slowly; Connor ruthlessly cut them down one by one.

"Let's go!" cried Yuri, snapping Kim back into the real world.

"Yeah, let's," added Connor, tossing his empty pistol aside.

Kim grabbed Connor's hand, and together, they dashed to Yuri's vehicle and dove inside.

A second later, Yuri placed his vehicle in reverse and sped back out of the hole he'd smashed through the warehouse wall, tearing off more wood and metal that gouged deep grooves into the side of the old truck. Yuri slammed the brakes, switched gears, and pressed his foot on the gas pedal. The tires shrieked on the cement road as the battered vehicle sped away from the warehouse and toward safety.

"I couldn't see you in the dark, but it sounded like you beat the crap out of that guard," said Connor, lying low in the back seat.

"What of it?" replied Kim, hunched down behind Yuri.

"Nothing, but where did you learn to fight like that?"

"It's called Israeli Krav Maga. Why fight fair when you can fight to win?"

"I hear you."

Kim grinned. "Now, Connor North, tell me you're happy to see me."

Connor relaxed and returned Kim's grin. "Yes, I'm happy to see you."

Kim winked and edged closer. "No. Tell me like you mean it."

Connor looked deep into her eyes. "You have no idea how happy I am to see you, Kim Swiftwater."

Kim's heart swelled. She leaned close enough to Connor that she could feel his warm breath on her face.

"Hey, what about me?" asked Yuri, shattering the moment. "Aren't you happy to see me, too?"

Connor and Kim chuckled.

"Yes, I'm happy to see you too, Yuri," said Connor. "By the way, where are we going?"

"A friend's place. You can get cleaned up there while I go and get everyone some food."

Kim sat up, looked at Connor, and smiled—*perhaps another day.*

28.

"Come again?" Connor blurted out, staring at Kim in horror.

"I lost the map. Or, more accurately, we lost it when that missile struck our Humvee, sending me flying through the air and into a creek," retorted Kim.

Connor let out a pent-up cry. "You're telling me this entire assignment has been for nothing?"

Kim waved her hands in the air. "No, no, you've got it all wrong."

"I do?" Connor snapped. "How so?"

"I made a copy."

"A copy?" Connor shook his head. "When?"

Kim picked up a drawing and handed it to Connor. "Voila, the Grenier map."

Connor looked over the picture briefly and reached for a chair. He dropped down on the chair and hung his head down. "My God, we could have died in the jungle. And for what? This drawing."

Kim gently placed a hand on his back. "But we didn't, and now we have a good idea where the scrolls are buried."

"Kim, this map includes Western Greenland, Canada, and the States."

"I know. The crudely drawn map we saw in Katarina's bunker didn't have Greenland on it. Now, why would Captain Moore have done that?"

Connor raised an eyebrow. "To keep the gold's location a secret?"

"Exactly."

Connor ran a hand over his stubbly chin and studied the map, looking for clues. "I don't know; there's not a lot of detail on it, nor a convenient X to mark the spot."

Kim let out an annoyed grunt. "Quit being so damned negative for a minute! It's a start. Just be thankful DuFour's people don't have it."

At the sound of DuFour's name Connor's gut clenched. "Kim, when I was being held hostage, Vallin made it quite clear to me that I was bait. He was after you and the map, not me."

"Yeah, but he can't get us now."

Connor looked down at his mud-stained clothes and examined the buttons. "Can't he?"

Kim's eyes widened. "You're wearing a bug. Your clothes, take them off and give them to me."

Without hesitating, Connor ripped off his vest and shirt and handed them to Kim. She quickly ran her fingers over every inch and then tossed them aside.

"They're clean. Your pants, mister."

Connor turned around and removed his trousers and socks.

"Spoilsport," Kim teased.

"Here," said Connor, tossing her his clothes.

Kim moved her fingers along the seams on Connor's dirty pants and then inspected the rest of the garment. "It's not there. Your underpants, please."

"What? You've got to be kidding."

Kim smiled and broke out laughing. She held up a tiny, button-sized GPS device between her thumb and forefinger. "I found it in your vest. I just wanted to see how far you'd strip down for me."

Connor shook his head. "Has anyone told you recently that you're a horrible person, Kim Swiftwater?"

"I know. Hurry up and get dressed," said Kim, dropping the tracker into the toilet and flushing it down the drain. "This place is compromised. I'll call Yuri and tell him we must move ASAP."

"This has to be the place," said Vallin, looking up at a run-down, three-story apartment building. A steady downpour didn't dampen Vallin's thirst for revenge. He couldn't wait to wipe the smug look from North's face when he got his hands on the map.

"I don't know, sir," said one of Vallin's three hired killers, checking his hand-held tracking device. "I'm not getting a signal anymore."

"Any number of things could have happened," countered Vallin, unholstering his pistol. "They're up there, I know it."

"Yes, sir," responded the mercenary, placing the tracker into a pouch on his vest and drawing his 9mm pistol.

Vallin crept forward, looked up the rickety stairs leading to the third floor, and then glanced back at his men waiting right behind him. He raised three fingers as a warning and slowly lowered them one by one. When the last finger fell, the four men rushed up the stairs. Vallin was the first to arrive and kicked in the door to Yuri's safe house. The next two shooters ran past him with their pistols at the ready and stormed into the tiny one-room apartment, screaming for North and Swiftwater to remain still.

Right away, Vallin could sense that something was wrong. The room was too quiet.

"Clear, sir," reported one of the men. "There's no one here."

Vallin holstered his pistol and walked inside. He dropped his shoulders and swore when he spotted a red balloon floating in the middle of the room with a note attached to it. Vallin walked over and grabbed the piece of paper.

Sorry, but you're late. Kim and I have gone out for dinner.
Better luck next time,
Connor North and Kim Swiftwater.

Vallin crumpled up the note and hurled it across the room. He clenched his jaw so tight that it hurt. His body shook with white-hot rage.

"I'm going to gut that man and watch him bleed out if it's the last thing I do," swore Vallin.

"Sir," said one of the men covering the door.

"What is it?" yelled Vallin.

"I can hear sirens coming this way. Someone must have called the police."

Vallin stood as still as a statue, grinding his teeth.

A tall, muscle-bound Asian man grabbed Vallin by the arm and shook him. "Sir, we've got to leave. Now!"

Vallin yanked his arm free and nodded bitterly. "Yes, yes, you're right. There'll be other times. Let's go, men."

The Asian merc rounded up his friends and led them down the stairs to their waiting car.

Vallin shuffled his feet, wondering how Rin was going to take the news. If she were half as brutal as her reputation, Vallin would rather blow his brains out than endure the pain she would inflict on him before beheading him.

"Oh man, I would have paid a million bucks to see Vallin's face when he found the safe was empty," said Connor.

"I'm sure he took it all in stride," added Kim, chuckling.

"Laugh all you want, you two," said Yuri. "But I had to pay good money for that room."

"I hope it wasn't a lot," said Kim. "Because, in my humble opinion, it wasn't fit for a rat to live in."

"True. But it was available. Unfortunately, I paid the owner for two nights in advance."

"And how much did that cost you?" queried Connor.

"Fifty dollars, but fifty dollars is still fifty dollars."

Kim and Connor broke out laughing.

"What's so funny?" protested Yuri.

"Yuri, it's not your money to begin with," said Connor. "It's Jason's, and I hope you bleed his bank account dry."

"You don't like Mister Hamilton very much, do you?"

Kim saw a flash of bitterness in Connor's eyes and decided to change the subject. "So, Yuri, how much is this new palatial mansion costing you?"

Yuri looked around the mid-sized apartment. "A bit more than fifty dollars, but I must agree with you, pretty lady, that last place sucked."

Kim smiled. "Do you know when our new clothes and food will arrive?"

Yuri checked his watch. "Any minute now."

As if on cue, there was a knock on the door.

Yuri drew his pistol and edged to the door. "Who is it, please?"

A man behind the door barked, "Yuri, it's me, Andrei. Open this friggin' door, or I'll kick it open and then kick your ass."

"I'd best do what he says. Andrei can be a handful when he's pissed." Yuri holstered his weapon and opened the door.

Kim and Connor both blinked in surprise. Instead of a mountain of a man, with knuckles dragging on the floor, Andrei was barely five feet tall, with a pleasant smile on his round face, wearing a purple velvet tracksuit with a thick gold chain around his neck.

"Evening," said Andrei.

"You're late," remarked Yuri.

Andrei looked up at Yuri and shook his head. "I'm late when I say I'm late."

To Kim and Connor's surprise, the two men raised their fists and moved around the room as if a fight were imminent. Instead, they dropped their hands and warmly embraced each other, as only true friends can.

"Yuri, you're as ugly as ever," Andrei said mockingly.

"And you're still short."

"But still good-looking."

The two comrades let go of each other, and Andrei motioned for two men standing in the hallway to enter the room. One of the young men carried a couple of suitcases while his partner's arms were filled with bags of take-out food. Andrei brought out a wad of hundred-dollar bills and paid his men before ushering them out of the apartment.

"Wow, what did you get?" asked Kim, smelling the mix of mouth-watering aromas in the air.

"Let me see," said Andrei. "There are salad rolls, beef satays, a couple of curry dishes, a sweet and sour stir fry, a ginger stir fry, a chili beef, and plenty of rice. And, of course, three bottles of vodka."

"What are you going to drink, partner?" quipped Yuri.

Andrei smirked. "You under the table, Yuri Uvarov."

Kim shook her head at all the male posturing and said, "The food sounds delicious."

"Come, let's eat," proposed Yuri, clearing off the dinner table.

"It all sounds nice and spicy," said Connor, inspecting the food.

Kim elbowed Connor in the ribs. "Get it into you, Captain. Trust me; you'll like it."

"Yeah, but I may not like it so much when it comes out of me."

After dinner, Andrei's associates returned with a large plastic container and laid it on one of the beds; as before, Andrei paid his men and sent them off to do other tasks.

"What's in the box?" asked Connor.

"A secure laptop, three new phones, a portable scanning device, IDs, and whatever else Yuri asked for," replied Andrei, patting his full belly.

"A black marketer's black marketer," quipped Kim.

"In a sense, yes," replied Andrei. "He scratches my back, and, from time to time, I scratch his."

"If it's none of my business, please tell me so, but I'd really like to know how you two vagabonds met," said Connor.

"That's easy. We used to work for the Horatio Group," explained Yuri, reaching for an open bottle of vodka on the table.

"I'm sorry...the what?" queried Kim.

"Mercenaries," explained Connor.

"Not just mercenaries, but well-paid ones at that," said Andrei proudly.

Yuri shot back a glass of vodka and continued. "At the time, I was a helicopter pilot, and Andrei was my crew chief. We were good—"

"Damned good!" interjected Andrei.

Yuri filled his and Andrei's glasses and toasted his comrade. "Yes, we were damned good at what we did. That was, until one day in Liberia when we were operating against some anti-government rebels. I was ordered to fire upon a group of insurgents. Only they weren't rebels. It was a wedding party, so I refused to open fire. I knew right there and then that a local warlord was trying to settle a score and had fed lousy intelligence to our people."

"That's horrible," said Kim, hanging off every word.

"Unfortunately, these kinds of incidents happen more often than you would think," said Connor. "It doesn't matter where you're serving or whose army you're in; someone will always try to exploit you for personal gain."

"Just the thought of being told to open fire on innocent civilians turns my stomach. What did you do next, Yuri?" asked Kim.

"I told my base what I could see and continued to refuse to fire. So my wingman was ordered to attack, and the bastard did so without hesitation."

"He at least got what was coming to him," said Andrei bitterly.

"What happened?" asked Connor.

"His chopper was hit by ground fire and crashed in the jungles of northern Liberia. We heard years later that he somehow survived the crash but was captured by some rebels who had lost loved ones at the wedding. They tortured him for days before dousing him in gasoline and burning what was left of him alive."

"Well, that's a gruesome way to go," commented Connor. "But as you say, he had it coming to him."

"So, what happened to you two when you returned to your base?" asked Kim.

"We were arrested and locked up in cells," said Yuri. "But Andrei and I had other ideas and broke out of jail. After a few small missions together, we finally made our way to Pakistan and decided to go our separate ways. I set up shop in Europe and the Americas, and Andrei in the Far East. And that's all there really is to tell."

"Wow, that's quite some story," remarked Kim.

"And every word of it is true," said Andrei, toasting his comrade.

"You two have lived quite the lives," noted Connor.

The two comrades filled their glasses and toasted each other. "To friendship."

Connor and Kim lifted their soft drink cans and said, "To friendship."

29.

The rhythmic but loud snoring coming from Yuri and Andrei passed out on the couch surrounded by empty vodka bottles and food cartons reminded Connor of his younger days when he and his fellow officer candidates would get a rare weekend to themselves. They'd cut loose and drink far too much, only to instantly regret their decision on Monday morning's run through the obstacle course.

"Connor, they're here," said Kim, turning the secure laptop so they could see Knox's and Hamilton's faces on the screen.

Hamilton waved at Kim. "Right off the bat, Henry and I want to say that we're so relieved that you're both still alive."

"Thanks," replied Kim. She and Connor had earlier agreed that she would do the talking to prevent him from saying something stupid out of anger. "Sir, have you had a chance to examine the drawing of the map I sent you an hour ago?"

"Yes and no," responded Knox. "I think we can both agree that the map is of Western Greenland and parts of North America; however, until a cartographer examines your rendition of the map in detail, it's nothing more than a drawing."

Kim was taken aback. "Sir, I can assure you that what you're looking at is a near-perfect copy of the Grenier map."

"We don't doubt that. But Mister Hamilton and I would both feel better if an expert looked it over."

Kim nodded. "It's your money. Do you have someone in mind?"

"Yes. We've already hired Professor Andrew Forest from the University of New York to examine the map. He's an expert in medieval cartography and has assured us that he'll get back to us within the hour."

"That's pretty fast," whispered Connor to Kim.

"If Professor Forest comes back and says the drawing mirrors the style of maps from the medieval period, then what?" asked Kim.

"Then we'd like you to try and find the treasure before anyone else does," said Hamilton.

Connor looked at Kim and rubbed his fingers together off-screen.

Kim paused for effect. "I don't know. I'm starting to feel like there's a target on my back."

Connor looked away, grinning. Kim was doing fine without him.

"I would naturally pay you and Connor well if you were to continue helping me," said Hamilton.

"We'll have to talk about it. I don't want to put words into his mouth, but I think Connor's nearly ready to pack his bags and head home to Africa."

Hamilton looked over at Connor. "Please don't leave. Stick with it until at least Professor Forest gets back to us."

"I'll think about it," responded Connor.

"Please do."

Kim said, "I don't think there's anything else we can discuss right now, Mister Hamilton, so I guess we'll hear from you in an hour or so."

"Yes, and we hope to have some positive news for you when we speak again."

The call ended, and the screen went dark.

"So, how did I do?" Kim asked Connor.

He smiled and said, "Brilliantly. I know you won't stop until you've found the treasure, but they don't know that. And if we're going to continue risking our lives, we should at least be well reimbursed for our efforts."

"I'd call you a mercenary like our two sleeping friends, but aside from the truth, I kind of like money, too."

Connor stood and rummaged through Andrei's jacket for some money.

"What are you thinking?" Kim asked.

"Coffee. I need a coffee and maybe something to eat that won't upset my stomach."

Kim's stomach rumbled. "Count me in."

Thousands of kilometers away, Vallin lay in bed, smoking a cigarette, watching the ceiling fan spin in circles. He saw it as a metaphor for his life that seemed to be going nowhere. The faint hint of perfume that hung in the air from the young prostitute he'd shared his bed with last night helped reinforce his existence's empty loneliness.

There was a knock at the door.

Vallin's heart beat faster. He slid out of bed and slipped on his boxers. Vallin drew his pistol from his holster hanging over a chair next to the rest of his clothes and warily approached the door. "Yes, who is it?" he asked.

"It's me, Rin. Open the door."

A cold chill crept down Vallin's back. He'd been expecting her all night long while at the same time foolishly hoping that their paths would never cross again. His mouth became dry. Vallin ran his tongue over his lips.

"Come on, Jean, open the door," demanded Rin. "I want to talk to you."

Vallin glanced over at the closed windows but knew that was a non-starter. He was ten floors up, and any fall from this height would be fatal. He was trapped. "Just one second," said Vallin, composing himself. If he was going to die, Vallin decided he would rather die on his feet, facing Rin, rather than shamelessly begging on his knees. So, he lowered his pistol, flipped on the lights, and opened the door.

"Took you long enough," Rin said, walking in and holding a cardboard tray with two large cups of coffee in it.

Stunned, Vallin moved aside and hurriedly threw on a T-shirt. "Uh, what brings you here so early in the morning?"

Rin put the tray on a table, revealing a pistol in her hand. "You do, Jean. Please drop your gun, or I'll be forced to kill you."

Vallin shook his head. He swore as he threw his pistol on his bed and raised his hands.

"I saw the girl you were with last night leaving the hotel," said Rin. "She looked like a lot of fun. A bit young and thin for my tastes, but hey, we're all different. Aren't we?"

"If you say so."

"Try not to sound so bitter, Jean. I didn't come here to kill you. I wanted to but was overruled by my superiors."

"Lucky for me."

Rin sighed. "Yes, it would appear so."

Vallin scrunched his brow. "If you're not here to kill me, then why are you here?"

Rin indicated at the chairs by the table. "We need to talk."

Vallin looked down at Rin's pistol. "At gunpoint?"

"Oh, this? This is life insurance." Rin lowered her pistol and laid it on the table. "I knew you'd be on edge when I arrived and didn't want to be accidentally shot by you. Now lower your hands, Jean, and take a seat."

Vallin cautiously sat. He kept one eye on Rin and the other on her pistol just out of arm's reach.

"There's no need to tell me about the fiasco at the warehouse. I was there right after you left and tidied up the mess you left behind."

The fact that she'd shot anyone left behind—wounded or not—angered Vallin. Some of them had families and didn't deserve to be coldly executed with a bullet to the head.

"I also know that you missed capturing North and Swiftwater by mere minutes. It would appear, Jean, that if you didn't have bad luck, you'd have none at all."

"So, I'm cursed with bad luck; what of it?"

"Well, that's the problem. My employers expect results, and so far, you and your boss haven't done spectacularly well in that regard."

"What can I say? You're right; I've had a run of bad luck recently, but I can feel that things are about to change."

Rin's thin lips curled into a smile. "I do hope so. For your sake."

Vallin wasn't sure where their conversation was going, so he took hold of a coffee, ripped off its lid, and sipped. "My compliments. How did you know I like cappuccinos?"

"I didn't. I like them and just happened to buy two this morning."

"Still, a good choice."

Rin's voice turned cold. "Jean, I didn't come here to discuss coffee. My employers asked me to find out how you intend to get hold of the map. If I don't think your next move is sound, I hate to say it, but I'll get my second chance to kill you," Rin picked up her pistol and aimed it at Vallin. "So, think fast."

"I don't have to. I already have a plan," Vallin replied calmly.

"That's fast."

"In the military, I was always taught to have a contingency operation in mind, just in case my original plan failed."

"Well, what is it?"

"What did novelist Walter Scott say was thicker than water?"

Rin's eyes instantly gleamed in the light. "Blood. Blood is thicker than water."

"That's right. So, while we idle our time away chatting and having cappuccinos, some men of mine are already on the move."

"To where?"

Vallin passed on his plan and then sat back with his hands locked behind his head and a satisfied grin on his face.

Rin placed her pistol on safe and put it down. "Well done, Jean, I must commend you. This scheme of yours might work."

"Oh, it'll work, all right."

"Like your boss, you've bought yourself some more time, but no more screw-ups, Jean. Okay?"

Vallin raised his hands. "I got it. I really do."

"I don't know what my people see in DuFour. There must be a blood connection between one of his ancestors and some members of The Order."

"What the hell is this order you keep talking about?"

"That is none of your business. Suffice it to say they pay me well, so I don't ask any questions. I suggest you do the same."

Vallin sat back in his chair. Outward, he looked calm and in control, while deep down, he knew he'd dodged another bullet. But, unfortunately, he knew fate wouldn't be so kind the next time. If it came down to him or her, Vallin knew who he'd prefer to die first.

30.

The second Connor opened the door to their safe house, he was hit by a pungent wall of stale alcohol and body odor. He pinched his nostrils and stepped inside. "Good lord, I hadn't noticed it before, but this place stinks."

"Oh God, yes," added Kim, also turning her head away from the smell.

Yuri and Andrei were still asleep on the sofa, snoring louder than a truck backfiring on the street.

"Let's clean up a little before breakfast," Connor suggested. Kim nodded and laid their food on the table. A few minutes later, the room was somewhat more liveable. Connor had fixed a fan, helping to clear the air.

They had just started to eat when a text message popped up on Kim's phone. She checked it and flipped open her secure laptop. "It's Knox and Hamilton calling us."

Connor glanced at the time. "They're early."

Kim crossed her fingers. "Not by much. Let's hope they have good news."

Knox and Hamilton's faces filled the screen. Both men looked like they had a secret they wanted to share.

"Good day, gentlemen," said Kim. "I take it you have news for us?"

Hamilton cleared his throat. "Professor Forest got back to us a few minutes ago and said your drawing was exquisite. He was pretty upset that you'd lost the original map, as he'd loved to have taken the time to examine it in detail. But that's not a realistic option now."

"No, it is not," replied Kim, tired of people constantly reminding her that the map was lost.

"Regardless of what the good professor thinks, I'd like you and Connor to fly to Greenland as soon as possible to look for the scrolls."

"Sir, aside from a few lines in Captain Moore's journal and my sketch drawing, we don't have much to go on."

"And just in case either one of you hasn't checked a map recently," protested Connor, "Greenland is one huge piece of real estate."

"We know that," said Knox. "That's why we've hired an expert on Norse settlements to meet you in Greenland's capital, Nuuk."

Kim sat back and patted Connor on the arm. "Yes, now I remember. The boy Moore found said they were shipwrecked near an abandoned settlement."

"And stayed there until some Inuit saved them from starvation," added Connor, recalling the conversation.

"Most known Norse settlements were located near Nuuk or on the southern tip of Greenland," Knox explained. "The ruins Grenier's people stumbled across centuries ago must be well to the north of any other known sites, or the treasure would have been found years ago."

"That makes a lot of sense," said Kim.

"So, when can you get going?" asked Hamilton.

"It's not that easy," said Connor. "We're wanted people. The minute we board a commercial plane the opposition will know where we're going."

"That's not a problem," said Hamilton. "I can hire a plane to get you to Nuuk."

"That's fine, but we'll need some up-to-date passports, and I'd like to bring Yuri with us."

"Why?"

"Because he has contacts neither Kim nor I have, and he knows how to fly a plane. Something tells me we're going to be spending a lot of time in the air looking for this settlement."

"All right, you can bring him," replied Hamilton reluctantly.

"Hey, don't get cheap on us, Jason," warned Connor. "We're the ones taking the risks out here, not you, so put a smile on your face and continue paying for everything that we need. Okay?"

"Of course. Please excuse my demeanor. It's been a long few days, and I'm tired."

"Not a problem, Jason. How long do you think it will take to arrange a plane to pick us up?"

"Give us a couple of hours, and Mister Knox will call Kim to tidy up the details."

Connor smirked. He'd knocked Jason down a peg, and his ex-father-in-law didn't like it one bit. That's why he handed over the rest of the negotiations to Kim, not him. "Talk to you later, Jason."

The screen went dark.

Kim looked at Connor and tutted.

"What? What did I do now?"

"You embarrassed Mister Hamilton in front of his colleague."

"So?"

"You could have been a little more diplomatic, and that's all I'm going to say on the subject."

Connor opened his mouth but closed it instead. Kim had a different view of Hamilton, and nothing he could say would change her mind. So, he sat back instead and reached for his food.

"There is no need to ask; I'll go," said Yuri groggily, raising a thumb.

"How much of our conversation did you hear?" asked Connor.

Yuri sat up and ran his hand over his face. "All of it. But I must warn you that Greenland is terra incognito to me. I don't have a single contact in that part of the world. But you're right—you're going to need a pilot, and I'm the best there is."

"Or that we can afford?" teased Kim.

"That too," replied Yuri, finishing off what was left in his glass from the night before and then reaching for a half-empty bottle.

Connor stood and took the bottle from Yuri's hand. "Sorry, mate, but I need you at your best. You can have a drink or two on me when this is all over."

Yuri put on a sour face. "But I am at my best when I drink."

31.

Nuuk International Airport – Greenland

"Oh, thank God for that," said Connor as the Nuuk airport terminal came into view. Unlike most international airports, Nuuk's was small and resembled an oblong metal warehouse at the base of a rocky hill.

"And that makes eighteen hours," said Kim, stretching her arms over her head.

"It could have been worse," noted Yuri.

"How so?"

"Count your lucky stars, pretty lady. Had we taken a commercial flight, we'd still be in the Netherlands, waiting for our connection."

Kim leaned forward and smiled at Yuri. "You know, I'm getting a little tired of being called *pretty lady* because I find it more than a bit sexist. Maybe it's okay where you grew up to speak to a grown woman that way, Yuri, but I don't like it."

Yuri sat back and furrowed his brow. "But you are a pretty lady."

"That may be so, but my name is Kim Swiftwater, and I'd like you to use it from now on."

Yuri nodded. "Okay, I'm sorry. You're right; I'll try to use your name from now on."

"Thanks, that's all a person can ask for."

The Learjet reduced speed and taxied toward the terminal.

"It looks overcast," noted Kim, peering out of the window at the gray sky. "I wonder if it's going to rain today?"

"Rain or not, I doubt we're dressed for the weather," said Connor.

"The first stop after checking in will be to the nearest store to buy some warmer clothes," said Kim.

"Sounds good to me," said Yuri, glancing down at his rumpled Hawaiian shirt and military-style combat pants.

The plane stopped, and the engines switched off. The flight attendant opened the front side door and greeted the ground crew. A young woman in a dark blue uniform boarded the jet, took the passports from the attendant, and quickly stamped them.

"Welcome to Greenland," said the customs agent. "Don't worry about your baggage; I have arranged for it to meet you inside the terminal. I hope you enjoy your stay."

Yuri smiled like a wolf and waved at the woman. "After meeting you, I may never leave."

"Then you'll need a longer visa and a better line than that," said the woman deadpanned before leaving.

"Ouch," said Connor. "Want some lotion for that burn? When will you learn how to speak to women?"

Yuri shrugged and grabbed an old canvas pack from the chair beside him. "It wasn't the first time, nor, unfortunately, will it be the last occasion that a future wife and I get off on the wrong foot."

Connor shook his head. "You're one of a kind, Yuri."

"*Da*, I know."

Connor clapped his hands together and announced loudly, "Okay, folks, it's time to get to work. They ain't paying us by the hour, so grab your bags and head for the terminal."

Kim looked at Connor and raised her eyebrows. "Since when did you care about how much this expedition costs?"

"I don't. I was just channeling my inner Marine."

"Well, don't. It doesn't suit you. I prefer the more sedate, retired-anti-poaching Connor North to your inner Marine persona."

"Okay, ma'am," said Connor, mockingly saluting Kim.

"And you can stop that, too. I'm younger than you by several years, old man."

The joking immediately stopped when they stepped onto the tarmac, and a cold breeze whipped by them. They hurried inside and were surprised to see a tall, handsome young Inuit man in his mid-twenties standing there with a sign in his hands, looking for the Fields, the couple's new alias.

"Good afternoon," said Connor. "I'm Mister Fields." He turned and introduced the rest of the party. "This is my sister Kim and our good friend Yuri."

"Good afternoon to you, sir," said the man. "My name is Gunnar Karlsen. I'm one of Professor Lang's graduate students. He sends his apologies, as both he and his wife are very sick with the flu. He asked me if I could help you, and I naturally said yes."

"That's too bad," said Kim. "Did the professor tell you why we've traveled all this way to Greenland?"

Gunnar nodded. "Yes, but if you're looking for evidence of Norse settlements near the Arctic Circle, I'm afraid you may be wasting your time. To date, the only evidence of habitation we've found in Western Greenland is here around Nuuk, in the Nuup Kangerlua fjord, to be precise. That's not to say there weren't smaller settlements to the north of here, but we've yet to find them."

Connor said, "Well, the one we're looking for is allegedly on an island."

Gunnar ceased his brow. "Sir, do you have any idea how many islands there are between here and the Arctic Circle?"

"No, but I'm sure it's in the hundreds."

"That's why you're here," said Kim, smiling at Gunnar.

"Ma'am, I don't mean any disrespect, but what makes you so sure that we're going to find evidence of Norse settlements to the north of Nuuk?" asked Gunnar.

"Please call me Kim. Ma'am makes me feel old."

"Sorry."

"It's all right. Now, as to your question, we'd like to keep what we know a secret for now."

"That's your call, but the more I know, the better I can assist you in your search."

"Excuse me," said Yuri, interrupting. "I'm just a humble pilot, not an amateur archaeologist. I know my request came out of the blue, but have you been able to rent a seaplane for us?"

Gunnar nodded. "That wasn't a problem at all. My uncle runs a small airline charter in town. Typically, his pilots do the flying, but he's agreed to rent you a Twin Otter for the next five days. After that, you'll have to bring it back to Nuuk for some scheduled maintenance."

Yuri nodded. "Five days should be plenty."

Connor checked the time. "It's getting too late in the day to do anything of value. So why don't we check in to our hotel and then do some clothes shopping before supper?"

"I'm all for that," said Kim.

"I have a van waiting in the parking lot to take you to your hotel," explained Gunnar. "I haven't anything else to do today, so I'll stick around and drive you wherever you want to go."

"Thanks, that would be nice," said Kim.

"So that settles it," said Connor. "Let's check-in."

Supper that night at the hotel was simple but tasty. Everyone had whatever choice of fish they wanted, as it had been caught locally that day and served with fried potatoes and vegetables. They sat in a quiet corner, drinking coffee and eating dessert while a piano player entertained some people at the bar.

"Gunnar, do you know what the weather will be like for the next few days?" asked Kim.

The young man nodded. "According to the news, we're in for some pleasant weather. The daily high will be around eight, with a low of only four Celsius."

"Sounds positively balmy," joked Yuri.

"That's forty-six to thirty-nine Fahrenheit for Connor," teased Kim.

"You're hilarious," he replied, faking a belly laugh. "Don't forget I was in the military, so I know the metric system and how to convert Celsius into Fahrenheit."

"When are sunup and sundown?" queried Yuri.

"This time of the year, we can count on a good nine hours or more of sunlight. Sunup is around 0800, and sunset is at 1730 hours," explained Gunnar.

"That's good. That means we can get a lot of work done before the sun goes down," said Connor.

"Just before coming down for supper, I called Gunnar's uncle to check on the plane," said Yuri. "It's only two hundred and forty kilometers to the Arctic Circle, and range will not be an issue as our plane can fly fifteen hundred kilometers before refueling. The owner said it was fitted with a LiDAR pod earlier today to help speed up our search. He claims that the system is accurate to within eight inches."

"Professor Lang suggested we rent one from the university," interjected Gunnar.

Yuri shook his head. "At twenty-five grand a day, I hope it's worth it."

"Oh, it is. I've used one in the past, and it proved to be invaluable."

"I'm sorry, what's a LiDAR?" asked Kim.

Gunnar looked over at Kim. "LiDAR stands for light detection and ranging. In layperson's terms, it is a highly sensitive 3D scanner that can see objects buried underground. So, as our plane flies over an island, we'll be able to see what's hidden from the naked eye. For example, in the past decade, archaeologists in South America have found hundreds of unknown settlements ranging from villages to cities lost in the jungle using LiDAR."

"That's amazing."

Gunnar wiped his lips with a napkin and sat back in his chair. "I may only be a university student without very much life experience, but I've been watching the three of you ever since you landed, and I want to tell you upfront that I'm not one for playing games. I know Professor Lang, and I are being paid a lot of money to help you, but I can't help but wonder who you really are and why you're here. It's clear to me that none of you are amateur archaeologists. And please don't insult my intelligence by continuing to pretend to be siblings. Ms. Fields is a closer relation to me than you are, Mister Fields."

"Fair enough," said Connor.

"I have to warn you that removing any artifact found in Greenland without permission is illegal. I may be here to assist you, but I'm also duty-bound to report you to the police if you were to take so much as a rusty belt buckle from a dig site."

"That's not exactly why we're here," said Kim.

The grad student scrunched his brow. "I don't understand."

Kim looked around and lowered her voice. "Promise not to laugh at us?"

Gunnar crossed himself. "I'll try my best."

"We have evidence that people from the early fourteenth century were shipwrecked on an island somewhere to the north of the main Norse settlements around Nuuk and only survived because of help from local Inuit hunters."

Gunnar's mouth twisted. "That's plausible, but I have never read any records of this happening."

"That's because the people found an already abandoned home and lived in it until disease and a bitter winter nearly killed them all. They even acknowledged that without help, they would have all died. Over time, they integrated themselves into the Inuit community, eventually becoming one."

"An abandoned settlement, you say?"

"Yes."

"And how do you know this?"

"Because we do," interjected Connor firmly, making it clear their sources were out of bounds.

"All right, for one moment, let's say I believe you. I'm not sure I do, but we'll skip over that for the sake of this argument. Why is it so crucial that you find whatever you're looking for?"

"In a word, money," said Connor.

Gunnar smiled. "Compared with you and me, the people of that era were dirt poor. Their currencies were ivory and livestock. There are no hordes of gold out there waiting to be found."

"And what if you're wrong?"

"I know Norse history like the back of my hand. Unfortunately, there's no pot of gold at the end of the rainbow. If there were, I'd know about it."

"Gunnar, why are you so sure you'd know about our missing settlement?" asked Kim.

"Because, over the past several years, Greenland has had unseasonably warm summers, which has led to the permafrost melting and revealing long-lost clusters of homes. But all of these have been close to Nuuk. Sadly, if these new sites aren't correctly excavated, any organic remains or manufactured materials found there will rot and be gone forever."

"So it could be out there, and you just don't know about it," proposed Connor.

"Maybe, maybe not. Just out of curiosity, how much money are you talking about?"

Connor shrugged. "It could be worth trillions, or it could just be a wild goose chase, and there's nothing there. We won't know until we find this settlement."

Kim said, "What we haven't told you so far is that we're in a race to find this alleged treasure before a man called DuFour can find it."

"So what if he finds it first?" asked Gunnar. "He'll still have to follow our laws governing cultural sovereignty."

Kim and Connor chuckled at Gunnar and shook their heads.

"What's so funny?" he demanded.

"Men like DuFour couldn't give a damn about your laws regarding the protection of cultural heritage," explained Connor. "He'll take want he wants, and no one here, other than us, can stop him."

"You're exaggerating. Surely the police could handle this man?"

"I wish I was exaggerating, Gunnar. I'm not joking when I say it's best to leave the police out of this."

"Why?"

"This man is dangerous."

"Very dangerous," stressed Kim. "Would you like their blood on your hands?"

"No, of course not," responded Gunnar. "But no one is above the law."

Connor looked Gunnar in the eyes. "DuFour and his people think they are. This man is connected and has more than enough money to buy whatever he wants, even the police and judges."

A young waiter approached the table to see if they wanted anything more but was brusquely waved off by Yuri.

Gunnar tilted his head. "Let me get this straight. You're telling me that you're in a race with this DuFour character to find this alleged settlement and whatever may be buried there, even though you have no real idea of what may be there."

"Now you're getting it," said Connor.

Gunnar shook his head and let out an exasperated sigh. "Whatever. If you were to ask me, I'd say you're all insane. But the money's good, and since I need money for a new car, who am I to question your motives? As long as you leave everything where we find it, I'm your guide for the next four days."

32.

Burkeville, Texas

Tiva Swiftwater walked home at an unhurried pace, talking and laughing with her two best friends, Sarah and Valeria. They had spent the better part of the day playing at another friend's house, but it was now time to come home. Just back out of earshot was her foster father, Darren Long, a retired police detective who had insisted on walking Tiva and her friends home before it got too dark. Tiva had protested that she and her friends could walk home by themselves. After all, she was almost eight years old and about to enter grade three. But her complaints had fallen on deaf ears, and here they were, approaching Valeria's house.

"Goodnight, Valeria," said Tiva. "See you tomorrow."

Valeria waved at her friends and jogged to the front door, where her mother awaited her.

"Thanks, Darren," said Valeria's mother, hugging her daughter and waving to the man.

"It's not a problem," he replied with a smile. "Walking the girls home gives me some exercise and a good excuse to get out of the house."

"Excuse or not, I really do appreciate your help."

"Like I said, it's my pleasure," he said, rubbing his right knee. Shot on duty with less than a year to go to his pension, Darren and his wife had called it a day and left Houston for a quieter life.

A couple of houses later, Sarah said goodbye, leaving Tiva and her foster father to walk one more block to their home.

Having respected Tiva's wishes to be treated more like a big girl than a child during the walk home, Darren moved up alongside her and smiled. "So, did you have a good time today?"

Tiva nodded and held up her make-up bag. "Jen's mom let us practice on her younger brother, Brian."

Darren chuckled. "I'm sure he really appreciated that."

"He didn't mind, but after a while, Brian got bored and ran away."

I can't blame him, thought Darren.

"Dad, what's for supper?"

Darren loved to hear Tiva call him dad. It made his heart warm. It had taken years after the abuse and trauma Tiva had endured to warm up to her foster parents, let alone call them mom and dad. Darren pretended to think for a few seconds. "I think Mom's making chicken-fried steak."

"Mmm, my favorite."

"Mine too; that's why Mom's making it."

A steel-gray van drove out of a side street and turned down the road toward Darren and Tiva. Years of police training resulted in an unconscious habit, and Darren idly cataloged the scene: tinted windows and an unfamiliar vehicle in general. Casually, he placed himself between Tiva and the road.

The van started to slow.

Darren frowned. He placed his hand over his Glock 19 pistol and mentally thanked Texas for its open-carry laws.

The van stopped, and the driver's side window came down, revealing a young blonde-haired woman holding a map. Her hair was a mess, and she looked perturbed.

"Excuse me, sir, but my boyfriend and I are lost." The blonde's voice had a hint of a Scandinavian accent in it. "Could you please tell me the best way to get back onto Highway 79?"

Darren relaxed and lifted his hand away from his sidearm. "Sure thing. Can I please see your map?"

"Here," said the woman, offering Darren the map. "I'm the worst navigator in the world."

"Let me see," he said, checking their location on the rumpled map.

Suddenly, the woman said coldly, "Sorry."

Darren looked back at the van. His eyes widened at the sight of a gun aimed at him. Before he could warn Tiva to run, the woman pulled the trigger, firing a tranquilizing dart into the former officer's neck. To Darren's horror, a side door on the van flung open, and two other women dressed in black ran outside and grabbed hold of Tiva. His vision narrowed a second later as his knees buckled, and he tumbled onto the pavement.

"Daddy!" screamed Tiva in terror as she was forced into the van, and its door slammed shut. Unfortunately, he could do nothing as the drugs surged through his blood. In seconds, he passed out and would remain asleep for hours.

"Go," yelled the blonde to the driver.

The driver slammed her foot on the gas pedal and dove the van out of the quiet, sleepy community onto a dusty back road where another vehicle awaited their arrival. Hours later, when the authorities found the abandoned van, there was no trace of Tiva or its occupants, only a new set of tires heading east toward Louisiana. It was now a matter for the FBI, but even they would be too late to help. Tiva and her captors were already safely outside of the country in Haiti, awaiting orders for their next move.

33.

Nuuk, Greenland

At precisely eight o'clock in the morning, on a calm sea, Yuri revved the engine of his rented, red and white Twin Otter, startling a handful of seagulls hovering near the busy pier, sending them squawking and flying skyward. Then, Yuri steered the floatplane into the harbor, increased speed, and took off. Connor sat in the co-pilot's seat, with a map spread out on his lap, while in the back, Gunnar and Kim operated the LiDAR via a laptop computer. Finally, Yuri banked the DHC-6 Twin Otter over and headed for their first search area just south of the Arctic Circle. Gunnar doubted any Norse family had ever lived that far north, so he suggested they eliminate that area first before heading south.

"I've never understood why they call this place Greenland when it's clearly not," said Kim to Gunnar.

Gunnar smiled and pointed to a map. "Hundreds of years ago, when the Vikings first settled here, the north went through a warm spell that lasted well into the early thirteen hundreds. The land back then was good for farming, and thousands of Norse families emigrated to Greenland to make a new life for themselves. Some, as you know, pushed on a little bit further to Newfoundland and settled there."

"So, what made them leave?"

"No one really knows, but I like to think that it was a combination of climate change and a decline in the value of walrus ivory in Europe. The ivory trade had been one of their chief sources of revenue for centuries, and when cheaper ivory from Russia and Africa began to arrive in Europe, the bottom fell out of the market. So, one by one, the families abandoned Greenland and sailed back home. The last recorded western settlement was abandoned in 1350. As for the southern settlements, there is a lot of scholarly debate as to when the last people left Greenland for Iceland. Some say 1408 and others as late as 1480."

"And what do you think?"

Gunnar shrugged. "I'm not sure. My area of expertise is on the western settlements, and there, we have definitive proof of when the last ship sailed for Iceland."

"What about the Inuit? Did they have an impact?"

"A good question, but once again, the records are sparse. But, most assuredly, there was contact. How much that played into the Norse's decision to leave Greenland has yet to be decided."

"Whatever happened, I find the subject quite interesting. How long is it until we can begin our search?"

Gunnar checked his watch. "If your pilot is as good as he says he is, we should reach the Arctic Circle just before nine o'clock, and then we can begin our search."

Kim smiled. The thought of finding a settlement lost for more than five hundred years excited her. She turned in her seat, looked down on the rocky coastline, and tried to imagine living in such barren and inhospitable terrain. A shiver ran down her back. Life would have been hard for Grenier, and the rest of the people marooned on a deserted island. No wonder so many died in their first winter trapped in the ice.

An hour later, Yuri turned the plane around and started to fly slowly south in a zigzag pattern over the seemingly never-ending islands that dotted the coastline. Some were no larger than a car, while others were kilometers across.

"*Yuri, the LiDAR works best at two thousand meters,*" said Gunnar into his headset mic.

"*Roger that,*" replied Yuri. "*Making our elevation two thousand meters.*"

Kim felt her stomach rise as the plane dropped from the sky to take up its new patrol altitude. She waited until the Twin Otter was level before asking, "Gunnar, do all of these islands have a name? Because there's a hell of a lot of them out there."

"I'm sure they do to the local Inuit, but most have yet to be recorded by the government back in Nuuk."

"Where does your family come from?" Kim asked.

"I was born in Oaanaaq," replied Gunnar. "Which the world knows as Thule. My family has lived there for generations. However, my parents insisted that I get an education and shipped me off to live with my uncle in Nuuk while I went to school and university. And you, where does your family come from?"

"I wish I knew my ancestry. All I can say with certainty is that I'm Cree, and I was born in the Eagle River First Nations Reserve in Alberta, Canada, and raised by my grandparents. I have a sister with a daughter, Tiva, whom I hate to say I haven't seen in a few years. I'm also embarrassed to say that this is all I know. One day I'm going to have to do one of those DNA tests to see where I come from."

A beep sounded from Gunnar's laptop, ending the conversation. He announced excitedly, "I've got something."

Kim moved over to better see the ground beneath the plane through the LiDAR imagery. The picture was a mix of blues, greens, reds, and yellows. She couldn't tell what had caught Gunnar's eyes in the myriad colors.

Gunnar keyed his mic. "*Yuri, can we take another pass over the large, crescent-shaped island we just flew over?*"

"*Can do; just give me a minute.*"

"*What did you see?*" asked Connor over the headset.

"*I'm not sure, but it looked manmade,*" replied Gunnar.

Yuri turned the Twin Otter around and slowly approached the island.

Everyone held their breath as they flew over the top of the bleak-looking island. The laptop beeped again.

"*There*," said Gunnar, pointing at a red oblong-shaped object.

"*Should I land the plane?*" asked Yuri.

Gunnar enlarged the picture and swore under his breath. "*No. It's a fishing boat that must have washed ashore decades ago and then rotted.*"

"*Are you sure?*" asked Connor.

"*Yeah. It looks like the kind my great-grandfather used to use back when he was a fisherman.*"

"Damn," said Kim, feeling the built-up excitement leave her stomach. "I was really hoping we'd found the treasure the first time out."

"It's never that simple," explained Gunnar. "The closer we get to Nuuk, the more false alarms we're bound to encounter. Your five-day plan may turn out to be a bit of an overly optimistic timetable."

Kim sighed frustratedly and muttered, "We're lucky if we have another seventy-two hours."

Gunnar leaned forward. "Sorry, I didn't catch that."

"Nothing. It was nothing; I was just upset that we hadn't found the treasure."

"Patience is the key to the game."

Gunnar's laptop beeped again as the plane flew over an island with a tall, flat hill at the northern end.

Kim sat back. It was going to be a long day, indeed.

34.

Paris, France.

It didn't matter which model walked past him wearing the newest fashions; Rene DuFour was growing bored and restless. His redheaded minder, Demi, sat beside him, raptly watching the models, not saying a word. Ever since Vallin had lost contact with North and Swiftwater in Thailand, it was like Vallin had dropped off the face of the Earth. DuFour thought a weekend in Paris, taking in the latest fashion shows, would prove to be a relaxing distraction. Regrettably, the exact opposite had occurred. The quieter Vallin was, the more agitated DuFour became. Finally, unable to take it anymore, he excused himself, exited his seat, and walked to the back of the exhibition house for some privacy.

A balding, pale-white man in a tuxedo with a pencil-thin mustache hurried over. "Is there something wrong, monsieur? Is there something else perhaps I could show you?"

DuFour waved his hand dismissively in the air. "No, Pierre, your exhibition is breathtaking. I just need some space for a few minutes to think."

"But of course, monsieur. Please let me know if you need anything."

"Some time alone will be fine right now."

Pierre bowed his head slightly and hurried back to the stage.

DuFour sat at an empty table and dug out his phone. He saw there were four unanswered calls and checked them. His eyes widened when he saw Vallin's name. DuFour cursed himself for turning his phone off when he sat down to watch the show. He hurriedly returned Vallin's call.

"Yes, sir," said Vallin.

"Do you have news for me?" demanded DuFour.

"Yes, I do." Vallin calmly explained that he had ordered some of his people to kidnap Tiva Swiftwater and hold her until she became a valuable pawn in the game.

"Excellent plan, Jean. But what of the map? Have you found Swiftwater and North?"

"No, sir, but it's only a matter of time before I do."

DuFour's phone beeped. "One minute, Jean, I have another call."

"I'll be here."

"Yes," said DuFour curtly to his private secretary back at his chalet.

"Sir, it's me, Dominic," said the other caller.

"Yes, what of it?"

"Sir, I just sent you a text message; I think you need to read it."

DuFour grumbled to himself. That was until he read the message. Then, in a flash, his mood changed. "Dominic, are you sure this is a legitimate text and not some hoax?"

"I thought the same as you," replied Dominic. "But I did some digging, and it would appear to be legit."

DuFour could barely contain himself. "My God, this is the best news I've received in weeks. Did he mention the map?"

"No, sir. He's not sure what they are looking for, only that they've been at it for the past two days and that whatever they're looking for is quite valuable."

DuFour paused. "How did he know to contact me?"

"He said he'd heard your name brought up in conversation and took it from there. Sir, he's asking for twenty-five thousand dollars to keep you in the loop."

DuFour grinned. "Reply immediately and let the person know I will pay their demand for twenty-five thousand dollars. Hell, I'd pay a million for news like this. But don't let him know that."

"Yes, sir," said Dominic.

DuFour hung up on Dominic and recommenced talking with Vallin. "Jean, stop whatever you're doing."

"Yes, of course, sir. Is there something you want to pass on to me?"

DuFour's eyes lit up. "They're in Greenland looking for the treasure as we speak. Assemble a team and bring the girl with you. It's time we put your plan into action."

"What plan?" asked Demi, standing like a vulture over DuFour.

DuFour's heart skipped a beat. "My God, woman, please don't sneak up on me like that. It's disconcerting."

Demi shook her head. "I don't care. The plan, Rene, what is it?"

DuFour stood and put away his phone. "Care for a trip to Greenland, my dear?"

35.

Connor strolled into the hotel restaurant, looking forward to some coffee and a bagel, when he spotted his compatriots silently sitting around a table. He pulled out a chair and sat down.

"Come on; it's not that bad," said Connor, attempting to cheer everyone up. "It's only day three. We still have two more days to come up with something before we have to return Yuri's plane. If we haven't found the gold by then, we'll hire a boat if we have to."

"What if we're wrong?" proposed Kim. "I only saw the map for a few seconds. What if we're supposed to be looking in Baffin Island, not Greenland?"

Connor shook his head. "No, it's here. And I don't give a damn if you only saw the map briefly. I'd trust your memory over a modern-day map with the exact GPS coordinates to the missing settlement on it."

Kim raised her head. "Really?"

"Really."

Gunnar yawned loudly and stretched his arms over his head.

"Burning the midnight oil?" asked Connor.

Gunnar nodded. "I haven't gone to bed yet."

"How come?"

"I spent the night at the university digging through old Norse records. I read that a small number of families were banished from the settlements around Nuuk for crimes relating to things like murder, theft, and adultery. Maybe one of them made it to a nearby island and lived there until disease, starvation, or predation wiped them all out."

A waiter approached with a fresh carafe of coffee and took everyone's order.

"That may be true, but it still doesn't narrow down the search," pointed out Yuri.

"I knew you'd say that, and I have come up with an idea," said Gunnar, placing a map of the coast on the table. "I say we flip our search on its head and start just north of the last known settlement and go from there. Using common sense, I've eliminated all of the islands that are too small to host a family or two on them and circled the rest as possible targets. I also called my uncle this morning, and he's willing to put off the Twin Otter's scheduled maintenance for one more day, giving us three full days to find the gold."

"It can't hurt," offered Connor. "All we've got to show so far are a handful of long-lost boats and a ring of rocks that looked like the outside of an old Norse home but turned out to be nothing."

"I'm okay with the new plan," said Kim. "What do you say, Yuri?"

"Me, I'm just the pilot," responded Yuri. "I'll fly wherever you want me to."

"Then it's decided," said Gunnar. "Let's toast to a better day."

The four companions lifted their glasses of orange juice and did just that.

"Yes, we've got contact!" announced Gunnar, pumping his fist in the air as they flew over a dark, circular island.

"What do you see?" asked Kim. They had been airborne for hours. Each island they had surveyed had turned out to be a dead end until, it seemed, now.

Gunnar waited for the information from the LiDAR pod to appear clearly on his laptop. Then, he picked up a pen and pointed at three circular rock shapes in the ground. "These rings are undoubtedly the outer rings of three old Norse homes."

"*Have we found it?*" asked Yuri excitedly.

Gunnar nervously tapped his pen on the laptop screen. "No, I don't think so. In my mind, I see three or more abandoned homes and a unique structure made by the people who were shipwrecked on the island where they lived and most likely buried the gold. I'm going to record this location for future considerations."

"*Okay, you're the specialist,*" said Connor. "*Where to next?*"

Gunnar keyed his mic. "There's a triangular-shaped island thirty kilometers to the northwest of here that might fit the bill. It's marked A-9 on the map."

"*Got it,*" replied Connor.

Kim felt the mood in the plane change; optimism replaced pessimism. Maybe today was their day. She crossed her fingers and glanced out a window at the dark gray sea beneath them. Then, out of nowhere, a wave of melancholy swept over her, and she wondered how her sister and niece were doing. Kim resolved to go and visit them when the mission was behind them, and she'd been paid.

"Here we go," said Yuri as he flew their Twin Otter straight over a triangular-shaped, rocky island.

Kim could feel the excitement building inside her as she watched Gunnar's laptop screen. She looked at Gunnar's face, looking for any sign of emotion. The young grad student could have been at a poker table, with his eyes fixed on the screen as the information poured in.

Red and blue images appeared on the screen.

"Yes!" hollered Gunnar, starling Kim. "This has to be it. I've got the outline of three homes, a larger communal house, and something substantial buried a couple of meters underground that looks like a massive turtle's shell."

"*Are you sure this is the place?*" asked Connor.

"I am," responded Gunnar. "Let's take her down and take a look."

"*You heard the man,*" said Connor to Yuri.

"*Yes, siree, taking her down.*"

Kim glanced out the window at the island. The land was flat near the water but gradually grew toward a large rocky hill that dominated the rest of the landscape.

"*Make sure you're buckled up back there,*" warned Yuri, bringing their airplane in for a smooth landing on the water. He decreased power and steered toward a black sandy beach. The aircraft suddenly stopped as the floats ran aground, and Yuri switched off the engine.

"All ashore; who's going ashore," joked Connor, removing his headset and opening his door.

Kim and Gunnar put on their Gortex jackets and joined the rest of the party on the wet sand.

Gunnar cleared his throat and waved a handheld GPS in the air. "Okay, remember what I said in the restaurant the first day we met? You cannot remove a single object we may find on this site. I'm going to treat this place with the respect it's due and record everything on my camera and GPS."

"You won't get any pushback from us," said Connor.

The grad student waved an arm over his head. "Okay then, let's go."

They fell into line and walked off the sloping beach onto a muddy, rock-strewn surface. Right away, they spotted a row of rocks laid out in an oblong shape.

"Wow," said Kim. "Just think, that was a house nine hundred years ago."

They walked over to the structure and saw the ground was about a meter below the surface inside the long-abandoned home.

"Gunnar, what gives?" asked Yuri, pointing at the sunken floor.

Gunnar lowered his camera. "It was common practice back then for the settlers to dig one meter down for insulation in the winter and to keep the home cool in the summer."

"I'm amazed that someone else hadn't already stumbled across this island," said Kim.

"Up until a month ago, I'm willing to bet all of these buildings were still buried under the mud," explained Gunnar. "With the warm temperatures and the tons of rain we've had this year, this place was most likely exposed in a matter of weeks."

"What about these tunnels?" asked Connor, standing in a passageway up to his waist that led from the first structure they found to one about twenty meters off to the right.

"Uh, that's not normal," said Gunnar, shaking his head. "The people who were shipwrecked here, where did they come from?"

"France," said Kim.

"And why did they leave France?"

"They were led by a man called Phillip Grenier, a member of the Knights Templar, who was fleeing a king's edict for the destruction of his order."

"My best guess is that they built these tunnels for protection from the elements or hostile outsiders. Either way, this is ground-breaking archaeology."

"They don't seem very deep," observed Yuri.

"That's because there's still mud and muck inside them," responded Gunnar. "They were probably five to six feet deep at one time and maybe even covered."

Yuri nodded. "*Da*, that makes good tactical sense to me."

Gunnar continued meticulously recording the ruins of the first dwelling before leading the team to the adjacent two homes. They were near copies of the first home, and the only thing they found, quite prophetically, was a rusty belt buckle.

Kim checked the time and nudged Connor on the ribs. "Gunnar's taking an hour or more per home. At this pace, it'll be dark before we finish cataloging the island."

Connor nodded. "I know, but what can we do?"

"Ask him to speed up. There's always tomorrow."

"Yeah, you're right." Connor touched Gunnar's on the back. "I know this is important to you, but could you please pick up the pace? We don't want to be out here in the dark, do we?"

"Sorry," he replied. "I must have lost track of time." He waved for them to follow him to the remains of a long house and hurriedly recorded its location.

"Time for dessert," said Kim, jogging alongside a passageway that seemed to lead nowhere. She stood there with her arms wide open and closed her eyes, imagining what lay beneath her feet.

Gunnar jumped into the tunnel and got down on his haunches. He ran a hand over the mud to reveal a pile of rocks. "Whatever you're looking for is gonna take time and hard work to reveal. According to the LiDAR, behind these rocks is a passageway leading underground into an open chamber. What's down there is anyone's guess."

"We've still got two hours of sunlight remaining," said Connor, "I say we start digging."

Gunnar waved a finger. "Not without permission, you're not. And before you ask, I don't have that kind of authority."

"Well, who does?" asked Kim, annoyed that Gunnar seemed to be throwing up roadblock after roadblock.

"Professor Lang might, but he's sick."

Kim handed Gunnar a satphone. "You knew we'd need permission before flying out here today. Now get us that permission! Call your boss and tell him we'll double whatever you're being paid if he grants us permission to dig."

"I don't know."

"Do it," said Connor firmly.

The call lasted less than a minute. Gunnar gave them a thumbs up; they had their permission and got to work.

Connor moved Gunnar aside, grasped the first rock, and handed it to Yuri, who placed it on the ground next to the tunnel. Then, taking turns, they slowly cleared the stones from the tunnel entrance until they were all sweating and covered in mud. Finally, Gunnar dug out a trowel and cleared the centuries of dirt away from a one-meter square stone.

"It's probably no more than an inch thick," he announced, gasping for air.

Connor poured some water over the stone and gently rubbed the mud away. Slowly, words came into view. "Gunnar, there's an inscription on the rock. Can you read it?"

Gunnar huffed as he dropped to his aching knees to examine the rock. "It's not old Norse, that's for sure. French, maybe?"

"Let me take a look," said Kim, replacing Gunnar in the passage. She read the words over and shook her head. "If it's French, it's unlike any I've ever read."

Gunnar snapped his fingers. "I'm such an idiot. It's French, all right, but it's Old French. Like all modern languages, it took hundreds of years before a common language was established. I'll take a picture of it and then send it to be translated." Gunnar dug out his phone and snapped a picture.

"Hey, I don't want to rain on anyone's parade, but it's getting late, and it looks like it might actually rain soon," said Yuri, holding out his hand as if he were ready to catch raindrops. "I say we stop for the day and pick up where we left off first thing tomorrow."

Connor lifted his head and looked up at the dark gray clouds. "I agree; let's get out of here before this tunnel turns into a river of mud."

"Shouldn't one of us stay here in case someone comes during the night and claims the treasure for themselves?" asked Kim.

"No one knows we're here," said Gunnar. "It would take a miracle for someone else in the dark and the rain to stumble across the island, let alone the treasure."

"Besides, we don't have any camping gear," said Connor. "In this environment, you'd catch hypothermia and die before the sun came up in the morning."

"All right, all right, you've convinced me," replied Kim, wiping a clump of mud from her jacket. "But I don't like leaving whatever is out here unguarded."

"None of us do, but what choice do we have?"

Reluctantly, they climbed out of the tunnel and returned to the plane in silence. Kim snapped her seatbelt in place and looked back at the long-abandoned village, praying she was wrong.

36.

Kim rolled over and smashed her fist into her pillow, trying to make it more comfortable. She hadn't slept a wink since crawling into bed after a long, hot shower. No matter how hard she tried, Kim couldn't relax. They'd abandoned a site that may be worth two trillion dollars to get some sleep. None of it sat well with her. Finally, she sat up and reached for her phone.

"No," she uttered in despair at the time. It was nearly five in the morning. She'd tossed and turned the night away.

Unexpectedly, her phone buzzed. Kim thought about ignoring the incoming call, as she hadn't shared her number with anyone other than her teammates. Curious, she brought the phone close to her tired eyes to see who was calling. Kim switched on a light and sat up. Her instincts told her something was wrong. She hesitantly answered the call. "Hello?"

"Hi, Aunt Kimy; I'm sorry to be calling so early, but I've been told to read a note to you, okay?" said Tiva. She sounded herself, and only Tiva called her Kimy. But who was telling her to read a note and why? It took all of Kim's energy not to lose her self-control. She took a deep breath.

"Sure, hon, let's hear it."

Tiva cleared her throat. "Good day, Kim Swiftwater. I want you to know that Tiva is being well looked after, and I would like to offer you a trade: Tiva for the treasure. We know you have found it, and we will arrive at the island twenty-four hours from now to collect it. Do not alert the police, or there will be conseekwenses. No, that's not right," said Tiva. "Consequences. Did I say that right, Kimy?"

"You sure did, hon. Are you sure you're all right?"

"Oh, yes. At first, I was really scared, but my new friends told me that Mom and Dad know where I am and that I'll be going home soon."

"That sounds nice."

"My new friend, Jenny, looks after me and dresses me up like a pirate because of my left eye."

"Could I please speak with the people looking after you?"

"Mrs. Wilson," said Tiva, handing over the phone.

"Yes," said a stern-sounding woman.

"Can Tiva hear our conversation?" asked Kim.

"No, she's in the other room."

Kim got to her feet. She grasped the phone so tight her knuckles blanched. "I don't know who you are, but if you harm a single hair on Tiva's head, I will kill you."

"Ms. Swiftwater, there is no need for threats."

"I'm not threatening anyone; I'm stating a fact. You people have crossed a line that there's no going back from. You don't ever threaten another person's family. Ever!"

"I'm just doing my job, Ms. Swiftwater. But I can assure you that Tiva is being looked after by one of my best people. This is not a complicated deal. Give my employers the gold, and we'll hand over Tiva to you unharmed."

"I wish I could trust you, but my heart tells me you're lying."

"Dead hostages are bad for my business," retorted Mrs. Wilson bluntly. "You do your part in this business, and I'll guarantee your niece's safety."

Kim glanced at the time. "I guess we'll see if you're telling the truth twenty-four hours from now."

"Until tomorrow," said Wilson, ending the call.

Kim looked down at the phone in her hand and started to shake. Then, unable to contain her rage anymore, Kim dropped to her knees and let out a tormented cry from deep inside her chest.

Bang, bang, bang.

"Kim, are you all right?" called out Connor, beating on her bedroom door. A split-second later, the door flew open, and Connor ran inside wearing boxers and a T-shirt. "Kim, what's wrong?"

Kim couldn't speak. Tears streamed down her face. Finally, she got to her feet and held out her phone.

"Did somebody call you?" asked Connor.

"Is something wrong?" Yuri asked, standing in the shattered doorway.

"I don't know," said Connor.

"Tiva," stammered Kim. "They've got my niece, Tiva."

"Yuri, please get Kim some water," said Connor, guiding Kim by the hand to a chair. He pulled a blanket from the bed and draped it over her shoulders.

Kim sat and placed her phone beside her.

Connor got on his knees and looked into her tear-filled eyes. Then, gently, he asked, "Kim, who told you they had Tiva?"

"I don't know," she replied, sipping some water. "I only heard one name, Mrs. Wilson, which I'm sure is an alias."

"What else were you told?"

"They said they know we've found the treasure and want to exchange Tiva for the gold."

"Did they say when?" asked Yuri.

Kim ran a hand over her cheek and wiped a tear aside. "They said they'll free Tiva twenty-four hours from now at the island."

"God, I'm going to make DuFour pay when this is all over," said Connor, banging his fist on the table.

"I'll call Gunnar and see if he can speak with harbor control and amend my flight plan so we can get going early today," proposed Yuri.

Kim wiped the rest of her tears from her cheeks. "Don't bother; he's got to be the person who sold us out."

"Let's not jump to conclusions," protested Yuri. "Gunnar seems like an okay guy."

"How else would Tiva's kidnappers know about the island? And yesterday, Gunnar said the writing on that stone was Old French."

"Yes, what of it?"

"It wasn't French; it was Latin. Any student of medieval history should have some understanding of the language. He knew exactly what was written on it but chose to lie to us."

Yuri scrunched his brow. "But you said it was French as well."

Kim turned her hands out as if to say, *oh, well*. "I thought he was dragging his feet yesterday, so I tested him."

"Clever," said Connor, grinning at Kim.

"Were you also able to translate the stone?" asked Yuri.

Kim downed the rest of her water. "Yeah, it's a warning not to disturb the dead."

"The dead? Are you sure?"

Kim nodded. "That's what it said. I even checked using an app on my phone."

"So, that's why they're giving us twenty-four hours," said Connor. "They're hoping we'll make it safe for them to loot the treasure."

"I normally don't get very involved with my clients, but this DuFour character is really pissing me off," said Yuri. "I don't want him to get the treasure, nor do I want Kim's niece to get hurt. But you have to listen to me. I've spent years working for people like this, and they can't be trusted to keep their word. As soon as they get their hands on the gold, Tiva's life will be forfeit, as will anyone else's on the island. So, what are we going to do?"

Connor stood and started to pace. "One thing at a time. First, Kim, you had best call Tiva's foster parents to let them know she's still alive. I'm sure they're going out of their minds with worry by now. Second, Yuri, after you drop Kim and me off on the island later this morning, I'll need you to come back here right away and do some shopping for me."

A hotel employee with a red, puffy face, dressed in a dark blue jacket, knocked on the doorframe. "What the hell happened here?"

"Sorry, this is all my fault," explained Connor. "I thought I heard a scream and got carried away. Please bill me for the repairs to the door."

"You're damned right I will." The man walked off in a huff, mumbling in Danish to himself.

Yuri waited until the hotel employee was gone. "Connor, this is Greenland, not New York City. Guns, ammunition, and whatever else you're considering will be hard to find."

"I know, but I also know you'll do your best," said Connor.

"*Da*, I will."

Connor turned and smiled at Kim. "So, Kim Swiftwater, thief extraordinaire, do you feel like breaking into a tomb today?"

Kim nodded and got out of her chair. "There's no time like the present. Let's get to work."

37.

Kim and Connor waved at Yuri as he banked their Twin Otter over the island and headed back to Nuuk. A light mist hung in the air, making everything feel cold and wet.

"I guess this is it," said Connor, heaving a heavy pack onto his back.

"Do you think Yuri's right?" asked Kim.

"About what?"

"About Tiva. Do you think they'll kill her once they have the treasure?"

Connor looked deep into Kim's eyes. "Let's try not to think about that right now. Let's see if the gold is here to start with. After that, we can brainstorm all we want to figure out a way to rescue Tiva. Okay?"

Kim nodded and picked up her pack. "If Tiva's life wasn't in danger, I think I could be having the time of my life right now."

"Then we'll just have to do this again another time."

Kim gave a watery smile. "You're on."

They walked off the beach and headed straight for the suspected treasure site. The mud stuck to their boots like cement, making walking laborious. Finally, Kim and Connor dropped their packs at the tunnel entrance and paused to catch their breath.

Connor slid a safety helmet on his head and unloaded a pickaxe from his rucksack. He stepped into the muddy trench, glad he was wearing knee-high rubber boots. He paused and glanced up at Kim. "I know we've got to help Tiva, but I can't help but feel that we're trespassing."

"I know. I feel the same way. I've suddenly lost all of my initial enthusiasm and wonder how my ancestors would feel, knowing I was about to desecrate a tomb."

"I'm sure they'd forgive you for Tiva's sake."

Kim glanced skyward. "I hope so."

Connor ran his hand around the edge of the square rock, blocking their path. "Do you think this place could be boobytrapped?"

Kim wrinkled her nose. "What, like in the movies?"

"Yeah, like that."

Kim shook her head and tutted. "Connor North, if there were any traps left behind to stop graverobbers, they have long since rotted or fallen apart."

"So, no rocks tumbling out of the roof or dozens of poisonous blow darts hidden in the walls?"

"No, none of that. But be wary of foot traps. I suspect those things are timeless."

"Wonderful," said Connor carefully, placing the chisel end of his pick behind the meter-square stone block. "Here goes nothin'," he said, digging in his feet and pushing as hard as he could.

At first, nothing happened, and then, with a loud wet thunk, the stone popped loose. A second later, it came free and slid to the ground, dropping into the muck. A chill shot down Connor's back. He was soon about to tread in a place that had closely guarded its secrets for centuries.

"What can you see?' asked Kim, trying to see past Connor.

Connor dropped to all fours and switched on his headlamp. All he could see was a stone passageway leading underground. "At least we didn't have to say open sesame."

"Quit screwing around. That's not what I asked. What can you see?"

"I think we've found the tunnel Gunnar saw on his LiDAR."

"How deep does it go?"

Connor shrugged. "Beats me."

"Well done," said a mud-soaked man, suddenly appearing out of nowhere, aiming a pistol at Kim's head. Steam rose from his body in the cold air. "Raise your hands, or I'll kill both of you."

Connor slowly stood. He and Kim raised their hands.

"Thank God that you showed up when you did. I've been lying in the mud for hours and was ready to quit."

"How did you know to come here?" asked Connor.

"Gunnar told me you'd be here," said the man with a strong Danish accent. "He also said that you're a pair of graverobbers wanted by the police."

Kim shook her head. "That's not true."

"Are you sure, lady? Because you sure look like it to me."

"Who the hell are you?" demanded Connor.

"You don't need to know my name," snarled the gunman. "Gunnar's paying me to make sure you two don't try and run off before he and the police get here tomorrow morning to arrest you both."

Connor scrunched his brow. "The police? He actually told you he was going to bring the police here to arrest us?"

"Yeah, why?"

"No reason other than he's lying."

"Screw you. I'll take his word over yours any day of the week."

"Whatever he's paying you, I'll triple it," offered Connor.

The man licked his lips. "Do you have the money on you?"

"No, of course, I don't, but I can easily pay you once we get back to Nuuk."

"I'd rather bank on Gunnar's five grand."

"Five thousand dollars," blurted out Kim.

"No, it's five thousand Euros," responded the man, trying to make it sound like a lot of money.

Kim lowered her hands. "You're insane. I'll give you twenty-five thousand Euros to drop your gun and walk away."

The man shook his head. "No, thanks. I think I'll stick with my five grand. I've got debts to pay, and if you two were to skip town and not pay me, then I'm as good as dead."

"I'd ask how you knew where to find us, but I suspect the answer would lie with Gunnar, a GPS, and a rubber boat," said Connor.

"Right on all three. Now, shut your mouths. I want to see this fortune in treasure Gunnar claims is buried here before the police arrive."

Connor lowered his hands. The man was greedy, so he decided to play for time. "We'd like to see the treasure, too, so you'll have to give us space to work."

The man brandished his pistol in the air. "All right, but don't try anything stupid because I know how to use this."

"I'm sure you do."

"Please, step aside," said Kim to Connor, "and let me take a look inside the tunnel."

Connor had barely moved to let Kim inside when she darted past him into the darkened tunnel. Connor shook his head and swore under his breath.

"What the hell's going on?" demanded the gunman.

Connor shrugged. "Sorry about that. Kim can get a bit excited."

"I don't care. Follow her. And remember, mister, I can't miss from this range."

Connor bent over and followed Kim underground. The passageway wasn't tall, forcing him to watch his head. The stone staircase had only ten steps. At the bottom, Connor stood beside Kim, speechless, as they stared into a large, circular room with a slate-tiled floor and a high-arched wooden roof. A musty odor hung in the air. Stacks of old furs, blankets, cooking utensils, packs, and a handful of weapons were spread along the walls. A pile of bundled ivory stood in one corner as if waiting to be taken to the markets back home in Iceland or Norway. Yet, everything appeared to be in near pristine condition.

On the wall to Kim and Connor's right was an intricately carved picture of a ship at sea fighting not to capsize as it was battered by waves as tall as the vessel itself. In the center of the room stood a waist-high, brass washbasin.

"Just think," said Kim, wide-eyed. "We're probably the first people to step foot in here in hundreds of years."

Connor shone his flashlight on the curved roof and let out a low whistle. "They must have used the bottom of their ship's hull to make the roof and then used whatever was leftover on the walls."

Kim stepped lightly on the floor and picked up a black bear pelt to reveal a medieval steel breastplate and helmet next to a small pile of copper plates. "Amazing, absolutely amazing."

"Move out of the bloody way!" ordered the gunman. "I want to see."

Not wanting to be shot in the back, Connor stepped aside but followed Kim's footsteps.

Kim moved her flashlight's beam along the tiled floor, looking for signs of a trap before treading lightly to the far end of the room. "Connor, look," she said, aiming her flashlight at the far end of the chamber.

Connor looked over and spotted another tunnel leading into the dark. "I wonder where that goes?"

"The gold," said Kim, winking.

Connor faced the thug. "Say there, friend, now that you're here, would you like to take the lead?"

The man jammed the barrel of his pistol in Connor's ribs, forcing him to wince. "No, you and the girl can carry on. I insist."

Connor glanced at Kim. "You heard the man. I'll follow you. You're lighter, more agile, and have a nose for these kinds of things."

Kim nodded, warily put a foot on a tile, then placed her full weight on it. When it didn't snap, she selected another tile and moved over. Regrettably, the passageway was lower than the stairs, forcing everyone to stoop over. Connor waited until she was a couple of tiles ahead before following her. Even though it was cold, sweat soon poured from Kim's face. Finally, the tunnel turned sharply to the left, and she pointed the way with her hand.

"How much longer does the tunnel go?" asked Connor.

"Maybe another ten meters," replied Kim. "It's hard to tell, but there's a beautiful tapestry hanging at the end of the passageway. I think it marks the entrance to the tomb."

"What's the holdup?" demanded Gunnar's stooge.

"Kim's looking for traps," said Connor over his shoulder.

The man burst out laughing. "Traps! There ain't no such things down here. You're just stalling."

"Kim and I would rather be safe than sorry."

"Idiots! Move aside!" The goon slammed Connor against the wall and shuffled past him.

"No, wait!" warned Kim as the man yanked her back and ripped down the tapestry, exposing a square-shaped room with a stone sarcophagus in the middle of the chamber.

"See, I told you there's nothing to be afraid of," said the man contemptuously. "Ghosts and ghouls are for kids."

The gunman spat on the floor by Kim's feet and waved his pistol in Kim's face. "Maybe when we're done down here, the two of us could put that bear rug back there to good use. Hey, darlin?"

Anger surged through Connor. He had seen enough and launched himself at the unsuspecting man. At the last second, he lowered his shoulder and struck the gunman hard in the back, knocking him off balance. The man staggered backward and tripped over his own feet. Then, in the blink of an eye, the floor gave way beneath him, and he fell back into an unseen pit. A horrid cry filled the chamber. Connor moved next to Kim and sucked in air between his teeth at the sight of the gunman skewered on a dozen centuries-old swords and spearpoints sticking out of the earth. One of the blades had severed the femoral artery in his groin, spraying blood everywhere. Unable to talk or move, the man lay there, slack-jawed, as his lifeblood drained from his body.

Kim reached down to help but was stopped by Connor. He shook his head and said, "No. There's nothing we or anyone else can do for him. He's going into shock and will be dead in the next minute or two from blood loss."

"Are you sure?" asked Kim.

Connor nodded. "One hundred percent. Don't forget, this man probably would have shot me and then raped you if he thought he could have gotten away with it."

"Connor, weren't you worried that the man's pistol could have gone off when you hit him and accidentally killed me?"

Connor picked up the assassin's pistol and wiped the dirt off the slide. He shook his head and showed the gun to Kim. "I saw that the safety was still on. The man truly was a fool."

Kim wiped the sweat from her forehead. "Thank God for that."

"What were you trying to tell our friend before he fell into the trap?"

"Back at the hotel, I did some reading and learned that if a trap was going to be present, it was almost always near the treasure."

"Haste makes waste," said Connor proverbially as he laid the tapestry over the open hole and the dead man's body.

Kim turned on her heel and took in the magnificence of the room. Everywhere her light shone, gold glinted back at her. Shields, plates, cups, swords, and life-sized animals were made from solid gold.

"Darn, I was really hoping to find the Ark of the Covenant in here," quipped Connor, looking around the chamber.

"That's for another day," replied Kim dryly.

"How much do you think all of this gold is worth?"

"Millions, maybe billions."

Connor shone his flashlight at his feet. "Do you think the floor's safe to walk on?"

"Yeah, I think so. But, if you let out a horrible scream, then I guess I got it wrong."

"Swell," said Connor. He warily walked toward the stone sarcophagus and looked down at a shield and sword chiseled into the lid. Connor reverently moved his hand along the shield, brushing away centuries of dust. A Templar's cross and words in Latin appeared.

"Kim, do you think you could decipher this writing?"

"If I can." Kim placed down a golden cup and joined Connor. She bent over and cleared some more dust away. "My Latin's rusty, but I believe we're looking at the final resting spot of Marc Grenier, formerly of the Knights Templar."

"So, we've finally found X on the map. All we need to do now is find those scrolls, and we'll be ready to trade them for Tiva in the morning."

Kim and Connor rummaged through the room for nearly fifteen minutes before both admitted defeat.

"They've got to be here," said Kim. "I can't believe we came all this way for nothing."

Connor didn't know where else to look until his gaze was drawn back to Grenier's stone coffin. "There's one place we haven't looked."

"Ghoulish," said Kim, "but I'm game to look inside if you are."

Connor quickly examined the stone lid and realized they would need some of their tools if they were going to move it even an inch. "I've got an idea, but we'll have to go topside for a minute or two to grab some tools."

Kim nodded. "We can call Yuri, too, and see how he's doing."

"Sure, but don't mention the gold."

"Why not?"

"Because our satphone isn't encrypted."

"Got it. All right, let's go."

38.

"So, what did Yuri have to say?" Connor asked Kim.

"He'll be here in a couple of hours with some of the equipment you requested."

"Some?"

"He warned you it was going to be hard to get his hands on black-market equipment in Nuuk."

"If he gets a third of what I asked for, I'll be happy. Now, I guess it's our turn to pull off a small miracle."

Kim placed the phone on her pack and picked up a pickaxe. "Lead on."

They carefully returned to Grenier's sarcophagus and stood side by side at the base edge.

"For Tiva," said Connor, jamming his pickaxe's chisel head under the heavy stone lid.

"For Tiva," repeated Kim, slamming her tool home, too.

Connor looked Kim in the eyes and said, "On three."

Kim nodded with fierce determination.

"One-two-three."

Kim and Connor bent at the knees, grunting as they tried to budge the stone cover. After a few seconds, Connor said, "Stop what you're doing and catch your breath. This is heavier than it looks."

Kim released her wooden handle and stepped back; her chest was heaving. "Okay, but no more than a minute."

Connor reached for a canteen on his belt. "You got it."

"What happens if we can't lift the lid?"

"Then we draft Yuri when he gets here to help us. One way or another, it's coming off today."

Kim spat on her hands and grasped hold of her pickaxe handle. "Let's do this."

Connor did likewise and mouthed, counting down from three. Finally, on zero, they dug deep inside their bodies and pulled as hard as possible.

Errrrrk!

The lid budged slightly and scraped across the surface.

"Yes!" said Connor, digging in his feet and pushing harder.

The top moved an inch, then another, and then suddenly, it slid to one side, exposing Grenier's remains.

Kim and Connor, taken by surprise, jumped back for a moment before composing themselves and peering inside the stone coffin. The late knight lay in full armor, with his shield and sword in his mailed hands. A purple cloth covered the man's face.

"I think we'll leave that there," suggested Connor.

"Yeah, that's a good idea," said Kim, not keen to see whether the man's face was mummified or not.

Connor looked over the remains and then respectfully moved Grenier's shield aside, exposing a canvas bag underneath. He took hold of the bag and picked it up. Connor moved away from the sarcophagus, and with his stomach tied in a knot, he opened the bag. Four copper tablets inlaid with writing in gold shone under his headlamp.

"Don't just stand there gazing," said Kim, "tell me what you've got."

Connor handed Kim the bag. "All I can say is B-I-N-G-O, we've done it."

"Oh my God, you're right!" exclaimed Kim, almost dropping the heavy bag. But instead, she sat on the floor and held one of the inscribed copper tablets aloft. Her eyes shone as bright as the tablet in her hand.

Connor let Kim revel in their glory for a few seconds before bringing her back to reality. "Now that we have Solomon's scrolls, what do we do with them?"

"Damn, just when I was starting to forget the real world." Kim slid the tablet back into its sack. "Before we do anything, we should close Grenier's sarcophagus to help preserve his remains."

"Yeah, that seems to be the decent thing to do."

Replacing the lid seemed easier than prying it loose. In under a minute, the deed was done, and Grenier's eternal sleep continued.

"Let's leave the scrolls here for now and go for a walk," suggested Connor.

"A walk! Why, what are you thinking?"

"Because I was always taught that it's always better to see your ground from the enemy's perspective before going into battle."

"A battle, what battle?"

Connor grinned. "The one to save Tiva's life and give DuFour one hell of a bloody nose."

Yuri brought the Twin Otter up onto the black-sand beach and switched off its engine. Before Yuri had undone his safety harness, Connor was already climbing on one of the plane's floats to get inside.

"Hold on a minute, partner," said Yuri, channeling his best John Wayne impersonation. "I'll be there in a minute to unload the inventory."

Connor nodded and stepped back out of the way. "Sorry, but it's going to be dark in a few hours, and I've got a lot of work to do."

"We've got a lot of work to do," said Yuri, tipping his hat in Kim's direction.

"Thanks," replied Connor, helping Yuri lift a couple of wooden crates out of the plane and onto the beach.

Yuri flipped open the lid of the first box. "Okay, you asked for an M4 with ten magazines and six hundred rounds." Yuri picked up a hunting rifle and handed it to Connor. "Instead, I present to you a Savage Model 110 bolt-action rifle with bipod and scope."

Connor grasped the rifle, ensured it was clear, and then looked through the scope. "Not bad. How many rounds did you get?"

Yuri tossed him two boxes.

"Forty rounds, great," said Connor, stuffing them into his pockets.

"It's all they could spare. Sorry."

"It's not your fault. What else did you get?"

Yuri grabbed an old ammo can and yanked it open. "You asked for Claymore mines. Unfortunately, the best I can do are two sticks of dynamite, two large glass jars, hundreds of tiny nails, blasting caps, and pull-pin fuses."

Connor nodded thoughtfully. "Okay, so far, not too bad. Pistols?"

"That was easier than I thought." Yuri put the ammo box aside and gave Connor a Glock 19 with a suppressor on the barrel. "I have two, plus one hundred rounds of 9mm ammo."

Connor looked back at Kim, who instantly shook her head.

"I'm no good with guns," said Kim. "I'd shoot myself in the foot if you gave that pistol to me."

"Okay, Yuri, it looks like the second pistol is yours."

"Suits me," he said, sliding it into his belt.

Connor nudged the second crate with his foot. "What's in the second box?"

"There's a camo jacket and vest for you. A pair of radios, binos, knives, traffic flares, thermite explosives, bungee cord, and two sets of coveralls. I still have the wood and old clothes for stuffing you requested on the plane."

"Coveralls?" asked Kim.

Connor grinned. "Scarecrows. We used them in Africa, and if timed just right, they'll scare the crap out of whoever is coming your way. I'm hoping they'll buy me some time to get my hands on an M4 so I can even the fight."

Yuri cleared his throat. "Speaking of that, the word on the street is that twenty men are headed this way first thing tomorrow morning. That's a lot of firepower to deal with, partner."

"I know"

"So, what are we going to do?"

"First, you're going to hide your plane and then return with Gunnar's dead friend's boat."

"And after that?"

"Pray for a miracle." For the next ten minutes, Connor outlined his plan. Finally, when he was done, he looked his comrades in the eyes. "Well, what do you think?"

Yuri shrugged. "Custer thought his plan was foolproof, too, but I can't think of anything better. So, I'm in. And before we go much further, where did you say that boat was hidden?"

Connor pointed off to the east. "That way, I think."

"Got it."

Connor turned and looked at Kim. "I need to know what you're thinking."

"Twenty men sounds like a lot," she said. "But I'm in, as well. Let's give them hell."

Connor smiled. "All right, my friends, let's get to work."

"This has to be the longest night of my life," said Kim. Wrapped in a warm blanket, she stared at the millions of stars in the clear night sky.

"I know what you mean," agreed Connor, tossing some wood on their small fire.

Nearby, Yuri lay under a tarp, fast asleep and snoring up a storm.

"The one good thing about being so far away from civilization is we get a spectacular view of the Milky Way," said Connor. "It's like this where I work in Africa. So beautiful and peaceful."

Kim glanced over at Connor. "You miss it, don't you?"

Connor nodded. "Yeah, I do. But my love for it also got me into this mess. I originally signed on to Jason's nonsense on the condition that he helps keep the anti-poaching team I work with operating for another ten years, keeping the mountain gorillas safe. Then, you came along and changed the equation. And lastly, Tiva, a girl I have never met, has brought us all here."

Kim smiled and shifted a little closer. "What do you mean, I changed the equation?"

"It's my clumsy way of saying I couldn't leave a friend in the lurch."

"When this is over, are you planning on heading back to Africa, or are you looking at taking some time off first?"

"I don't know. I guess it depends on how tomorrow goes."

Kim tilted her head. "How so?"

"First, we have to survive the day, and secondly, I have to live with what I'm about to do."

Kim looked away at the fire. "Sorry, I hadn't thought of that."

"It's all right. Most people never do. If this were only about money, I'd walk away and never look back, but it's not anymore. My only real quarrel is with Vallin and DuFour. If I can get the rest to leave without killing too many of them, and Tiva is safe, I'll have done my job, and my conscience will be clear."

"It all sounds so simple."

"I know, but it rarely ever is. Tomorrow is going to be hell."

39.

Rene DuFour sat quietly at the front of the Griffon hovercraft as it skimmed over the cold, dark waters of the North Atlantic at close to fifty knots an hour. A light rain fell from the leaden sky, making it hard to see through the windows. Not that DuFour cared. His mind was filled with dreams of the unimaginable wealth that would soon be his. Next to him sat Demi, The Order's red-haired minder, in an all-green leather outfit, absentmindedly loading and unloading her 9mm Glock 17 pistol.

"Sir, we're five minutes out," reported Gunnar, sitting behind DuFour with his hands tied behind his back. The poor grad student's face was a mess. He had two black eyes, red, puffy cheeks, and a split lip.

"Thank you," replied DuFour. He looked over his shoulder at his assault team leader, "Jean, get your people ready."

"Yes, sir." Vallin undid his seatbelt, stood, and slung his SMG over his shoulder. Like the rest of his team, Vallin wore a mix of military and civilian clothing.

"Do you need me to do anything?" asked Gunnar meekly.

"No, just sit there and keep your mouth shut!" snapped Vallin, showing him the back of his gloved hand. "That's unless you want me to help rearrange your face again."

Gunnar looked away and meekly shook his head.

Vallin glanced down at Tiva, sitting next to Jenny, a black woman with a thick, British accent and a slightly round face. The young captive wore warm clothes, a comical patch over her left eye, and a pirate hat canted on her head. For a brief second, Vallin felt uneasy about ordering Tiva's kidnapping, but that was nothing compared to what awaited her if her aunt and Connor North didn't play ball and hand over the tablets. He cleared his mind of such thoughts and instead focussed it on the mission at hand.

Vallin walked back to the crew compartment, brought his fingers to his lips, and let out an ear-piercing whistle. His team was a mix of ex-military and police officers who had been kicked out of their respective services for a variety of charges. He waited until everyone's eyes were on him and him alone. "Oy, everybody, listen up. We land in five. I don't expect any trouble today, but if there is, don't hesitate to kill anyone who gets in your way. You can't collect your money if you are dead."

"It's okay; I was planning on spending Santiago's anyway," said a tough-looking woman with a short ponytail.

"You wish, Gabrielle," replied her partner, a broad-shouldered man with curly black hair and a neatly trimmed beard.

A gruff chuckle filled the cabin.

"I'm serious," stressed Vallin. "Shoot to kill."

"And what if your plan goes awry?" asked Rin, unbuckling herself from her chair.

Vallin was tired of Rin's face. In fact, he despised everything about her. "It won't. Trust me."

"It's your life."

"Yeah, and I intend on being around to enjoy my retirement. Now, get out of my way. I have a job to do."

Kim stood alone on the sandy beach beside the dead man's Zodiac. She wore a blue ball cap and had her jacket done up to her neck to keep the rain out. Kim silently prayed to her ancestors for their help in protecting Tiva today. She knew she was far from pious, but for the next hour or so, she hoped the spirits would overlook that fact. Then, the faint noise of an engine caught her attention. Her stomach instantly tightened. Kim brought up a radio to her lips. "They're coming."

"*Can you see them?*" asked Connor.

"No—wait, I think I can see them now." A dark shape drove through the fog and sped toward the beach. "It looks like they're in a hovercraft."

"*Remember what we talked about and do whatever they say, and this will all soon be over.*"

"I hope so."

"*So do I.*"

"Keep your head down, Marine."

"*You too.*"

"I've got to go…they're here."

The hovercraft slowed and then drove up onto the beach. The driver maneuvered his craft alongside Kim and switched off its engines, deflating its air-filled skirt. A second later, the hovercraft's side doors flung open, and Vallin's mercenaries rushed out of the craft and quickly established a cordon.

Gabrielle dashed over and pointed her Swedish-made compact SMG at Kim's stomach. "Hands up."

Kim slowly raised her hands.

Gabrielle quickly searched Kim for any hidden weapons. All she found was Kim's Motorola, which she looked over and tossed back to her.

Vallin and Rin followed his people out into the rain.

"Is she clean?" Vallin asked Gabrielle.

"Yeah," replied the killer. "She's only packing a radio."

Vallin stepped uncomfortably close and glared at Kim before pulling back on his weapon's charging lever and loading a 9mm round into its chamber. "Where's North?" he asked.

"He's at the burial chamber, waiting for my signal that DuFour has agreed to release Tiva in exchange for the tablets," responded Kim.

Vallin looked back at the hovercraft and yelled, "Hey, Karlsen, get your arse out here now!"

Gunnar tripped over his feet exiting the craft and fell end over end onto the beach. He stood, avoiding eye contact with Kim. "Yes," he said to Vallin.

"How far away is the burial chamber?"

Gunnar raised his bound hands and gestured inland. "It's about three hundred meters from here. The closest ruins, however, are just off the beach."

"I never bloody well asked that," snarled Vallin, slapping Gunnar across his face.

Gunnar staggered back and lowered his head. "I'm sorry." The poor grad student had fallen afoul of Vallin the instant they met. Angered by Rin's continued presence, Vallin had taken out his pent-up frustration on Gunnar.

Vallin looked past Kim at the Zodiac. "Where's Karlsen's contact?"

"Dead," replied Kim. "He fell into a trap and was skewered to death."

Vallin chuckled. "Figures. Did you set the trap?"

"No, it was already inside the tomb."

"Jean, what's going on?" DuFour asked, stepping foot on the beach with Demi a step behind him.

The tough-looking mercenary turned to face his boss. "I'm just getting the lay of the land, sir."

"Well, whatever you're doing, hurry up. I don't like being cold and wet."

"Sir, Ms. Swiftwater's partner is waiting about three hundred meters inland to trade the scrolls for the girl."

"So be it. Bring the girl out."

Kim bit her lip and held her breath.

"Aunty Kimy," cried Tiva, sprinting out of the hovercraft and running into Kim's arms.

Kim swung Tiva in the air and held her tight in her arms. "Hey there, sweet peach, how are you feeling?"

"I'm okay. I miss Mom and Dad, but Jenny has been really good to me."

Kim placed Tiva back on the ground but held onto her left hand for dear life.

A black woman stood a few feet away with her hands by her sides. "I'm Jenny," she said with a brief smile.

Kim sized Jenny up. She didn't look dangerous, but looks could be deceiving. "Thanks for looking after Tiva."

"It wasn't hard. She's a good kid."

"Okay, I've had enough of this touchy-feely crap," said Vallin. "Handcuff the two women together."

"Hey, this wasn't in my contract," protested Jenny.

"I don't care," replied Vallin. "Gabrielle, cuff them."

Jenny turned to leave. "Screw this!"

Vallin swung up his SMG and aimed it between Jenny's eyes. "Sorry, I didn't hear that."

Jenny took a step back. "Okay, mister, you win. Please don't shoot me."

Tiva's eyes widened. "Kimy, what's happening? Why are these people being so mean to you and Jenny?"

Kim put on her best face as she and Jenny were cuffed. "It's all right. This will all be over soon, and when it is, I'll take you home. Would you like that?"

Tiva nodded.

"All right, Jean, let's get this over with," ordered DuFour.

Vallin paused. "Sir, I must advise caution. I don't trust North or Swiftwater. They're up to something."

"Of course they are. But you've got twenty of the best mercenaries I could hire for you against one. So do your job and get me those scrolls."

Vallin cursed his boss' impatience and grabbed Gunnar by the collar. He dragged the helpless grad student off the beach until they could see the first ruins through the rain and mist. Vallin opened a pouch on his tactical vest and brought out his binoculars. He searched the grounds for any sign of North or what he might be planning. A shiver shot down his spine. The island looked barren and cold.

"How exactly is this village laid out on the ground?" demanded Vallin.

Gunnar pointed into the fog. "The first set of ruins is about one hundred meters straight ahead. You can't miss it."

"And then?"

"The encampment is shaped like a triangle with houses on each corner. At the back of the triangle are the remains of a long house, and then just a bit more is the burial mound."

Vallin shook Gunnar. "Are you sure?"

"Yes, sir. I'd bet my life on it."

"Well, that was a poor choice of words," said Vallin, flipping his weapon's safety to automatic and firing a burst at point-blank range into Gunnar's head. The doomed man was dead before he hit the soggy ground.

"You should really watch your temper," said Rin, walking out of the mist. "Anger can cloud your mind and make it hard to make good decisions."

Vallin swung around and glared at Rin. "I don't need your damned advice!"

Rin grinned. "Be careful today. It would be a shame if you were accidentally shot in the back."

Vallin gnashed his teeth. He stepped over Gunnar's body and waved his squad leaders to his side. "Okay listen up; this is how I want this to go down. Alpha squad, you will clear the left side of the settlement. Bravo squad, you'll clear the right. While Charlie squad will remain in reserve under my command. There are four ruins we must clear before we get to the gold, so stay alert."

The squad leaders responded with a thumbs-up and then spread their people out, ready for action.

Kim watched the lead teams advance up the beach and slid her left hand into a pocket on her jacket. She made sure her guard wasn't watching her and keyed her radio three times.

The enemy was coming.

40.

Connor heard the clicks. A mix of adrenaline and fear surged through his body. No matter what happened next, he was ready. Connor adjusted the camouflage tarp he was using as a ghillie suit and laid his rifle's sights on a man in the center of a group of mercenaries advancing out of the mist next to the first ruins. He gently laid his index finger on the trigger and took up some of the slack. Connor took a long, deep breath and slowly let it out to calm his heart rate.

The man in the middle shouted out an order, identifying him as the team leader.

Connor laid his scope's reticle pattern on the man's chest and lowered his aim until it rested on the mercenary's right thigh. It was time. Connor held his breath and pulled back on the trigger. There was a loud bang as the rifle fired. Connor felt the recoil, cocked his rifle to eject the spent casing, and loaded a fresh round into this weapon. A grin crept across Connor's lips. The team leader was down on the ground, begging for help. Connor moved slightly and waited for the first person to try and take command before firing another round, seriously wounding the next in line.

Pained cries for help traveled on the winds.

"For the love of God, did anyone see where the shots came from?" yelled Vallin, lying in the cold, wet mud.

"Sweet Jesus, help me," pleaded Santiago, only meters away from Vallin. His body was covered in a cold sweat. He ripped open a pouch and dug out a field dressing. Santiago was desperate to staunch the blood shooting out of his leg with his every heartbeat.

"Be quiet," ordered Vallin, raising his head slightly to try and spot North. A second later, the whip-like crack of a bullet flying right over his head forced Vallin to duck.

"I think I see something," hollered a mercenary carrying a grenade launcher.

"Kill him!" yelled Vallin.

Connor knew it was time to change locations when he heard the distinct popping sound of a grenade launcher firing a 40mm projectile in his direction. He hunched low and hurried for the muck-filled passageway between the two furthest houses when the grenades struck home in his old position and exploded. Thousands of razor-sharp, jagged metal pieces cut through the air where Connor had been lying only seconds ago. He hurried along until he was in the last building's ruins. The only things behind him now were the longhouse and the tomb.

A sharp pain shot through Connor's left leg, causing him to wince. He dropped low in the remnants of the old building and checked his leg. *Damn, a deep cut.* He thought he'd escaped the grenades unscathed, but the blood seeping through his clothes told him otherwise. *It could have been worse*, thought Connor, happy he was wearing his liquid body armor under his shirt. Connor guessed he had, at best, a minute before Vallin and his men sorted themselves out and continued their advance. He poured water from his canteen over the wound to clean it before wrapping a field dressing around it. Connor rolled over and rested between a pair of boulders. He'd hurt the first squad. Now, it was the second's turn.

Kim heard the grenades explode and pulled Tiva in tight.

"What's going on, Kimy?" Tiva asked, scared.

Kim wasn't sure how to reply but knew lying wouldn't help anyone. "These people are trying to hurt my friend."

"Why?"

"Because they want something."

Kim looked at her niece and, for the first time, noticed that she had a fake scar on her cheek. "Tiva, do you have your makeup bag with you?"

Tiva smiled and held up a small pouch. "Jenny, let me keep it. She even helped me draw this scar. Do you like it?"

"Yes, I do. Could I please see your makeup bag?"

Tiva undid her jacket and pulled out a small pouch packed with cosmetics. "What do you want this for, Kimy?"

Kim glanced over at their guard, whose whole attention was fixed on the sounds of gunfire coming from the ruins. Kim winked at Tiva and helped herself to a bobby pin. "This ought to do."

"Do what?"

Kim got on one knee and looked deep into Tiva's eyes. "Hon, when I tell you to, I want you to close your eyes and cover your ears until I tell you it's safe. Okay?"

Tiva nodded and adjusted her pirate hat.

"What's going on?" asked Jenny.

Kim lowered her voice. "Something's about to happen. If you want to stay alive, you'll listen to me."

"What are you talking about? We're handcuffed together, or did you forget?"

"Am I?" Kim asked, removing the restraint from her wrist. Her eyes narrowed. "Do as I say, and you'll live."

"Help!" pleaded a female mercenary, writhing in the mud, with a wound blasted through her stomach and out her back.

"No, don't help," warned Vallin. But his orders fell on deaf ears, as another hired killer fell right next to her with his right kneecap turned to a bloody pulp.

"Four. That's four, God damn it," snarled Vallin.

"I'm no soldier, Jean, but you appear to be losing," said DuFour.

Vallin rolled over on his side and was astonished to see DuFour and his minder, Demi, kneeling next to him, seemingly oblivious to the danger. "Sir, get the hell down before North shoots you."

"In the mud! I don't think so. North's hit everything he's aimed at so far. If he wanted me dead, I'd be dead by now."

"Damn it, I'm hit," cried another merc.

"Five," said DuFour mockingly.

Vallin wiped the muck and rain from his face and swore. Then, as loud as he could, Vallin yelled, "Anyone who has been hit and can crawl should try and make it back to the beach. If you can't, just stay where you are, and we'll come for you. Everyone else move up into line with me. We're going to flush this son of a bitch out."

The surviving assaulters crawled through the cold mud until they formed a rough line.

"Who has the grenade launcher?" asked Vallin.

"I do," responded a man with a scraggly, blond beard on his face.

"We need cover. Can you lay down a smoke screen for us to use?"

The grenadier nodded and loaded a smoke grenade into his weapon.

"All right, fire them until you're out of grenades."

The man raised his launcher slightly and pulled the trigger. The first projectile landed just behind Connor's position and discharged a cloud of red smoke. In seconds, three more grenades hit the ground, helping to create a wall of multi-colored smoke.

Vallin jumped to his feet with his SMG in his shoulder. "With me! Advance!"

"Game's up," said Connor, knowing his position was vulnerable. In a minute or less, Vallin's people would be on him. He glanced back at the longhouse and knew it was there—that's where he'd have to make his last stand.

Connor ducked down and ran through the knee-deep mud in the passage back to the ruins. The odd shot or burst of gunfire told Connor that Vallin's people were spooked and firing at anything that looked like a person. He counted down in his head until he was reasonably sure the mercenaries were closing in. Then, Connor lifted a rock revealing a pair of pull-pin fuses. He yanked the first one and watched it catch alight before arming the second. Connor slid down in the mud and took cover behind a thick rock that had once been part of the longhouse's foundation and waited with bated breath.

"Let's go," said Vallin, trying to encourage his people. "Keep moving."

The hired killers walked into the fading smoke screen dragging their feet, unsure of what awaited them on the other side.

"Come on, come," urged Vallin.

The smoke parted, and the medieval stone ruins of the longhouse came into view.

The hair on the back of Vallin's neck shot up. It was the perfect spot for an ambush.

A loud snap immediately followed by another startled Vallin.

Suddenly, two figures released from their elastic bungee cord triggers shot out of the ground. The traffic flares attached to the back of the scarecrows activated. Smoke and bright, burning light silhouetted the scarecrows.

Before he could stop them, Vallin's spooked people opened up on the figures as if they were real people.

Connor waited one more second and then said, "Surprise."

Regrettably, only one of the dynamite sticks in the glass jars packed with tiny nails hanging from the scarecrow's necks exploded. But one was more than good enough, as it launched hundreds of projectiles at waist height, straight at Vallin's line. People screamed in agony and surprise as the nails tore through flesh, killing and wounding half of the mercenaries still on their feet.

Kim turned Tiva toward her and held her close. "Don't look, baby."

Gabrielle turned her head and saw Kim wasn't cuffed to Jenny anymore. "What the hell?"

Kim closed her eyes, knowing what was coming next. Two silenced shots made her cringe. Slowly, Kim opened her eyes and let out her breath. Gabrielle lay dead with two holes in the side of her head.

"Is everyone okay?" asked Yuri, tossing the tarp aside and climbing out of the Zodiac.

"Yeah, we're fine," replied Kim. "Thanks."

"Can I look now, Kimy?" asked Tiva.

Yuri scooped up the tarp and laid it over Gabrielle's body.

"Now you can, dear," said Kim, letting go of her.

"Who are you?" Tiva asked the strange man standing next to Kim.

Yuri hid his pistol behind his back and smiled. "My name is Yuri, and I'm here to make sure nothing bad happens to you."

Tiva looked up at her aunt. "What about you, Aunt Kimy? Aren't you staying with me too?"

Kim got on one knee. "Hon, my friend is in danger, and I have to help him. Yuri will take good care of you until we can meet again."

"What about me?" asked Jenny.

"What about you?" said Kim brusquely.

"I'm not one of them. So, please, I'm begging you; don't leave me here."

"Jenny's a good person," said Tiva.

"I'll watch her," offered Yuri, picking up a heavy canvas bag and throwing it over his shoulder.

Kim nodded. "Okay, it's time to go."

With tears in her eyes, Tiva threw her arms around her aunt. "Be careful."

"I will. By the way, do you have any black makeup?"

"Here," Tiva replied, handing Kim her compact.

Kim hugged Tiva one last time and faced Yuri. "All right, you've done your part and then some. Please take Tiva to safety, and don't forget the bag Connor wants you to take and call the cavalry as soon as you can."

"I won't. Here, take this," said Yuri, holding out his pistol.

Kim shook her head. "I already said I'm a crap marksman. But I will take your knife."

"It's your call," Yuri said, handing over his combat knife.

Kim flipped open Tiva's compact and ran two fingers through the black makeup. She winked at her niece and then ran the fingers from one temple to the next over her eyes.

"I love you, Aunty Kimy," said Tiva.

A lump formed in Kim's throat. "I love you, too. Now go."

41.

"Jesus," uttered Vallin, staggering back and forth on his wobbly legs. He looked down and saw three nails lodged in his chest. Without thinking, he reached down and plucked them out, one by one.

"Help me," begged a man on his knees, with nails and glass embedded in his face.

Vallin shook his head. For a brief second, he thought he saw someone looking at him from the longhouse and threw himself to the ground just as a gun fired, killing the man to his right. Vallin had had enough. He crawled into a depression filled with wet mud, opened a pouch, and brought out a hand grenade. He yanked off the safety pin and lobbed it at the longhouse.

Splash!

Connor heard the grenade land in the mud barely a meter from his head. His combat instincts kicked in. He spun about and sprinted for the passageway leading to the burial chamber. Connor was almost there when an explosion of mud, rocks, and metal knocked him off his feet. He landed facefirst in the muck. Connor rolled over and felt a shooting pain in his left wrist. He glanced down and saw he'd shattered his wrist. Connor knew there was no time to try and splint it. The enemy was closing in. His problems only grew when he couldn't see his rifle anywhere. He searched in vain for a few seconds, but it was lost under a sea of mud.

"Go!" Connor urged himself, feeling like a mule had kicked him in the chest. Finally, he pulled himself to his feet, slipped his broken wrist into his jacket, and staggered down the tunnel. With only a pistol left, Connor knew the odds had suddenly swung against him. He stumbled his way to the burial chamber's entrance and prepared to make his last stand there.

"Jean, Jean, can you hear me?" asked DuFour, nudging Vallin with his foot.

Vallin flipped around and glared at his boss. How the hell the man was still alive was beyond him. Vallin blinked; there wasn't even a speck of mud on DuFour's or Demi's clothes.

"Jean, North ran off toward the crypt. If you hurry, you should be able to get him before he kills any more of your men."

Vallin's body ached everywhere. He stood and looked around at the carnage at his feet. Rivers of blood mixed with the mud. There were only six people from his original team left to fight.

Rin, her face covered with scars from the homemade claymore mines, crawled out of the mud and stood. She wiped the muck from her hands and looked at Vallin. "I'll guard Monsieur DuFour while you take care of that son of a bitch."

For once, he agreed with Rin. Vallin nodded and waved for his people to follow him. A couple of men hesitated for a moment before falling into line. Even Vallin wasn't sure of his odds anymore. But, he figured the day wouldn't be wasted if he got to kill North.

Connor jammed himself as best he could behind a tall boulder and waited. He figured he could get two, maybe three mercs before they would be on him. He hadn't expected to die on a cold, desolate island off Greenland, but he was buying time for Kim and Tiva to escape. There were worse ways to give one's life.

A dark shape stepped into the passage and warily moved toward the crypt.

Connor calmly laid his pistol's sights on the man and fired twice. The mercenary tumbled onto his knees and then slid into the muck. A second person let loose with his SMG, spraying bullets down the trench in a wasted attempt to hit Connor. The man swore as he ejected his empty magazine.

"Good night," Connor said, putting a single round between the man's eyes.

"Screw this!" yelled a man with a Slavic accent. "Keep your damned money."

Other voices joined in.

Connor smiled. They'd had enough and were mutinying.

A burst of automatic fire abruptly silenced the discussion.

Kim sprinted as fast as her legs would carry her through the thick mud. Everywhere she looked were dead or dying mercenaries.

"Water, please," begged a man with a stomach wound.

Kim didn't stop. The man could go to hell for all she was concerned. He'd made his bed and could lay in it until he died. Kim heard shots from up ahead and dug deep for whatever strength she had left in her body. She had to help Connor.

At the last second, Kim spotted DuFour and two women looking toward the burial mound, but not her. With a war cry on her lips, Kim dove at Rin, knocking her to the ground. Kim rolled over on her shoulder and came up with her knife still in her hand. Rin saw her SMG sinking in the mud and quickly drew her blade.

"I'm going to enjoy gutting you," snarled Rin, standing.

Kim had no intention of dying and took a step back, giving them space between each other.

Rin smiled and lunged at Kim's face.

Instead of jumping back, she remembered her Krav Maga training and turned her body. Simultaneously, she slashed at Rin's outstretched arm, cutting a deep groove.

Rin winced in pain and spat on the ground. Blood trickled down her right arm onto the mud. "Okay, you bitch. That's going to cost you."

Kim stayed silent, her mind and body focused on the next move.

Rin clumsily thrust at her opponent's stomach. Kim saw the move coming and blocked it with her left hand. A split-second later, Kim swung her blade across Rin's exposed neck—a bright, crimson spray shot from the doomed woman's severed carotid artery. Rin jammed her left hand over the wound, trying to stop the bleeding. She staggered on her feet and weakly thrust his knife at Kim's face before falling straight back into the mud, unable to stand anymore.

"Drop your knife," demanded Demi, placing her pistol against Kim's head.

Kim swore and tossed the bloody blade aside.

"Good girl," said DuFour. "Now, let's go and get those scrolls."

"North!" bellowed Vallin. "Show yourself."

Connor chuckled. "Why so you can shoot me down like you did to your men?"

Vallin walked out into the open and dropped his SMG and pistol. "I'm unarmed. Let's settle this man to man with knives."

Connor glanced down at his shattered wrist. A hand-to-hand fight was the last thing he wanted right now. "I don't know. Maybe another day."

"The game's over, Mister North," said DuFour, moving next to Vallin. "I've got your friend."

Connor got to one knee and felt his stomach drop at the sight of Demi aiming a pistol at Kim's head. He gritted his teeth and stood.

The pain shooting through his body reminded him he wasn't as young as he used to be. Connor slowly climbed out of the passage and stood beside the burial chamber.

"Are you okay?" Connor asked Kim.

"Yes, for now," she replied.

"Tiva?"

"Gone. Yuri should be most of the way to Nuuk by now."

Vallin took a step. "So, Captain North, what do you say? Shall I kill you in front of your girlfriend and then maybe have my way with her?"

Connor shook his head. "She's not my girlfriend, and I'm friggin' exhausted."

Vallin spat on the ground. "Coward."

"Sure, whatever."

Vallin thought he had the drop on an exhausted Connor and brought his hand back to throw his knife at his adversary's chest. He was, however, a fraction of a second too slow. In one smooth move, Connor dropped to one knee, raised his pistol, and shot Vallin in the head. The dead legionnaire crumpled to the ground.

Kim saw her chance and thrust her head forward while simultaneously shooting her left hand across her body, pushing Demi's gun hand back. A second later, Demi pulled the trigger, missing Kim's head by inches. Kim spun on her heel, grabbed the weapon with both hands, and twisted it up and out of Demi's hand.

"Surprise," said Kim, aiming the pistol at Demi's head.

"What the hell!" uttered Demi, staring wide-eyed down the barrel of a gun.

"Krav Maga," replied Kim. "It works. Now place your hands on your head and sit down in the mud."

Demi contorted her face. "I will do no such thing."

"Now!" warned Kim, inching the barrel of her pistol closer to Demi's face.

Demi's face blanched. Her hands shook as she put them on her head and sat in the cold muck.

Connor limped over. "You'll have to teach me that move someday."

"Sure, why not? It's easy to learn."

Connor looked at Demi and let out a tired sigh. "I don't know or care who you are, but let's hope this is the one and only time our paths will ever cross."

Demi looked up. "So do I, Mister North. So do I."

Connor pointed at Kim's face. "What's up with the makeup?"

"Oh, this. I thought it made me look like a Cree warrior."

Connor nodded. "Nice touch."

"I suppose you'd like to renegotiate a new offer for the scrolls?" mused DuFour.

"I didn't think we ever had one to begin with," said Kim.

"Well, maybe we can come up with something now."

"No," said Connor bluntly. "No more money. No more death. If you want the scrolls, you can have the bloody things. But be careful what you wish for. Someone somewhere will always be looking for them. Are you sure they're worth the danger?"

DuFour's eyes lit up. "Of course I am. Where are they?"

Connor moved aside to reveal a canvas bag on a rock behind the burial mound. "You can have the scrolls. There's more than enough gold in the crypt for Kim and me to live on for the rest of our lives quite comfortably. What do you say? We keep the gold, and you get the scrolls?"

"What are you waiting for, Rene?" said Demi. "Go and get the bloody scrolls."

"Remember, DuFour, this is what you asked for," said Connor, wrapping an arm around Kim to help steady his aching body.

DuFour hurried over and ran his hand over the canvas bag. His heart raced in excitement. "I'm rich," he said euphorically, picking up the bag. DuFour flipped open the cover and lustfully looked inside at four copper plates.

"Goodbye," said Connor, waving at DuFour.

For a second, DuFour was confused. Then, with a bright flash, the thermite boobytrap inside the bag ignited. The thermite soared to well over two thousand Celsius and instantly melted the copper onto DuFour's hands, burning and tearing the skin and bones from his limbs. He let out a horrified howl and fell to his knees as his body burned alive.

Kim turned her head into Connor's chest. "Oh God, what a horrible way to die."

"He had it coming," replied Connor, holding Kim in his arms.

"Yes, he did." Kim was about to check on Connor's wounds when the enormity of everything that had just happened hit her like a speeding train. Her stomach turned. Kim barely had time to bend over before she threw up.

"Easy does it," said Connor, comforting her. "It's been a rough day for everyone, but it's over."

Kim caught her breath and wiped her chin. "I've never killed anyone before."

"It was you or her, and I'm glad you are the person standing here with me."

"Thanks." Kim smiled weakly, unsure if she would be sick again.

Out to sea, the sound of helicopter rotor blades cutting through the air heralded the arrival of the police. Connor and Kim looked skyward as two dark-blue police choppers flew over the island and prepared to land.

"It looks like we've got a lot of explaining to do," said Kim.

"Yeah, I hope Jason has deep pockets because there's no way we're going to bluff our way out of this one."

42.

Connor North slowly opened his tired eyes and breathed deeply through his nostrils. Then, he gingerly sat up in his hospital bed and glanced down at his bandaged left wrist. It had been three days since the incident on the island, and Connor was still coming to terms with everything that had transpired.

There was a light knock on his door.

"It's open...I think," said Connor.

The door opened. Kim and Tiva walked in, accompanied by Henry Knox, of all people.

"Morning, sleepyhead," teased Kim.

Connor couldn't help but smile. "You try having surgery on your wrist. It's not as much fun as it sounds."

Tiva waved. "Good morning. Aunt Kimy says you got hurt helping me. I'm sorry if it hurts."

It was Connor's first time meeting the bright, young girl, and he could see in her eyes how she and Kim were related. "It's okay, hon. It'll heal, and I'll get better."

"I hope so. Aunt Kimy says that you're her special friend."

Kim blushed and gently pulled Tiva toward her. "That's enough for now. Why don't you take a seat and play a game on my phone."

"Okay." Tiva took the phone and sat. In seconds, she was oblivious to the adults in the room.

"So, Mister Knox, what brings you all the way out here?" asked Connor.

"You do," he replied, smiling.

Connor groaned and rolled his eyes. "Not this again. No, really, why are you here?"

Knox and Kim grabbed a couple of chairs and dragged them over to the bed. "I'm here to let you know that your lawyer should be arriving shortly from Denmark. I hear she's damned good at her job, so the two of you should be on a plane back to the States in the next day or two."

Connor raised an eyebrow. "You couldn't have called Kim and passed this on?"

Knox raised a hand and shrugged. "Yes and no."

Connor's small reservoir of patience was rapidly drying up. "Knox, please, no more riddles. Why are you here?"

Knox nodded. "Sorry. Mister Hamilton asked me to speak with you."

"Yes. What about?"

"The scrolls. Did you actually melt them with a thermite charge?"

Connor grinned. "I sure did, and I'd do it again in a heartbeat. The information on those scrolls belongs to everyone, not just billionaires who don't care how many people have to die to get them what they want."

"And now nobody has it," said Knox disappointedly.

"I agree with Connor," said Kim. "It's better that they're gone."

"Well, at least the remainder of the treasure is still intact."

"Speaking of that, have the Danish authorities taken possession of the cache?" asked Connor.

"Yes, they have, and that's why Mister Hamilton is in Copenhagen arguing that he should get a 35% finder's fee."

"A what? He didn't find the treasure. We did."

"Yes, but you were acting as his agents when you found the burial mound, so legally, whatever was found belongs to Mister Hamilton."

Connor ground his teeth and prepared to turn the air blue when he remembered Tiva was in the room. He simply shook his head instead. "I always knew Jason was a piece of work. This just confirms it." For once, Connor noted, Kim didn't jump to Hamilton's defense.

"There's one last thing I have to tell you, and it involves the woman arrested on the island with you."

"The redhead?" asked Kim.

"Yes, her."

"What about her?"

"She's gone."

Connor furrowed his bow. "What do you mean she's gone?"

"Yesterday, she vanished somewhere between the police station and the courthouse where she was to be arraigned," explained Knox.

"So what? That's the Danish police's problem, not ours," remarked Connor.

Knox shook his head. "Demi Collins is not a person to take lightly. She and her Order are the antitheses of everything Mister Hamilton and I believe in. I'd be careful if I were you. She was taken down a notch the other day, and she'll be back, this time, looking for blood. You should have killed her when you had the chance."

Connor was done talking. "Okay, Knox, we're finished. I expect Jason to live up to his end of the bargain and pay us what we're owed, or he'll find out the hard way how persuasive I can be. Got it?"

Knox got to his feet. "There's no need to worry about that. Your money is already in your respective bank accounts. I wish you and Ms. Swiftwater a good day."

Connor watched Knox leave the room, praying that was the last he would ever see of him.

"So, what are you going to do with your money?" Kim asked.

Connor shrugged. "I don't know. Until my wrist is healed, I doubt I'm going anywhere."

Kim smiled at Tiva. "Well, I know what I'm going to do. First, I'm taking Tiva home to her foster parents, and then I'm going to see my sister. It's been far too long since we last saw one another."

"That sounds like a good idea. Maybe when you're done, you can meet me in New York?"

Kim provocatively lifted her eyebrow. "New York for the weekend, eh?"

"It's not what you think," replied Connor, smiling.

"A girl can dream."

Suddenly, the door swung open, and a woman with a tall, athletic build strode into the hospital room. "Mister North, Ms. Swiftwater, my name is Sonja Steel, and I have been retained by Jason Hamilton in case you require the services of a defense lawyer."

Kim stood and offered her hand. Then, out of the corner of his eye, Connor noticed a red Templar Knights tattoo on the inside of Steel's right wrist and burst out laughing.

"What so funny?" Kim asked.

"Nothing. I just have this feeling we'll be packing our bags sooner rather than later."

43.

New York City

A light rain fell from gray clouds covering the city.

Kim and Connor stood silently under their umbrellas, each lost in their thoughts. Both were well-dressed. Connor carried a bouquet of flowers in his hand while Kim held a single eagle's feather. Both were nervous about what was to come next but knew it had to be done.

It was Connor who eventually broke the nervous silence. "So, how was your trip to Texas?"

"Fine. My sister's doing better than expected, and Tiva couldn't be happier to be home again," said Kim.

"That's good to hear." Connor paused and looked around. "And the scrolls?"

"Yuri flew into Houston and handed them to me. They're hidden in an old trunk in Tiva's foster parents' attic."

Connor grinned. "Excellent." He offered his arm to Kim. "Shall we do this?"

"When you said you were going to take me to meet someone special, I thought you meant your mom."

Connor looked at Kim and smiled. "Not today."

Arm in arm, they approached Rachel North's headstone and stopped a few feet shy. Connor laid his flowers over her grave and cleared his throat.

"Hey there, Rachel, I've brought someone I'd like you to meet. Her name is Kim Swiftwater."

Not sure what to do or say, Kim reverently placed her eagle feather on the tombstone. Finally, she mustered a small smile. "Hi. You've got a good man here."

Connor continued. "It's a shame you two never met; I'm positive you'd get along. In many ways, Rachel, she's a lot like you." He slid his hand over and took Kim's in his. "She's intelligent, brave, single-minded, and full of life. She's my friend." Connor squeezed Kim's hand tight. "She's my good friend."

END